Rhaynel Murray

Gerald's Ordeal

A novel. Part 2

Rhaynel Murray

Gerald's Ordeal
A novel. Part 2

ISBN/EAN: 9783337048723

Printed in Europe, USA, Canada, Australia, Japan

Cover: Foto ©Andreas Hilbeck / pixelio.de

More available books at **www.hansebooks.com**

GERALD'S ORDEAL.

GERALD'S ORDEAL.

A NOVEL,

BY

RHAYNEL MURRAY.

Magna est veritas—et prævalebit.

IN THREE VOLUMES.

VOL. II.

LONDON:
THOMAS RICHARDSON AND SON;
DUBLIN, AND DERBY.
NEW YORK: HENRY H. RICHARDSON AND CO.
MDCCCLXXII.

GERALD'S ORDEAL.

CHAPTER I.

PARIS on a hot day, is not the coolest place in the world, and so Charles Lethbridge thought, as he strolled slowly along under the colonnade of the Rue de Rivoli, at two o'clock in the afternoon of the sixth of August, 186—. Having obtained a few days leave, he had come over with one of his brother officers for a "lark" to the French capital, and began to think he had been a decided ass for his pains.

"How on earth is a fellow to keep cool in such a furnace as this?" had been his constant exclamation ever since he arrived. "I declare it is worse than London a hundred times."

On this particular morning, the young guardsman had breakfasted at a late hour, in what could scarcely be considered as full dress, and finding it next to impossible to breathe in the atmosphere of his rooms at the hotel, he had completed his toilet and sauntered down to the Champs Elysées, in hopes of being able to endure existence with more equanimity in the open air. With the aid of a "Tauchnitz" novel and his cigar case, he had contrived to get through a couple of hours under the trees, stretched at full length on a bench, an object of admiration to all the *bonnes* who passed with their young charges that way.

That "lazy beggar, Mortimer," had not made his appearance when he came out, and would probably have gone off somewhere on his own account before this, Charles thought, and so not caring to go back immediately to the hotel, he crossed the street and entered the garden of the Tuileries at one of the side gates. Here, for some time, he remained wandering up and down the shaded alleys, or reclining on one of the seats, until a sudden longing for an ice took possession of him, and he summoned sufficient energy to return to his hotel for the purpose of getting one.

A number of waiters and underlings belonging to the establishment, were crowded about the entrance of the courtyard of the Hôtel de Louvre as he approached it. A departure of some importance had apparently just taken place, and the carriage and pair which was bearing away the travellers was still in sight, although rapidly vanishing in the distance. A tremendous 'chatteration' was going on between the *filles de quartier*, and the lady at the Conciergerie with respect to *la belle Anglaise*, who it seemed it was a *nouvelle mariée*, and to catch a glimpse of whom as she left the hotel with her husband for the continuation of their wedding tour—they had all with one accord left their posts above, and collected in the *cour* below.

Charles made his way through the throng, and throwing himself on a chair at the foot of the grand staircase which leads up to the house from the courtyard, he desired a " garçon" to bring him an ice and to make haste about it.

" Halloa, Lethbridge.   Where have you been ? You look rather warm than otherwise, my dear fellow !" cried a voice from the gallery above, and looking up, Charles perceived a young man leaning over the parapet, in whose features the reader would have recognized those of Sir George Hamilton, who was also in Paris, on his way back to England from Switzerland, where he had been touring for a short time with a friend.

" I've been wandering about," answered Lethbridge, " and trying to keep cool, but I can't say that I have exactly succeeded.   Do you know anything about that fellow Mortimer ?"

Sir George came down the stairs and took possession of a vacant chair by Charles's side.

" No, I haven't seen him at all to-day," he said. " But I say, Lethbridge, you've just missed the departure of the bride and bridegroom.   They hadn't been gone two minutes when you came in. Everybody in the place turned out to have a look at them."

"What bride and bridegroom?" enquired Charles, putting down his empty glass on the table, and calling to the waiter for another ice. "I didn't know there was any such interesting couple in the place."

"Oh, you may always reckon on meeting two or three sets of them in this house at any time of the year," rejoined the other, laughing. "These only arrived yesterday from England, and were married the day before, I imagine. They are going up the Rhine for their honey-moon, and only took this place on their way."

"What was the name? Did you hear it?"

"Yes. The Howards were talking about them just now, when I was in their room. They knew him. His name is Graham."

"Scotch, I suppose," remarked Charles with a yawn. "Was she nice-looking? Did you see her?"

"An uncommon pretty girl, I believe. I only just caught a glimpse of her as they came down the stairs, but that is what they tell me."

"Indeed! And do you know who she was?"

"She was a Miss Lennox; and by the way, Lethbridge, I think you must know something about them. Is not Wentmore, her father's living, near you in Southshire?"

"Wentmore!—Lennox!" cried Charles, starting up, as if he had been shot, "Impossible.

Who told you so? I should have heard of it. There must be some mistake."

"My dear fellow, I only know what Mrs. Howard told me. I thought she might be a relation of my friend, Ferdy Lennox, and it was for that reason that I asked if she had anything to do with the Wentmore family. Mrs. Howard said she had heard Mr. Graham say that his wife, (who was his cousin by the way,) had lived at Wentmore in Southshire, and as I knew Lennox had a sister, that settled it."

"Yes. It can be no other," muttered Charles. "You did not hear her Christian name, I suppose?"

"I did not. But now I think of it, Mrs. Howard showed me a note which was lying on her table, and which she said the bride had just sent her, and the signature was 'B. Graham.' So it must be something beginning with B," answered Sir George.

"I have known the Lennoxes all my life," said Charles, with an assumption of indifference, "and I am sorry I did not see her. But it does not signify, and I shall hear all about it from home before long, I daresay."

Then nodding to Sir George, he slowly mounted the staircase, and took the way to his own room.

The young baronet looked after him, and gave utterance to a low whistle as he did so. "Poor fellow!" he said to himself. "It looks very much

as if there was something in the news I have just
given him, which he didn't quite like. I shouldn't
wonder if he had been in love with her himself.
Eh bien! telle est la vie!"   And lighting a cigar, Sir
George betook himself to the Palais Royal, where,
for the next half hour or so, he amused himself
by wandering up and down the arcades, admiring
the pretty things which were offered for sale, and
the pretty girls who sold them.

In the meanwhile, Mr. Charles Lethbridge had
shut himself up in his room, "Au Troisième,"
and was pacing up and down it in no enviable
frame of mind. There could be no doubt that
Blanche Lennox was married then, and to that
odious cousin of hers, whom he had seen at
Christmas when the private theatricals took place
at Lethbridge. He remembered hearing something of the kind talked of, as likely to take place,
one day when he was calling at the Oaks, but he
had taken no notice of it, and set it down as a
piece of gossip, originating probably with the
people who were alluding to it.   "How could
I be such a fool!" he exclaimed angrily to himself.   "Such an ass, as to suppose that she would
not be snapped up by some one, even if this Scotch
cousin, (be d——d to him!) had not come in her
way! But, how very odd of Cissy not to say a
word about it, when she must have known. I
will write to her directly. Stay—I will go myself and hear all about it at once. I shall just

have time to do so, and get back to London when my leave is up. As to staying here, that is impossible."

Yes, it was impossible, after what he had just heard, that he should remain quiet anywhere. In one word, Charles Lethbridge loved Blanche Lennox, had done so ever since he had said goodbye to his private tutor and his books, and had returned home for a few weeks ere joining his regiment, shortly before our story began. He had not seen her for some time, and when they met accidentally one day, soon after his return, he felt that he had never known how beautiful, how altogether lovely and lovable she was, till then. But from that moment he had resolved, that, if possible, he would win her for his own, and ever since, he had worshipped the very ground she trod upon. He had never breathed a word on the subject to her or to anyone. He had always thought of her as so safe at Wentmore, so completely out of the way of the world and of others, who might be attracted by her in the same way as he had been himself, that with this conviction he had remained content. He had not heard of the visit to London this season, or else he would not have felt so easy on that score, but Cissy, who usually kept him *au fait* with regard to all that passed at Lethbridge and its neighbourhood, had not been so good a correspondent of late, and he having been on the sick list for more than a fortnight before getting his leave, had not himself met Lady Frances and her daughter at parties, as he otherwise must have done.

No sooner had he resolved upon returning at once to England, than he set to work to make the necessary preparations for his departure. He had plenty of time to catch the evening mail to Calais, and he determined to cross by the boat that night. His next care was to find Mortimer, and acquaint him with his determination, but this he was not able to do so easily. " Meester Mortimerre," the waiter who spoke English, informed him, " had gone off to the Bois de Boulogne with some friends, and had left word for M. 'Lethbreedge' that he should be back for the seven o'clock *table d'hôte*, but he need not expect him sooner." Charles, therefore, ordered some dinner for himself in the " Restaurant," and scribbled a line which he desired might be given to Mr. Mortimer on his return, acquainting him with his reason for leaving Paris so suddenly, which he alleged to be a desire to " see the governor at Lethbridge upon some business matters, which he should just have time to do before his leave was up, if he set off at once."

When Mr. Mortimer took his place at the *table d'hôte* that evening, he glanced down the table, and seeing Sir George Hamilton within speaking distance on the opposite side, he told him that Lethbridge had gone off and left him to his own devices for the next two or three days, "when I shall have to return to London myself," he added. "I hope you will stay till I go? I had no idea Lethbridge was likely to cut off like that. It must have been a very sudden resolve. He never said a word to me about it last night."

Sir George laughed, and shrugged his shoulders. "He's a funny fellow," he said. "I think he was rather upset today altogether. I'll tell you what I suspect was the reason bye and bye!"

The day following, as Cissy Lethbridge was returning through the park to her home, from visiting a poor woman in the village, she saw a fly approaching the house by the drive, and wondered who its occupants could be. It was too early for visitors, being only half past twelve by her watch, and she did not remember hearing that anyone was expected to luncheon. But it soon passed out of sight, and she did not disturb herself further on the subject. Cissy was in a very bright and happy mood. The world from her point of view, and everybody in it, was praiseworthy and delightful. Nature seemed to attune itself to her cheerful frame of mind, and everything was *couleur de rose* for her. As she tripped along the path which led by a short cut to the house, she looked round her every now and then with a smile which spoke of the gladness of heart within.

She passed through the garden, and stepped into the drawing-room through a window which

opened upon the terrace. As she did so, the
sound of a familiar voice struck upon her ear. It
was that of her brother Charles. It came through
an opposite door, which led into a corridor communicating with the entrance hall.

In one moment, Cissy was amongst the group
which had already collected round him. The
Colonel and Mrs. Lethbridge had been in the
garden with their Vicar's wife and daughter, who
were paying a morning visit, and the Colonel had
caught sight of his son's face as the fly drove up
to the door.

Cissy, of course, reiterated the questions the
others had been asking, as to " Where he came
from ? and how long he was going to stay?" She
was so delighted, and they had not expected him
in the least.

" I was so utterly tired of Paris. An awfully
stupid place at this time of year, and as hot as the
infernal regions. I had two or three days of leave
left, and thought I might just as well have a look
at you here."

Charles repeated this a dozen times in reply to
all the exclamations of surprise and delight which
met him, and everyone ·was quite satisfied. He
was a dear good fellow for coming at all, and they
must make the most of him while he was there.
Cissy had a hundred things to ask about Paris,
and what people were wearing there just now.
"Now, Charley, don't pretend you don't know,

but tell me," she said, as she and her mother, (Mrs. and Miss Lawrence having taken their leave,) carried him off into the drawing-room, and placed him on a sofa between them. The Colonel following, and telling them that he had hurried on the luncheon as he was sure Charley must be ravenous, and that it would be ready directly.

"I did not know Cissy was such a one for the fashions," laughed Charles, as she looked up in his face eagerly, awaiting his reply. "I suspect you have been taking a leaf out of Mad Vernon's book, Miss? And as to asking me, you could not get hold of a worse person for telling you anything about what people have on, especially ladies, for I never know by any chance."

Cissy looked disappointed, and her father and mother laughed.

"Ah! but when young ladies get in a sort of a way engaged,—*in a sort of a way*, mind you," said the Colonel, "they are apt to think more of such things than formerly. Eh, Miss Cissy?" and the old soldier chucked his daughter under her chin as he spoke.

"Engaged!" exclaimed Charles. "To whom? Not really? Why you have none of you ever said a word about it?"

"No, no, it is a secret at present, and besides, we do not call it an engagement," said Mrs. Lethbridge. "But Cissy shall tell you herself, and I am sure you will be very pleased."

"Come into the conservatory, Ciss, and let us have the whole history from beginning to end. I don't even know the name of my brother-in-law that is to be, as yet! He's a deuced lucky fellow whoever he is, that's all I can tell him."

So saying, Charles got up and passed through the glass door, which led into the conservatory at the further end of the room. Cissy only lingered behind to kiss her mother, and whisper, "Of course he ought to know," and then she followed him into a recess, where a seat was charmingly placed near a back ground of orange trees.

"Well Cissy?" said her brother, pulling her down beside him, and giving her a kiss as he did so. "Who is it?"

"Ferdinand Lennox."

Cissy's voice was very low, and she turned away her head to conceal the blushes which suffused her cheeks and brow.

"You don't say so!" exclaimed Charles, and then, instead of the congratulations, and expressions of satisfaction and interest, which Cissy had prepared herself to hear, he went on in a hurried excited tone. "I do think, Cissy, that it was unkind of you, especially as you must have known so well what was going on at Wentmore, to keep me in ignorance about this marriage. I can understand your being chiefly taken up with your own affairs, but it is not as if we had been strangers, and, of course, I—I" here Charles stammered and became rather incoherent. "You might have felt certain that any idea of the sort concerning her, would have been of interest to me. Why did you not tell me?"

Cissy stared at her brother in amazement.

"What marriage are you speaking of? I don't understand you," she said.

"Nonsense," cried Charles, impatiently. "Do you mean to say, you do not know that Blanche Lennox is married?" And he got up and stood before his sister, awaiting her reply.

She looked perfectly bewildered.

"Blanche!—Blanche Lennox!" she repeated. "My dear Charley, what could have put such an idea into your head? *Married?* Of course I should have known it, if it had been true. She is no more married than I am."

"That shows all you know about it. I tell you she is. She has married that cousin of hers, Mr. Graham, and they were in Paris only yesterday, at the very same hotel as myself. I know it as a fact. And they have gone up the Rhine or somewhere, on their wedding tour."

It was now Cissy's turn to be impatient, and she started up from her seat half angrily, exclaiming,

"I don't believe a word of it! There must be some mistake.—Mamma!" And she burst into the drawing-room in quest of Mrs. Lethbridge as she spoke. "Do you hear what Charley says? Tell him it is all nonsense. I never heard of such a thing!"

But Mrs. Lethbridge was not there. The room was empty, and Cissy was about to run in search of her, when her brother who had followed her, laid his hand on her shoulder.

"Don't be silly, Ciss, but listen to me. How many daughters has Mr. Lennox of Wentmore? How many sisters has Ferdinand? You know as well as I do, that Blanche is the only one, and George Hamilton, who heard all about it from some friends of Graham's who were staying in the hotel, told me that she was *the daughter of Mr. Lennox of Wentmore.* There is no possibility of a doubt, and besides that, Hamilton himself saw a note from her to Mrs. Howard, signed, 'B. Graham,' and you know it was reported everywhere last spring, that she was engaged to him. Don't you remember my mother being asked if it was true, over and over again?"

"You say she was in Paris yesterday, at the Hotel de Louvre? All I can say is, that if she could get married in London and arrive in Paris the same morning, she is a wonderful person. Here is a note which I had from her by this very post, and which was written in London *yesterday,* and if you will look at it you will see for yourself that it is signed, 'Blanche Lennox,' as plainly as possible."

Cissy had crossed the room whilst speaking,

and opened an escritoire at the further end of it,
from which she extracted a letter, which she
held up to her brother in triumph.

He snatched it out of her hand, devoured it
with his eyes, and then suddenly seizing Cissy
in his arms, he nearly smothered her with kisses.

"Charley! Charley! be quiet," cried she,
laughing, and struggling to free herself from his
embrace. "Are you mad?"

"Yes, I think I am mad," he returned. "Mad
with joy,—and you are a darling for showing me
that letter!" And again he caught hold of her,
and kissed her repeatedly.

"Charley!" she exclaimed, tearing herself away
from him at last, and retreating a few steps, whilst
she fastened a look of keen inquiry upon his face.
"Charley! you don't mean?—Why, I do believe—
Oh! I am so glad!" and then, in her turn, Miss
Cissy sprang to her brother and returned the
kisses he had bestowed upon her with interest.
Mr. Charles did not attempt to deny the soft im-
peachment, which her incoherent exclamations had
implied, but coloured up and laughed, and said
he thought she was the more mad of the two.

"I am *so glad!*" repeated Cissy, seating herself on her brother's knee, and looking up into his
face with a radiant smile. "I understand now
why you were in such a state, at the thought of
her being married! I suppose I have satisfied
you about that anyhow?"

"Well, I suppose you have," answered Charles, whose countenance reflected the satisfaction of her own. "But, still, I can't quite understand it all. There must be some wonderful mistake somewhere. Hamilton was so positive about the name, and there is no other Miss Lennox of Wentmore."

"Why,—yes there is!" cried Cissy, springing up, as if struck by a sudden inspiration. "How stupid of us not to think of that sooner. There is Miss Barbara Lennox, who has lived at Wentmore so long—ever since her father died, you know—their cousin, and Mr. Graham's cousin too! Why Charley! how stupid of you not to think of her!" And in her superior wisdom, Miss Cissy drew · herself up and regarded her brother with a look of surprise.

"Of course! That explains it all," exclaimed he, with an air of conviction. "What an idiot I must have been not to remember her. B. stands for Barbara, as well as Blanche, and as to their saying she was Mr. Lennox's daughter, that was a very natural mistake for strangers to make, especially if they knew he had one, and had never heard of his niece. But, surely, Cissy, you must have known of the likelihood of such a thing? Has Blanche never said anything about it? Surely she must have told you if there was an idea of anything of the sort?"

"No; she has never said a word, nor has—nor has Ferdinand," said Cissy, blushing. "I can't make it out. But if it was Barbara Lennox, you must have known her directly? She is not in the least like Blanche."

"I never saw her. I knew nothing about their being at the hotel till yesterday morning, when I came back from a walk, and they had that moment left. They had arrived the night before, having been married in England in the morning."

"But did not Sir George Hamilton describe her to you?"

"He had only caught a glimpse of her, and did not know whether she was dark or fair, or what she was like really, in the least. The Howards told him she was nice-looking, and that was all he knew about it."

"Well, I must say I am astonished," said Cissy, "at their never having told us a word about it. Lady Frances and Blanche and Mr. Lennox are in town, you know, and Barbara went off into Warwickshire, to Leamington I think, on a visit, when they went up to London. Perhaps—it is just possible—that they did not know what was going to happen themselves? That is not likely, but I can't think why Blanche—why they none of them, ever hinted at such a thing being in any way even probable!"

"What are you talking about?" asked Mrs. Lethbridge, at that moment entering the room.

"What is it Blanche never hinted at?" And she patted Cissy fondly on the cheek as she spoke.

" Oh, mamma !" exclaimed Cissy, " only fancy! Barbara Lennox is married, and to Mr. Graham, their cousin, you know." And then she told all that she had heard from her brother on the subject, Mrs. Lethbridge giving utterance to various exclamations of surprise, as she proceeded.

"But that is not all," Cissy added. "I have found out something, mamma, about a certain young gentleman who was nearly out of his mind, because he thought it was Miss *Blanche* Lennox who was married instead of Miss Barbara !"

" Cissy ! don't be foolish. Hold your tongue," cried Charles, laughing, and putting his hand before his sister's mouth. " Don't attend to her nonsense, mother, but let us go into luncheon. I am sure it must be ready by this time."

Mrs. Lethbridge smiled and shook her head. " You are a pair of naughty children," she said, and as the butler just then came in to say that lunch was on the table, she led the way into the dining-room.

" I tell you what, Ciss," whispered Charles to his sister, as they followed their mother arm in arm, " I shall be off to London the first thing tomorrow, and you may guess where I shall go when I get there."

" Darling, darling Blanche !" returned Cissy, giving his arm an expressive squeeze. " There is no one I would rather have for a sister in the whole world, and she will be doubly my sister now, you know!"

Charles laughed and muttered something about "its not being so certain as all that comes to," and then began to scold her for never having told him the Lennoxes were in town. "Although I went nowhere else, of course I should have called on them," he said, "and certainly I should not have gone tearing off to Paris in that way, the moment I was out of the doctor's clutches."

"No one would think that you had been very bad, to look at you now, my boy!" observed the Colonel, filling his wine glass and nodding to his son across the table. "Your trip across the channel has set you on your legs again, there's no doubt about that."

"He was quite right to come and have a peep at us though, before returning to his duty," said Mrs. Lethbridge, looking with fond admiration at her handsome son. "Lethbridge air always set him up, when he had anything the matter with him, at school or at any time, and I think he looks better than when he first came, now."

"Nasty, deceitful boy," whispered Cissy, who was sitting next her brother. "As if I didn't know the reason you came over in such a hurry indeed! And poor mamma thinks it was for the pleasure of seeing us!"

Charles gave her a pinch in return for this

little speech, and assured his mother, that it was the hope of getting a week or so's longer stay at home, that originated many of his boyish maladies, he believed. Upon which the Colonel laughed, and said, he had "No doubt of it,—the young dog!"

That night, when Mrs. Lethbridge was alone with her lord, she asked him how he would like a double alliance between the Lennox family and their own, and she told him that hearing a report of Blanche's marriage, their boy had come over to ascertain the truth of it, and that he was so anxious to secure her for himself, she believed he was going up to town the next morning, on purpose to hear whether there was any hope for him or not. "I know how pleased you are at the prospect of Cissy's marriage, and how highly you think of them all," she said, looking up into the Colonel's face, "and a sweeter girl than Blanche does not exist, I am sure of that. She is the wife of all others I would choose for my Charley, pure-minded, lovely, well-born, and I think they will be equally fortunate if it can be arranged. He is worthy of her, dear fellow, indeed there are very few *I* should think good enough for him!"

"Well, I confess you have taken me somewhat by surprise," returned the Colonel, after a moment's pause. "So that is what the young rascal is up to, is it? She is as nice, as good and as pretty a girl as ever I set eyes upon, there's no doubt about that. The Lennoxes are a family one must feel proud to be connected with, and the double alliance would be no drawback in my eyes,—far from it. Charley will be a lucky fellow if he gets her, that's my opinion, and almost as fortunate as his father was before him."

So saying, the gallant old gentleman stooped down and kissed his wife's still smooth and comely cheek, with fond affection.

The next morning, our young guardsman took leave of his family, and was in London before one o'clock, having had a private interview with his father beforehand, which Cissy divined from his animated countenance as he came out of the Colonel's sanctum, had been no unsatisfactory one. He hurried to his barracks immediately on his arrival in town, where he deposited his traps, and then throwing himself into a hansom, desired the driver to take him as fast as possible to No. — Grosvenor Square.

CHAPTER II.

Mr. Lennox was very angry, when first informed of his daughter's wish to become a Roman Catho-lic. To Ferdinand, had been committed the task of communicating to him the unpleasant tidings, Lady Frances having written to her youngest son, imploring him to hasten up to town, as soon as she had herself become aware of the state of Blanche's feelings. The father's displeasure was chiefly directed against Gerald. This was *his* doing, he was certain, notwithstanding his positive commands that no attempt at proselytising was to be made with either of his other children by his renegade son,—but what were promises worth, made by anyone under the thumb of the Jesuits? Of course he was dispensed from observing them, and he had no doubt been inoculating Blanche, with all the "pernicious nonsense" he had himself imbibed, in his letters, if he had not been able to do so otherwise. In vain Ferdinand, who was himself utterly bewildered and shocked by this resolution on his sister's part, assured him that he was certain Gerald had had nothing to do with it, he might as well have talked to the winds, and Mr. Lennox declared that he would write to Gerald and tell him what he thought of his conduct. Then, again, his anger would change into sorrow, and hiding his face in his hands, he would lean back in his chair, and sobbing aloud, ejaculate, " Oh, Ferdinand, I cannot bear it. She was my pride,—my darling,—my only daughter, and to lose her too ! It is too much !"

And poor Ferdinand was a sorry comforter. He had been utterly unsuspicious of the blow that was in store for him. When his mother's hastily written and somewhat incoherent letter, acquainting him with what Blanche had told her, reached him, he had taken it for granted there was some mistake, and that he should find on inquiry that some particular development of ' Catholic' doctrine which the High Church party held in common with Rome, and which Blanche might have broached, had frightened Lady Frances into believing that she was on the point of secession. But when he found not only from her, but from his sister also, that the latter was actually bent upon becoming a Roman Catholic, he was completely taken aback and confounded for a time.

How it had all come about, was what he could not understand. To reason with her, he saw was

out of the question ; she was too unwell and unhappy to enter into any discussion on the subject,
and he did not attempt to press one upon her.
He merely said, " Blanche, my darling, is this
true ?" and she had answered, " Yes, Ferdinand,
it is, but do not speak to me about it now, only
try and comfort poor papa and mamma. It is
their suffering which breaks my heart, and I can
bear anything better than to see them so miserable."

And in the midst of all this sorrow on Blanche's
account, came the news of Barbara's intended
marriage. She had written once or twice since
her arrival at Leamington, and in one of her letters had mentioned that Sidney Graham was at
the hotel there for a few days, and that she saw
him very often, but never a word of what was im-
pending. The morning of Ferdinand's arrival in
town, Mr. Lennox received a note from his nephew,
informing him that although no doubt he would
be surprised, he hoped that it would not displease
him to learn that his cousin Barbara had consented to become his wife, and that the wedding,
which was to be a very quiet one, would take place
as soon as possible at Leamington. Mr. Lennox
at once took the letter to his wife, and his first
question to her was, " Has Barbara written to you
on the subject ?"

" No," answered Lady Frances. " It is most
astonishing. She seldom writes to me, but in

her letters to Blanche she has never hinted at such a thing. I never was more surprised in my life !"

"Did you know that it was in any way likely to happen? Did you ever notice anything between them, which might have led you to think they were attached to each other ?"

"Certainly not, or else I should have told you. They always seemed on a very proper cousinly footing together, but nothing more. I cannot make it out, my dear Reginald, at all."

"Well," added the Rector, walking out of the room, "I shall write to Master Sidney, and I think you had better do the same to the young lady. Why they are in such a hurry to be married I can't think, and I do not at all approve of the non-mention of settlements. I think I shall go down to Leamington myself, and have a talk with them both about it. She will expect me to give her away, of course. Poor Alice and Geof.! to think that their children should come together in this way! but I do not approve of cousins marrying as a rule."

And then he went off to write to his nephew, whilst Lady Frances sought Blanche and Lady Margaret, to acquaint them with what she had heard. Blanche's amazement was even greater than her mother's had been, for reasons of which Lady Frances knew nothing. She had never mentioned the fact of Sidney's proposal to herself, to any one excepting Barbara, she had always intended to tell her mother about it some day, but other matters had occupied her thoughts of late, and she had not felt inclined to enter upon the subject. But now, the recollection of that scene, of his passionate declaration of love, and of his subsequent anger, came back upon her with startling force. And how was it possible, she asked herself, that Barbara, knowing as she did what had passed between them, could have accepted Sidney afterwards? She was in ignorance of his having already proposed to and been accepted by Barbara, before she had told her of his previous offer to herself. Barbara had never hinted a word on the subject either then or since, and it was this utter silence on her part, which puzzled Blanche most of all.

"I must write to her at once, mamma," she said, her voice trembling, and the tears filling her eyes as she spoke. "It is so odd of Bibi not to have told us herself. I hope she is happy, but I never thought she cared for Sidney so particularly. I wish I could see her,—I can scarcely believe it is true."

Lady Frances noticed her emotion, but attributed it to the weakness produced by the agitating scenes she had recently gone through, concerning her religious difficulties.

"Poor child," she said to Lady Margaret, as Blanche sat down at the writing-table. "She is so easily upset now. I am sorry I told her so abruptly, but Barbara's conduct in keeping us all so entirely in the dark, is equally puzzling to me. She never was thoroughly open and confidential with me about anything, but she and Blanche were such great allies, that I cannot understand her not having told her. Your uncle wishes me to write to her, and I shall do so, but I shall tell her that after having been to us as one of our own children for so long, I think she certainly ought to have intimated the likelihood of such a thing, so that we might in some sort have been prepared for its announcement."

"I have seen so little of either of them," observed Lady Margaret, "that I cannot say whether I think them suited to each other or not. If it was not for their being first cousins, however, I suppose there could be no real objection to the marriage in any way? She has some money of her own, I believe, and he is well off?"

"Oh yes," answered Lady Frances, "as far as that goes, it is all very well, and they may be very comfortable and happy, but they each of them have a temper, and I should not have thought he was the sort of man to be attracted by a girl of Barbara's disposition. Indeed, I never thought that he took much notice of her, but it only shows that one never can tell."

When Ferdinand arrived that evening, and had ascertained the truth of what his mother had informed him about Blanche, he was also told of the news which that morning's post had brought respecting Barbara. "However, we shall say nothing about it at present to anyone," said Lady Frances, "until we have heard from her. I think it would be better not. She ought to have written to me, it was not treating me with proper respect or attention, not to do so. To tell you the truth, Ferdinand, I always thought she cared for you more than anybody, and I had no idea that she had the slightest *penchant* for Sidney."

"Cared for me?" said Ferdinand, smiling. "As a sister, perhaps, but nothing more, though I confess that I had no suspicion of Sid's being in such favour. Altogether, it has taken me quite by surprise."

This was Blanche's letter to Barbara.

"My Darling Bibi,

"I suppose I ought to congratulate you? but I am so astonished I hardly know what to say. Sidney's letter has taken us all so utterly by surprise. And what both mamma and I feel is, that you deserve a scolding for not having written to us yourself. I do think it was not behaving quite well to me, dearest Bibi, your own sister, not to say one word about it in any of your letters, and I cannot help wondering whether you are perfectly happy? Do you really love him very much ? Forgive me, for asking such a question, but I cannot help it. If you tell me you do, then I shall be satisfied. Of course, he never could have cared for me, and I wish now that I had not told you, dearest Bibi, what passed between us. It was foolish of me to believe he was in earnest. I was not well, and I believe he frightened me; at another time I should have seen, I daresay, that he was joking, and only have laughed! Write to me and tell me everything, just as if you were speaking to me. Surely, there can be no necessity for hurrying on the marriage so? Sidney says it is to take place very soon. You will come back to Wentmore first of all, will you not? I long to see you again. God bless you, dearest Bibi. Remember that I am always your own loving sister,

" BLANCHE."

And this was Barbara's answer.

" DEAREST BLANCHE,

"You must have thought it odd of me not to tell you of my engagement, but Sidney's letter informed you that we were going to be married, and there was nothing more to say. We are both of age, and can please ourselves. I shall not return to Wentmore, and I do not know when I shall see any of you again, as there are very good shops here, and I can get all I want without even going to London. I hope you have been enjoying yourself. My love to my uncle and aunt.

" Your affectionate cousin,

" BARBARA LENNOX."

Blanche was both startled and shocked. She felt at once that something was wrong, but if Barbara refused her confidence, she could do nothing to help her. Barbara also wrote a few lines to Lady Frances in answer to her note, in which she said that she hoped her uncle would not think of coming down to give her away, as he had proposed doing in his letter to Sidney. The gentleman in whose house she was staying, and who was a distant connection of her mother's family would do that. No day as yet was fixed for the wedding, and she had only one thing to beg, which was, that they would say nothing about it to anyone just yet, as she had no time for answering congratulatory letters, and she did not want to be troubled by any, so she would consider it a favour if they would remember this.

Blanche did not show her note from Barbara to Mr. Lennox, she thought he would be even more vexed by its tone, than by the rejection of his offer to give her away, which annoyed him considerably. "I shall certainly not go, if I am not wanted," he said to his wife, after reading Barbara's letter to her, ". and by all means do not tell people about it, since she would rather we did not do so. They seem both disposed to treat us somewhat cavalierly, and if they prefer keeping it quiet, I don't see why we should publish it. I think Sidney might have consulted me before speaking to her, but young people are so very independent now-a-days, that I suppose there is nothing wonderful in his not having done that."

Blanche wrote again to Barbara. This sudden engagement between her and Sidney, coupled with Barbara's reticence on the subject, had something mysterious in it which troubled her. She did not really think that Sidney had been otherwise than in earnest when he proposed to her, although she had made light of it in writing to Barbara, and this immediate transfer of his affections to another, she could not understand. She felt that it augured ill for Barbara's future happiness, and yet, as she knew all about his real or pretended attachment to herself, and chose to accept him in spite of it, it was, of course, her own affair, and she, Blanche, had no power, even if she had the wish, to interfere. Still, the whole affair was a perplexity to her, and it saddened her, and just now she had sadness enough to contend with on her own account.

Lady Frances and Ferdinand agreed that they would allow a day or two to pass, after this business of Barbara's engagement had transpired, before saying anything to Mr. Lennox about Blanche.

She, poor child, recognised, and at the same time, shrank from the necessity of informing him of her intense desire to be admitted into the Catholic Church. She explained this to Ferdinand with tears in her eyes.

"You know, dearest," he answered, "I would not say anything to pain you for the world, but I do not like to hear you speak as though you had never been in the Catholic Church. If your heart is set upon joining the Church of *Rome*, I can understand your not being content to remain out of her communion, but, you know," he added gently, "*we* consider ourselves as part of the One Catholic Church, and it distresses me to see that you have apparently forgotten that."

"I feel," said Blanche, with an effort, for it pained her inexpressibly to find herself opposed in argument to Ferdinand, for the first time in her life, "that in being admitted into communion with the Church of Rome, I am only returning to the Church of my Baptism, if ever I was baptized, and my reason for leaving the Church of England now, is because I believe that she is not a part of the One Catholic Church *at all*, and that as long as I remain in her, I am out of visible communion with the True Church of Christ. You must see, dearest Ferdinand, that this is my only standing ground, and that to recognize the Catholicity in any sense, of the Church I am leaving, would be simply suicidal."

Ferdinand made no answer. He told himself
that it was useless to say anything when his sister
was evidently primed with arguments by the
priests; and pressing one long fervent kiss upon
her forehead in silence, he quitted the room.

"Ask your mother to speak to me," Mr. Lennox said, as Ferdinand was leaving him, after the
interview in which he had acquainted his father
with Blanche's resolution.

When Lady Frances came to him, she found
her husband pacing the room with agitated strides.
Going up to him, she took hold of his arm, and
commanding her voice with an effort, she said,
"Calm yourself, Reginald, and do not be angry
with that poor unhappy child. She does not
know what she is saying, and only wants to have
the truth quietly put before her, to see how wrong
and mistaken she is. You can do this better
than anyone, but if you are severe you will only
frighten her and do no good. Take my advice,
and be very gentle with her. She is over-excited,
and not herself just now. A little quiet reasoning
will convince her that she has been deceived by
the priests, and in time she will see for herself
how false all their arguments are."

"Deceived by the priests!" exclaimed Mr. Lennox, "that is what angers me so! How did any
priests ever get hold of her? Where and when
did she place herself within reach of their arguments and deceits? What have you been about,

Fanny, that the child has been able to fall into the hands of Roman Catholic priests, or have anything to do with them? That is what I don't understand, and what I can't make out, and Ferdinand is as much surprised at it as I am."

Lady Frances turned from him, and sinking into a chair, burst into tears.

"You cannot blame me, Reginald, more than I blame myself, but I was so utterly unsuspicious, I trusted her so thoroughly. It seems," continued Lady Frances, as Mr. Lennox, moved as he always was by the sight of his wife's tears, placed himself by her side, and took one of her hands tenderly in his own—"It seems that she has been constantly in the habit of visiting the Church in Farm Street, although neither Margaret nor I knew anything about it. To what she has seen and heard there, as well as to the Roman Catholic books she has been reading and using of late, may be ascribed the mischief that has been done. All we can hope for now, is to arrest its progress before it is too late."

"Ferdinand tells me that she refuses to listen to any arguments, or replies to them in a manner which shows that she will only look at the subject from one point of view, and that she reiterates her determination to become a Romanist at all costs. I always thought Blanche was a sensible child, Fanny, and what she can see to like in their mummeries, or how she can bring herself to believe all that farrago of nonsense about the Virgin, and the Saints, and Purgatory and Indulgences, I can't imagine!" And the Rector with a fresh burst of indignation, jumped up, and began again walking up and down the room.

Whilst this scene was passing between his father and mother, Ferdinand was having a conversation on the same subject with his uncle in a room below. Lord Norwood had at first been incredulous when informed by his daughter of the new convert to Popery in his sister's family, but when Blanche herself had assured him that she could never be happy until she had become a Catholic, every other feeling had been absorbed in one of pity and concern for the " poor misguided child" herself, as he considered her, and for her father and mother and brother as well. He had come upon Ferdinand unawares, and had found him in an agony of grief, which for the moment he seemed unable to control. " Oh, Uncle Norwood!" he cried, " I thought when Gerald left us, that my heart must have broken, but Blanche's going too, is worse, far worse. How are we, any of us, to bear it?" And he laid his head on his arm which rested on a table, and sobbed aloud.

" My dear, dear boy," said Lord Norwood, controlling with some difficulty his own emotion, " God knows I feel for you. But do not give way like this. Remember that your father and mother depend mainly on you at this moment for comfort and support. Surely, it is not so utterly hopeless? No one has more influence over poor Blanche than yourself, she loves you so deeply and truly. Bye and bye, when she is calmer and able to listen to reason, you will convince her of her folly, and she will attend to you, when she would not to another."

"I do not think it," answered Ferdinand, despondingly. "By some unhappy chance she became possessed in the winter of some books which were intended, I believe, for Gerald, and their onesided view of things she has adopted as the true one. You do not know Blanche as I do, Uncle Norwood, but if once convinced that the Church of Rome was the only True Church, and the only safe one to belong to,—nothing would deter her from entering it."

"But how can a woman,—a child like that,— pretend to set up her own opinion, against that of so many wiser and older persons than herself?" exclaimed Lord Norwood. "She must know that the claims and pretensions of Rome, have been met and confuted over and over again? She has read her English History,—she can't suppose that the Reformation was brought about for no reason under the sun? By heaven! it is too preposterous after three centuries of deliverance from the bondage of Popery, to find one person after another going back to a system which our ancestors died rather than submit to! If men like Newman and Faber, and others had not led the way, we should not have so many foolish boys and infatuated women following their example now."

"True," said Ferdinand, but not coinciding fully in his uncle's views with regard to the Reformation, he rose from his chair, and by way of changing the conversation, proposed to accompany him to the House, if he was going to walk down.

Accordingly they departed arm in arm, and turning down Charles Street, took their way across Berkeley Square, and along Berkeley Street into the parks.

It was a fine day, and Ferdinand felt in better spirits, as he returned alone, having parted with his uncle at Storeys Gate. The carriage was standing at the door when he reached Grosvenor Square, and his mother was getting into it. Lady Margaret and Blanche were following out of the house, and as soon as the former saw him, she begged him to accompany them. Blanche's veil was drawn down, and she stepped quickly into the carriage without speaking, but Ferdinand fancied from the glimpse he caught of her face that she had been crying. Lady Margaret lingered behind to whisper, " I have persuaded them both to have a drive. They want cheering,—do come !"

Ferdinand hesitated. " Where is my father ?" he said. " He may want me to go out with him."

" He is gone off somewhere with the Dean of

Hexham, who called for him," answered Lady Margaret.

"In that case I shall be delighted," said Ferdinand, and jumping in, he took possession of the vacant seat beside his sister, and the carriage drove off.

That evening, Mr. Lennox had an interview with his daughter, and told her very distinctly that he would not hear of her becoming a Catholic. She was ignorant and deluded, and utterly incapable of forming a correct opinion as to the respective merits of the Church to which she belonged, and of the one she fancied was so superior, but which, as anyone who knew anything about it could tell her, was full of error and corruption; and deceived no one with its pretensions, and groundless assertions of infallibility, but weak men or silly women like herself. The Rector spoke quietly and dispassionately, and as if he considered that having declared his mind on the subject, it was sufficient, and Blanche would understand there was nothing more to be said one way or another.

She listened in silence, and having paused, and waited in vain for some remark in reply from her, her father inquired rather impatiently if she was convinced?

Rising from her seat and coming towards him, she laid one hand on his arm, and looking up into his face, said, "Dearest papa, I am convinced that there is only one course for me to pursue. However it may be for others, it is no longer safe for me to remain in the English Church. I cannot plead invincible ignorance,—I have heard all that is to be said in her favour, and also what is brought against her, and I must do as my conscience bids me, and submit to the Church which is in communion with the Bishop of Rome, the successor of St. Peter."

She was very pale, but she did not tremble, and there was a certain dignity in her manner as she spoke, which impressed her father in spite of himself. Leading her back to her chair, with an air of authority and determination, he said,

"Blanche, this is obstinacy. Listen to me." And standing before her, he repeated his assurance that she knew nothing in reality of what was to be said on the Anglican side, and was utterly deceived as to the real character and tenets of the Roman Church on the other. He gradually worked himself up into a state of great excitement, and spoke loudly and angrily. Blanche said nothing, but sat leaning her head on her hand, in an attitude of deep dejection. At last her father paused, and in a somewhat quieter tone, asked her if at length she was satisfied.

Blanche did not look up or answer, and he repeated the inquiry. Then hastily stooping over her, he took her hand in his. Her head fell forward, and he uttered an exclamation of alarm. She had fainted.

Placing her gently back in the chair, Mr. Lennox rang the bell, and in one moment, in his anxiety, forgot his late asperity and impatience with his darling child. Lord Norwood and his daughter were dining out, and he had requested Lady Frances and Ferdinand to leave him alone with Blanche, but they were on the alert, and the bell had not done ringing before Ferdinand was in the room.

"Do not be frightened, dearest mother," he said, turning to Lady Frances, who was following him down the stairs. "It has been rather too much for her, but she will be better directly." Then with his father's aid, he laid Blanche's inanimate form on the sofa, and restoratives being speedily applied, she soon opened her eyes, and smiled faintly on them all.

Lady Frances looked somewhat reproachfully at her husband. He stooped down and pressed a kiss on Blanche's forehead, then taking his wife by the hand, he whispered, "It was my fault,—I forgot she was not strong, poor darling, but it shall not happen again." Lady Frances thanked him with a smile, and soon after, Blanche pronouncing herself able to go upstairs, she was supported into the drawing-room between her father and brother, and established on a low couch beside her mother's chair. And the rest of the evening passed very quietly, the subject of religion being carefully eschewed by all.

The next morning, Mr. Lennox and Ferdinand had a long and earnest talk together, and the result of it was, that the latter sought Blanche in her room, and throwing his arms round her neck, he whispered, "Make yourself quite happy, my darling. My father wishes to see you, but it is only to tell you that as far as he is concerned, you may be 'received' to-morrow if you like! Come with me. He is waiting for us down stairs."

Blanche was petrified; she looked at her brother as if she scarcely comprehended him. Then without speaking, she followed him into her father's presence.

"Papa!" she exclaimed, in a half-bewildered manner, and going up to him, she hid her face on his shoulder, unable to utter another word.

Mr. Lennox pressed her fondly to his heart.

"God bless you, my child," he said. "Become a Hottentot, if you like,—only remember— *I will not have them make a nun of you.* I will never consent to that."

That evening was a peaceful one at Norwood House. The Earl and Lady Margaret, when they heard the turn affairs had taken, on the whole approved, and the latter whispered to Ferdinand her belief that "Now that opposition was withdrawn, he would see that Blanche was in no such great hurry to become a Papist, and would perhaps change her mind after all." Lord Norwood laid aside his anti-Roman feeling for the nonce, and declared that for his part he thought "a good Catholic had as fair a chance for the next world, as a good Protestant," a statement which drew a grimace from Ferdinand, whose eye met his cousin's at the moment. Mr. Lennox and Lady Frances were not happy, but did not say much, and hoped that all would turn out for the best. Contention with their children was at all times a thing so utterly repugnant to their feelings, that anything seemed better than that.

The next day, after breakfast, Lady Frances went upstairs, and presently returned with her bonnet on; an unusual thing with her at so early an hour. Lord Norwood and Ferdinand were waiting for her in the hall, and as soon as she appeared, the latter opened the door, and Lady Frances taking her brother's arm, they all went out together. Mr. Lennox watched their departure from the dining-room window, but it was unobserved by Blanche and Lady Margaret, who were still sitting at the table.

The three took their way to Hill Street, and notwithstanding its being an unusual hour for morning visits in that fashionable locale, they evidently had one in view. The Jesuit Fathers, attached to the Church in Farm Street, lived at No. —, and it was at that house they stopped.

On inquiring for Father Clifford, they were at once admitted, and for a long time remained closeted with the man who had obtained so strong an influence, over both Gerald and Blanche.

When they left, and slowly took their way back to Grosvenor Square, they agreed that their darling could be in no better hands, if she was to be guided by a Roman Catholic priest at all, so favourable an impression had he made upon them.

And he, for his part, knelt long and earnestly in prayer, after they had left him, on behalf of these simple but misguided souls, who might themselves be won, he trusted, by the example of one so sweet and saintly as his latest convert.

CHAPTER III.

FERDINAND's earnest solicitations had prevailed with his father so far, that he had consented, although not without great reluctance, to offer no further opposition to Blanche's wish. Ferdinand's tender love for his sister had determined him, when he saw how thoroughly bent she was upon entering the Roman Catholic Church, to make smooth, if possible, the way for her to do so, and remove such difficulties in her path as might still present themselves. Not that he was in any way reconciled, himself, to the step she meditated. To him, with his firm faith in the truth and sufficiency of the English Church, the thought of her leaving its communion was one of unmingled pain. But Ferdinand's nature was a thoroughly unselfish one. At first, his own misery at losing her (for he knew that it would be losing her in great measure) had overpowered every other consideration, and he had urged every motive he could think of, whenever an opportunity presented itself, without absolutely tormenting his sister, to induce her to change her mind. But when he saw that she was inflexible, when he became alarmed, (as he soon did,) for her health, and felt that her strength might give way altogether under the struggle, he resolved to forget himself and his own feelings in the matter entirely. He did not think she was imperilling her salvation by joining the Church of Rome; he could not, consistently with his own principles, think that; and so great was his dread of the effect a prolonged contention with them all might have upon Blanche's delicate frame, that he resolved to obtain, if possible, his father's consent to her change. Mr. Lennox, as we know, idolized his daughter, and had himself begun to feel uneasy on the score of her health. Ferdinand, therefore, found his task an easier one than he had anticipated, and great as was the Rector's horror and dislike of "Popery and Priests," he gave way at last, and Ferdinand was told he might bring his sister down, and she should have permission to be "received" if she wished it, from his own lips.

In a subsequent interview with his wife and son, it had been determined that the latter should go to Father Clifford, the priest with whom Blanche had placed herself in communication, (and who was the same that had admitted Gerald into the Church, a twelvemonth before,) and arrange with him what further steps were necessary to be taken in the matter. "I will not go myself, or have anything to say to him," said Mr. Lennox, "but as I have given my consent,—though God knows how reluctantly I have done so,—to her being admitted into the Roman Church, it is right that some member of her family should come forward and appear in the matter. Gerald would be the proper person to do so there is no doubt, but he is not here, and I do not choose to send for him. Ferdinand must therefore see this man, and explain to him that I have given leave for the ceremony to take place, since the child's heart is set upon it, but that I wish it to be done as quietly as possible."

Lady Frances expressed a great wish to accompany her son, to which her husband somewhat unwillingly yielded, and when Lord Norwood heard of their intention, he volunteered also to go with them. Mr. Lennox felt glad that he should do so, although he would not have proposed such a thing himself, and accordingly it was so arranged.

But Blanche and Lady Margaret, were, as we have said, in ignorance of this intended visit to Hill Street, and when the three set forth, they were still seated at the breakfast table, discussing the contents of that morning's post-bag. It had brought with it, a piece of news which afforded them plenty of matter for conversation. Barbara and Sidney had been married the day before, and the latter had written to his uncle, acquainting him with the fact.

"I feel," said Blanche, leaning her head upon her hand, "as if one's past life was receding away from one. Bibi and I, of late years, have been so exactly like sisters, and her marrying and going off in this way so suddenly, and so—oddly altogether, is a kind of shock to me. I am sure mamma feels it too."

"I know," observed Lady Margaret, "that you were very fond of each other, and it seems strange that she should have acted in this sort of way. I am going to ask you an odd question, perhaps, Blanche. Do you like your cousin Sidney?"

Blanche looked up at the speaker for a moment, and then answered,

"No, I do not like him. I never thought that Bibi did much. It is that which bewilders me about the whole thing. I do hope she may be happy, but I do not feel certain that she will be."

"They have gone abroad, have they not?" asked Lady Margaret.

"Sidney says they were to be in Paris last night, and intended going either to Switzerland or up the Rhine, as they felt inclined," replied Blanche.

Soon after, she rose and left the room, and Mr. Lennox, who had been sitting with a newspaper near the window, got up, and approaching the breakfast table, where his niece still sat, looking over her letters, he took a chair by her side, and informed her of the expedition to Hill Street, on the part of her father and aunt, and of its purport. "Blanche will be wondering where her mother is," he said, "and so you had better tell her. I wish now, to interfere in the matter as little as possible. I would rather never discuss it or even think about it, if I can help it. It is one full of pain to me, Margaret, and although for the poor child's sake, and also for your aunt's, I have withdrawn my opposition, and allowed her to do as she wishes, I do feel it very deeply, and must try to forget it—if I can."

Lady Margaret gathered up her letters, and then bending over her uncle, she kissed him fondly on the brow.

"Dear Uncle Lennox!" she murmured.

"God bless you, my dear," said Mr. Lennox, whilst a tear glistened in his eye.

"I will tell Blanche," said Lady Margaret, and then, with another kiss, she left him.

Blanche's spirits for a time recovered themselves wonderfully, after her father's consent to her becoming a Catholic had been obtained. She felt now, she might allow herself to be perfectly happy. The kindness and affection with which she was treated by those who suffered most by the step she contemplated, touched her inexpressibly. She felt as if she could not do enough to show her gratitude and sense of their forbearance. But those generous hearts considered themselves amply repaid, by witnessing the smile which once more hovered on her lips, and the gladness of soul which spoke in her every word and action. This visit to Father Clifford, on the part of her mother and uncle, surprised and delighted her above all. That Ferdinand should have gone to him, would not have surprised her,—she would have expected such a proof of brotherly regard from him, knowing him as she did,—but that her mother and Lord Norwood would have accompanied him, she had never supposed for a moment, it was so very, very good of them, and now there would be no further difficulty about making the final arrangements for her reception with Father Clifford. Lady Frances and her brother, had, in Mr. Lennox's name, given permission for it to take place, and Father Clifford had laid so much stress upon her obtaining her father's consent, that without it, she feared he would have refused to admit her into the Church altogether.

Every morning, after this, whilst they remained in town, Ferdinand walked with his sister to the early Mass at Farm Street, although he did not go beyond the door of the church himself. In the afternoon, too, at her request, the carriage would often take her round that way, or to the Oratory, for Benediction, and once out of curiosity, her mother and Lady Margaret entered with her, and witnessed this solemn and imposing rite at the latter church. Blanche glanced at the former when the bell rang at the moment of Benediction, and her heart overflowed with thankfulness and deep emotion as she did so.

It was on the afternoon of the second day after the news of Barbara's marriage had arrived, and the visit of Lady Frances Lennox and her companions to Hill Street had taken place, that on returning home from her usual drive with Lady Margaret and Blanche, Lady Frances was informed by the butler who assisted her to alight from the carriage, that Mr. Lethbridge was in the drawing-room, having called and requested permission, on hearing that they were out, to wait until they came in, as he wished particularly to see them.

"Charley Lethbridge, dear," said Lady Frances, turning to Blanche. "He is upstairs, Harrison says. I was thinking it strange he had never been to see us, but I daresay he has been out of town. We must make him stay to dinner. How pleased Ferdinand will be."

Lady Frances did not look particularly at her daughter, or she would have thought that somebody else seemed rather pleased, at the thought of meeting their young friend and country neighbour again. But after all, it was very natural that Blanche should like to see him, he was although young, such a *very* old friend, and Ferdy's brother-in-law elect as well; surely these were sufficient reasons to cause that look of pleasurable surprise which lent an additional charm to the sweet young face, and lighted up those deep blue eyes with a still softer brilliancy, as she followed her mother upstairs ?

"My dear Charley, I am so glad to see you !" exclaimed Lady Frances, as she entered the drawing-room, and the young guardsman who was standing near the window, advanced to meet her. "We were wondering what had become of you. You have not been in London all this time have you, without ever coming near us ?"

"I never knew you were in town till yesterday," answered Charles, grasping her hand warmly. "I have just come over from Paris, and took Lethbridge on my way back. Cissy told me you were here to my great surprise, and I scolded her well for not having done so sooner. I had no idea you were 'doing the season' this year. Have you been in town long ?"

"We came up on this child's account," said Lady Frances, turning to Blanche, with, whom Charles had already exchanged an *empressé* though silent greeting. "She was ordered a little gaiety and dissipation, and I hope on the whole it has done her good. But we shall soon be going home now, I am glad to say, as most of the gay doings are over. A good many people have left town already, and I am longing for my garden and the repose of Wentmore again."

"Cissy told us you had been unwell," said Blanche, and a bright colour suffused her cheek as she spoke. "Are you feeling quite strong again? Your trip to Paris seems to have done you good."

"Oh, I am all right again," replied Charles, who flattered himself that an especial interest in his well-being was manifested in this speech, and felt proportionately elated. "But I don't think Paris had much to do with my recovery. To go there from London at this time of year, is going from the frying-pan into the fire, with a vengeance. The heat is something awful. But I must tell you something that will amuse you greatly. Whilst there, I heard that you were married !"

"I!" "Blanche!" exclaimed Blanche and Lady Frances together.

By this time they were comfortably seated in a semicircle ; and Charles continued,

"Yes; and what is more, I felt convinced of the fact from a number of confirmatory circumstances. You were supposed to be with your husband, at the very same hotel where I was myself. I did not see you, it is true, or I should have found out the mistake," he added, laughing, "but I was told that I had just missed seeing a lovely English bride, who had set off with her bridegroom, (it was the day before yesterday,) on the continuation of their wedding tour, having been married in England, and come over to Paris the day before. The gentleman's name was Graham, and the young lady was—Miss Lennox of Wentmore ! So how could I doubt it was you ?"

" How very curious !" exclaimed his listeners.

" Of course," continued Blanche, "it was Barbara; our cousin, you know. She has married Sidney Graham, our other cousin, whom you must remember ? and they were going to Paris immediately, on their way elsewhere. How very odd, that you should so nearly have met them like that ! I daresay you were very much surprised ?"

" I was surprised," replied Charles, " and very indignant with Cissy for having kept me in ignorance, as I imagined, of the probability of such a thing. It was not until I reached home and had talked over the matter with her, that we arrived simultaneously at the conclusion that it must have been your cousin Miss Barbara, though even then she could not understand how it was that they had heard nothing about it."

" We were almost as much surprised ourselves," said Lady Frances. " It was all arranged in such a hurry. We had never seen either of them since the engagement took place, and as they did not wish it talked about, we did not tell anyone. If Blanche had seen Cissy, she would no doubt have confided the news to her, but she did not mention it in writing, as we thought it better not to do so. Now, of course, it is in the papers, so everyone will know. I always think myself, it is absurd to make mysteries about such things, but some people prefer it, and, of course, everyone has a right to please themselves."

For some time .longer they continued to converse about Barbara's marriage, and to laugh over Charles's mistake as to the identity of the bride; and then Lady Margaret coming in, it was arranged that he should return to dinner, which he was only too happy to do. Lord Norwood was dining out, but the others would all be at home, and Ferdinand would be so delighted to see him, Lady Frances said, adding with a smile, " especially as you have just come up from Leth-. bridge !"

Of course, it was solely on Ferdinand's account that Charles felt so eager to return to Norwood House, after hurrying back to his barracks and putting himself into evening attire ! Of course, it was the thought of meeting his old friend as his sister's *fiancé* for the first time, that made his heart beat and his eyes sparkle with pleasure, as he ascended the stairs for the second time that day at No. — Grosvenor Square ! He was very glad to see Ferdinand again. They had not met since the winter, and Charles Lethbridge was unfeignedly delighted with the choice his sister had made of a husband ; but still, we question if all the satisfaction he felt, at being invited to spend the evening with the Lennox family in this friendly way, was entirely to be ascribed to his future brother-in-law's account. We rather think that a certain blue-eyed damsel, who was standing near her brother when he entered the room, and who smiled sweetly upon him as he returned that brother's warm grasp of the hand, had something to do with it.

Ferdinand had a good laugh over Blanche's supposed arrival at the Hotel de Louvre, some few days before, with the "man of her choice," but confessed he should have been puzzled himself, if he had heard the description of "Mrs. Graham," that was given to Charles.

"It sounded very like, certainly," he said, giving his sister a kiss as he spoke, "and the initial 'B' too, in the note. I declare I should have set it down as a runaway match on Miss Blanche's part, if I had been in your place. As it is, I think Master Sid is a lucky fellow to have got such a nice wife as Barbara, only I confess I had no suspicion that there was anything of the sort on the *tapis* when last I saw them together."

"No more had I," observed Lady Frances in a low tone, as if speaking to herself.

At that moment, Mr. Lennox entered the room. He had heard of Charles's appearance on the scene, and as that young gentleman was a favourite of his, he was much pleased to see him and to hear a good account of all the Lethbridge party.

"Blanche is in constant communication, I know, with Miss Cissy, and so is someone else, I have no doubt," said the Rector, with a sly glance at Ferdinand, "but those long confidential letters contain very little news for the general public, so that I am kept pretty much in the dark as to what is going on, all the same."

Dinner was shortly after announced, and Charles who looked hesitatingly at Blanche as if in doubt as to whom to offer his arm, was told by her to take down Lady Frances. He did so, of course; Mr. Lennox following with his niece, and the brother and sister bringing up the rear. But when they got into the dining-room, and Charles had deposited Lady Frances in her place on one side of the table, he managed to slip round himself to the other, and so took possession of the chair next Blanche, leaving the one beside Lady Frances for Ferdinand. Blanche was not unconscious of this manœuvre on his part, but she did not remonstrate, and no one else seemed to notice it. Mr. Lennox seemed to have recovered his usual spirits which had flagged considerably of late, and each one took their share in the conversation, which soon became general and animated. Charles was unconscious of any cause for depression which the party around him might have, and only knew that he had not felt so happy himself for a long time, and the others were all glad to forget that smiling faces had not been the rule in that house for the last ten days or so.

Mr. Lennox did not keep the two young men

downstairs long, after the ladies had withdrawn, but allowed them to follow shortly into the drawing-room, whilst he remained for a while to take his customary nap below.

Lady Margaret was playing the accompaniment for Blanche in a song, at the piano, and Charles hastened to turn over the leaves, which gave him an excuse for standing near it. When it was over, he and Ferdinand took possession of a sofa on which they sat, each with an arm over the other's shoulder, in true brotherly fashion, whilst the ladies brought out their work, and the plans for the next few days were discussed.

"By the way, Charley," exclaimed Ferdinand, "have you anything to do to-morrow afternoon? Anything particular, I mean?"

"No," answered Charles, looking at Blanche, and thinking how lovely she was.

"Then why shouldn't you meet us at Kew? We are all going down there about five o'clock, it is really jolly under the trees there, and one can breathe something like pure air, instead of being choked with dust and stifled with heat, as one is in London," said Ferdinand.

"I shall be only too delighted," replied Charles, and he looked as if he meant it. "I will ride down and be there when you arrive. About five o'clock you say?"

"Yes," said Lady Frances. And so it was settled. That night, as Blanche kissed her mother and wished her good night, she said, "This has been a very nice happy evening, but I feel sometimes as if I had no right to be happy or enjoy myself ever again, after making you all so unhappy." And she turned away her head to conceal the tears that fell in spite of her efforts to restrain them.

"Charley's coming has done us all good, I think," answered Lady Frances, "and it was a comfort to hear papa laugh, and join in the conversation more in his old cheerful strain again. God bless you, darling, I know you are acting up to what you believe to be His Will, and that upholds me, although we cannot see things as you do."

The next day, as Lord Norwood's carriage, containing the three ladies and Ferdinand, drew up at the entrance of the gardens on Kew Green, Charles Lethbridge stepped forward and assisted the former to alight. "I have put up my horse," he said, "and been waiting about ten minutes. I was half afraid you might have arrived and gone in before I got here."

"I said you would be here first," cried Ferdinand, clapping him on the shoulder. "And now come along. Let's get out of this sun, for goodness sake. I know where there is a capital seat in the shade, if no monsters have taken possession of it already."

"Give me your arm, and do not walk too fast,

my dear boy," said Lady Frances. "I don't see many people about, which makes it all the pleasanter."

Ferdinand led the way with his mother, and Charles followed with Lady Margaret and Blanche. They were fortunate in securing a bench in a retired spot, and the ladies established themselves very comfortably upon it, the two young men taking up their position on the grass at their feet.

"This is what I call jolly," said Ferdinand. "Now, mother, I hope you will stay a long time. Dinner is not till quite late, and there is no occasion to hurry back."

Lady Frances smiled, and assured him that she enjoyed being there too much, to leave before it was necessary to do so. Presently, Ferdinand started up, and asked his cousin Margaret to go with him to the Palm House. He was seized with a sudden desire to look at some ferns, which he remembered the last time he was there.

"My dear Ferdinand, how can you think of such a thing," remonstrated his mother. "I cannot let you drag Margaret off there, it would be enough to kill her, one cannot breathe in that place."

But Lady Margaret assured her aunt she should like to go, and Ferdinand hurried her away before anything more could be said. Charles then rose from his recumbent position, and placed himself on the bench by Blanche's side, remarking that for his part he thought the Fernery a very good place to visit in cold weather, but at that particular season of the year he preferred a shady spot in the open air. Blanche laughed, and agreed with him. Lady Frances asked if he knew anything about the arrangements for the Archery season in South-shire, one meeting, she had been told, having already taken place.

"I heard my mother say they were all to be at Lord Maplescombe's, and the balls at the Assembly Rooms in Hillsborough afterwards," answered Charles. "I believe the two next meetings have been fixed, but I don't remember for what days."

And so they continued chatting for some time, until Lady Frances taking out her watch, exclaimed at the lateness of the hour, and begged Charles to go and look for the others. "I can't think what they are about," she said, "they must have gone off somewhere, and have forgotten all about the time. I must have a little rest before dinner when I get home, so do find them if you can."

"May I go too, mamma?" asked Blanche, "I am tired of sitting here, and should like a little walk. I am sure Charles will never find them by himself."

"Very well," answered her mother. "Only make haste back both of you, and take care the others are not kept waiting for you."

Blanche laughed, and assured her there was no fear of that, then telling Charles that she knew which way to go better than he did, they set off together down a side path, the young guardsman thinking that with such a companion to aid him in his search, he did not care how long that search was prolonged.

Lady Frances watched them as they disappeared in the distance, and the tears filled her eyes as she did so. It was long since she had seen her darling look so bright and smiling and like her old self as she did that afternoon, and a longing which was painful in its intensity took possession of her, that all might be with that darling once more as it used to be. If only this Roman Catholic fancy could be got out of her head, how happy, how thankful she, her mother, would be! She blamed herself for having been so blind to the progress such ideas were making in her child's mind, and yet she had been told so often both by Blanche and others, that the more "Catholic" members of the Anglican Church became, the less likely they were to go over to "Rome," that she had gone on trusting and believing all was as it should be, and that she need have no fear whatever on that score. It would have been different if her poor mistaken Gerald had been thrown more in her way, both she and Mr. Lennox would naturally then have been somewhat on their guard, but Blanche had seen so little of him since his 'perversion,' and the subject of religion had been so absolutely interdicted in their correspondence, that she was sure he had had no direct agency in the matter. As she gazed on the forms of Blanche and her companion whilst they remained in sight, Lady Frances could not help wishing that some other interest might arise in her daughter's mind, and take the place of the religious one which had lately absorbed her, and the idea presented itself that such an one as Charles Lethbridge, young, handsome, well-born, and excellent in every way, was just the person to create such an interest in any girl's mind. A double marriage with such a family as the Lethbridges could not be considered objectionable in any way, and Lady Frances smiled to herself as though well pleased with the thought as it entered her head.

In the meanwhile, the objects of her reverie proceeded on their way. The path which Blanche had chosen seemed an intricate one, and did not lead out on the open space near the Broad Walk as soon as she had expected. Charles did not object to it on this account, and seemed quite content to follow its windings wherever they led. Blanche was in high spirits, and amused herself with telling her companion amazing histories as they went along, of all the persons they saw either near or at a distance, assuring him at intervals of every two minutes that she knew they would see

the Palm House somewhere immediately. At
length she paused in front of a bench, and declared
that she was tired and must rest for a moment.
"And I give you leave," she said, "if we do not
come upon the Fernery directly, to ask the way of
the next person we meet."

"All right," replied Charles, placing himself on
the seat by her side, "it is delightful here, and I
agree with you, we had better rest a little."

They were quite alone. No one seemed to be
passing near, and the only sound which broke the
stillness of the summer afternoon, was the singing
of the birds in the trees overhead. They sat for a
while in silence, enjoying the beauty of the scene
and the softness of the air, which was sweet with
the scent of flowers.

"Blanche," said Charles, suddenly, and there
was a seriousness in his voice which caused her to
look round somewhat in surprise. "I wonder
why it is that some good people tell us, there
is no real happiness to be found on earth. It
seems to me that under certain circumstances, one
might be perfectly happy in this world. At least,
I know *I* could be."

"Very happy, no doubt," answered Blanche,
"if one always did right, but I suppose there are
few who do that, and therefore as a rule, this is
not such a happy world as it might be."

"I don't know what you mean by *always doing
right*," rejoined Charles, "but I, for one, would

ask for no greater happiness than I believe this world would afford, if—if—"

" If—what ?" asked Blanche.

" If I had always such an angel as you near me, to be my companion and my guide, and to show me what was right, and how I might try to do it."

Blanche's heart almost stopped beating. She became very pale for a moment, and then the colour rushed back and suffused her cheeks and brow. She trembled and could not speak, but she did not withdraw the hand which Charles had seized and held within his own.

" Blanche !" he continued in a low tone, standing up and bending over her, " would you act such an angel's part for me ? Blanche, darling Blanche, I love you with a love too great for words. To gain your love has been my ambition for long, but I did not know how impossible it would be for me to live without it, until the day when I thought I had lost you for ever, and that you had become the wife of another man. Blanche, I cannot bear to wait longer in suspense,—answer me."

She looked up at him, and that look was enough.

" My angel ! my angel !" he cried, " I am the happiest man in the world !"

And what happened next, was something I fear very indiscreet and inexcusable in so public a place as Kew Gardens; but happily, they were alone and unobserved, and in another instant Blanche had sprung up, and blushing deeply, she hurried half laughing and half crying from the spot.

She had not gone far, however, when she stopped, and turning to her lover, who in spite of some slight resistance had drawn her arm within his, and who was looking fondly down on her face, she said,

"But there is one thing I ought to tell you. I am—at least I am going to be—a Catholic. Perhaps when you know that, it may—make a difference."

She could not conceal the trembling anxiety with which she spoke. He noticed and recognized it, as a proof of the sincerity of her love.

"Going to be a Catholic, are you?" he said. "Whatever you were going to be, would make no difference to me! I have never thought much about it, but I daresay, if you think the Catholic religion the right one, that it is so, and I may become a Papist myself someday,—who knows?"

Charles had been accustomed to hear his sister and others talk of themselves as "Catholics," and he had himself at certain seasons publicly professed his belief in the "Catholic" Religion, as required by his Church, but when Blanche spoke, he knew at once that she was alluding to the Faith of Rome, and to no other.

She rewarded him with a smile of grateful relief, which made him feel, if possible, happier than before. A turn in the path suddenly brought them face to face with Ferdinand.

"Why! Here you are!" he cried. "Where have you been? Mother said she sent you to look for us ever so long ago, and we were tired of waiting for you to come back, so I set off to find you in turn. It is getting late, and their ladyships are impatient to start."

Blanche somewhat confusedly answered, that they had lost their way, and then ran on towards Lady Frances and her cousin, whom she saw advancing in the distance.

Charles took Ferdinand by the arm, and whispered something in his ear which caused him to start back with a shout of delight, and exclaim, "You don't say so? My dearest fellow, how glad I am!"

"Hush! Be quiet. Don't say anything now," said Charles, smiling, and in another moment they came up with the ladies.

Ferdinand was sent forward to look for the carriage, and Charles gave his arm to Lady Frances, who scolded him playfully as they walked towards the gates, for keeping them waiting, and said she should know better another time than to send him to look for anybody.

Charles did not make any very intelligible response, or attempt to defend himself in any way. He felt as if he was treading on air, and judging from his radiant smile and look, a passer-by might have thought Lady Frances was praising him for something, instead of blaming him, however mildly. After handing her into the carriage which was waiting for them at the entrance, he turned towards Lady Margaret and Blanche who were following behind, and if he held the little hand which the latter placed in his, as he stood at the carriage door before mounting his horse, a moment longer than was necessary,—it was only natural under the circumstances.

Lady Frances was tired, and did not talk much on their way home, and Blanche drew down her veil and leaned back in her seat, leaving Margaret and Ferdinand to keep up a laughing conversation between them.

She was very happy, and that was all she felt quite certain about. It seemed like a dream, and she almost feared to awake and find it one. Ferdinand got hold of her hand and kept it in his the greater part of the way, and she fancied there was something meant by the affectionate squeeze he gave it every now and then, but he did not speak, and she felt grateful to him for diverting her cousin's attention, and leaving her to herself.

Charles had whispered to her when he said goodbye, that he should call the next morning after breakfast and see her father. In the course of the evening, Ferdinand gave her to understand that he "knew all about it," and assured her with mock gravity that he was delighted to have her for a "sister-in-law." She begged him not to say anything to the others until the next day, and kissing her fondly, he promised to do as she wished. Even with her mother, she felt a reluctance which was almost insurmountable to enter upon the subject, but ere she parted from her that night, she hid her face on her shoulder, and with tears and blushes told her that Charles Lethbridge had asked her to be his wife, and that she had not said No, and further, that she had told him of her intention of becoming a Roman Catholic, and he had said that would make no difference, and if her mother would only tell her she approved, she should be very very happy.

Lady Frances pressed her to her heart, and murmured, "Be happy, then, my darling. He is a good man, and though I suppose there is no one I should think really worthy of you, I would sooner give you to him than anyone else I know."

CHAPTER IV.

"Blanche Lennox has become a Roman Catholic, and is engaged to be married to Charles Lethbridge."

Such was the great and exciting piece of news, which spread from group to group, at the last Archery meeting of the season that year in Southshire, and furnished the friends and acquaintance of both families, with ample matter for comment and conversation, during the dinner in the tent, and at the ball in the Assembly Rooms of Hillsborough afterwards. Neither of the young people were present themselves on the occasion, but both Lady Frances Lennox and Charles's mother and sister, had driven upon the ground in the course of the day, and as no secret had been made by them of either event, they were easily credited as facts.

And it was true. Two days after Charles had obtained the consent of her father to his engagement with Blanche, she had been admitted into the Church by Father Clifford, at the altar of the

Sacred Heart in Farm Street. In silent gratitude she had poured forth her thanks to God, feeling indeed that there was no " Good Thing" which He had withheld from her, praying earnestly for strength to persevere herself, and for the grace of conversion for those dear ones to whom the Light so clear for her, was still impenetrable darkness.

The party in Grosvenor Square, broke up soon after the ceremony of Blanche's reception had taken place. She did not return with her parents to Wentmore; a Catholic lady who was an old friend of her mother's, having begged permission to carry her off with her into the country for a short time. Mrs. Lewis had acted as god-mother at her confirmation, which had taken place as soon as possible after her reception, and the proposal on her part to take Blanche down to her pretty place in Leicestershire, where there was a chapel and a priest, and everything that the new convert could desire, was the more readily agreed to, as Mr. Lennox and Lady Frances shrank as much as herself, from the thought of their return-ing together for the first time to their Rectory home after the step she had taken. Lady Margaret and Ferdinand went with them, and Blanche de-parted the same day with Mrs. Lewis for Beaulieu.

The pleasure which the Rector and his wife felt in Blanche's engagement to Charles Lethbridge, was a comfort to them under the sorrow which her " perversion" caused them both, but whilst gladly giving his would-be son-in-law the consent which he sought from him, the Rector warned him that the Colonel might not be so pleased at having a Papist for his daughter-in-law. However, Charles assured him that he knew his father well enough to feel positive he would raise no objection on that score, and he was right. Colonel Lethbridge pulled a long face when informed of Blanche's secession from the Church of England, and Mrs. Lethbridge and Cissy both shed some quiet tears over it, but each of them felt that if Charles was satisfied, it was after all his affair and not theirs, and the old Colonel even went so far as to prophesy that now she had something else to think about, "she would give up all that sort of nonsense, and settle down into a plain honest Protestant again." But this sentiment did not seem to approve itself to his auditory, especially to Cissy and Ferdinand, who utterly declined being called Protestants themselves, and remarked to each other that " Blanche could not do that, as she had never been one !"

But if, as a rule, Blanche's conversion was a cause of regret and annoyance to her various friends and relations, there was one at least amongst the latter, to whom it brought joy and satisfaction beyond words. Her brother Gerald had been in Brussels all through the summer, working hard at the translations which he was preparing for the press, and which the vacation time gave him more leisure to attend to. He was kept *au courant* with regard to affairs in England by both Blanche and Ferdinand, who wrote constantly, and had been informed by the latter of his engagement, (although it was not to be called one as yet,) with Cissy Lethbridge. His mother was also a good correspondent, and from her letters he had gathered that Blanche had not been looking or feeling well of late. He had heard of the visit to London, and had wondered in himself at the fatigue and excitement which a young girl in his sister's position, would have to go through during the season, being thought desirable for her. No one had hinted to him that she was supposed to have any care upon her mind, which it was hoped that distraction might remove, for the idea was one which had scarcely presented itself to any excepting Mr. Findlay, the doctor, who recommended the change, and Lady Frances who was at a loss to account for the evident depression in her daughter's spirits at times. Gerald was therefore totally unaware of there being any feeling of the kind.

So afraid was Blanche, of Gerald's incurring blame on her account, that she had carefully avoided the subject of her doubts and misgivings on the subject of religion, when writing to him. Indeed, all controversy had been expressly forbidden by her father as a condition of their correspondence being allowed, and earnestly as Gerald prayed and trusted that she would in time attain to a knowledge of the truth, he had as yet had no grounds for supposing that she was more likely to become a Catholic, than any other of those dear ones for whom he offered the same unceasing prayers. It was his father's letter, reproaching him for having tampered, as it was assumed he must have done, with his sister's faith, that first led him to imagine that she had any serious thoughts of following his example. His surprise, therefore, was almost as great as the delight which the idea of her probable conversion afforded him. He had instantly replied to his father, assuring him that he had never once attempted in any way, directly or indirectly, to influence Blanche's mind upon religious subjects, and had at the same time written to Ferdinand, begging him to let him know if there was any reason to suppose that Blanche was inclined to become a Roman Catholic. Ferdinand's answer, accompanied by a few lines from Blanche herself, assured him of the fact that she had made up her mind to join the Church of Rome, and that her father, although most reluctantly, had at length given his consent to her doing so.

Gerald's thankfulness may better be conceived than described. He seized his hat, after reading the letter, and hurrying to the nearest church, he knelt before the altar and blessed and praised God for His unutterable Goodness and Mercy. Then rising from his knees, he flew in search of Mr.

Fitzroy, and from him to Father Anselm at the Carmelite Convent, from Father Anselm to the Abbé Beaufort, and every other Catholic friend and acquaintance he had in Brussels, informing them of the good news. And how warmly they entered into his feelings, how entirely they sympathized, how truly they rejoiced with him! Amongst Catholics, it is remarkable how literally the Apostolic saying is verified, that "*If one member suffer anything, all the members suffer with it; or if one member glory, all the members rejoice with it.*" Catholics of every clime, are knit together in a bond of fellowship, which obliges them to feel and care one for another. It was enough for even those who were personally unacquainted with Gerald Lennox, to know that one of his family had been received into the Church, and they were eager to congratulate and express their felicitations to him on the event.

But Gerald, amidst all his own overpowering feelings of joy and happiness, did not forget that to everyone belonging to her, excepting himself, this change in his beloved sister must be a matter for lamentation and regret. About distant relations and ordinary acquaintances, he did not concern himself, but when he thought of his parents, who had already suffered so much on his own account, and of Ferdinand, his heart ached within him, for he knew what a sorrow it must be to them. He wrote to Blanche; he did not say much, but what he did say was sufficient to convince her that he had never been so happy, perhaps, in all his life before, and the brother and sister, dear as they had always been to each other, did indeed feel from that moment drawn in a special way together.

He also wrote to his mother and to Ferdinand. To the former, without pretending to disguise the unfeigned pleasure and satisfaction which Blanche's conversion caused him, he said how entirely he entered into what must be her feelings on the subject, begging her at the same time to believe that the hearts of her Catholic children were hers, if possible, more than ever. With Ferdinand, he ventured to express a hope that the separation (so far as any existed) between them, might come to an end ere long, even as it had already done with him and Blanche. Blanche had told him of Ferdinand's kindness and generous interference in her behalf, and he thanked and praised him for this, most warmly. The recipients were both much touched with these letters, and agreed between themselves that it was a comfort to feel that what had cost them so much sorrow, was at any rate a source of unqualified rejoicing to one so dear to them as Gerald. Knowing how devotedly attached to one another were her three children, Lady Frances could not help looking wistfully at Ferdinand as he stood beside her with Gerald's letter in his hand, and reminding him that he was now the only one left to them, and that if he forsook their Church, it would be a blow which neither his father nor she could bear. "Never fear, mother," was his answer, "never fear. As long as I believe the Church of England to be a true and living Branch of the One Catholic Church of Christ—as long as I believe in her Orders and her Sacraments, which I do most thoroughly—every friend and every relation I have in the world may desert her Communion, but I never will."

And close upon the news of her conversion, followed the announcement of Blanche's engagement to Charles Lethbridge. She wrote herself to Gerald from Mrs. Lewis's country place, after she had left town, and told him of it. He was somewhat startled, and not altogether so pleased with the intelligence, as at any other time he would have been. He could not help asking himself whether she had done well, in engaging herself to marry a Protestant, so soon after her own conversion to the Catholic Faith. He was very fond of all the Lethbridges, and Charles had always been his particular friend as we know, but he had never seen anything but misery arise from "mixed marriages," and as he had no reason to suppose that Charles was enamoured of his sister's religion, as well as of her, he feared that no good could result from this one. Nevertheless, he was so fully aware of how greatly an engagement which met with his parents' approval, would smooth Blanche's path at this moment, and soften the blow of her secession to them, that he could not find it in his heart to say anything about his own misgivings on the subject to her, but added to his expressions of satisfaction at the alliance from every other point of view, that he hoped, on the most important one of all, they would be of one mind eventually. Blanche replied by telling him that she felt certain Charles would become a Catholic himself, before long, and entreated him to obtain prayers for his conversion from all his Catholic friends in Brussels, and especially from the Poor Clares, who she found had been praying for her, and on whose prayers she had the greatest reliance. She was evidently so happy and so confident herself, that it would be as they wished, that Gerald gradually became persuaded that it would be so too, and ceased to trouble himself on the subject.

"How many changes have taken place," he thought one day, as he wandered through the shady walks of the Bois de la Cambre, having spent the whole morning at his writing-table in the Rue d' Idalie, and rushed thither in hopes of getting rid of the headache, which confinement to his little room for so long a time had brought on, "since I was last at Wentmore! Blanche a Catholic,—both she and Ferdinand engaged,—and Sidney and Barbara actually married!" This last event. had surprised him more than all the others. Sidney had written to him just before it took place, and he in reply, whilst expressing every hope for his and Barbara's happiness, had not hesitated to say how much astonished he was, since during all the time they were so much together he had never heard him allude to her otherwise than in the most casual way, or seen him evince any peculiar interest when her name was mentioned.

He had also written to Barbara, and she had answered him in a short note, dated from the Hôtel de Louvre at Paris, in which she thanked him for his good wishes, and informed him that they had been married the day before, and were undecided as to the exact line they should take in their wedding tour, and wondered whether by any chance they should come across him in their wanderings, before returning to England. " They are not likely to do that, unless they come this way," thought Gerald. "Poor Barbara! I wonder if she likes me any better than she did, or whether she has forgiven me yet, for becoming a Catholic ?"

He was very lonely that summer in Brussels, and had it not been for the work with which he was kept so constantly supplied by his friend the publisher, he would often have found the dullness of the Belgian capital at that time of year, irksome in the extreme. As it was, the hours during which he sat pen in hand in the close and heated atmosphere of his lodging, began to tell upon him, and day by day as the sultry weather continued, he felt less able to bear up against it, until ·at length he could no longer conceal from himself, that his health was suffering from such severe application. His weary and languid air, when he carried his manuscript on Saturday evenings to Monsieur Poisset, made that gentleman remonstrate with him, and beg him not to work so hard.

"Glad as we are to have your invaluable assistance, my dear sir," he would say, "I would rather, much rather, you did less, and took more time over it. We shall have you laid up if you do not take care, and then we shall be deprived of your services altogether. For our sakes, therefore, I beg of you to take matters more easily."

But Gerald could not be persuaded. During the vacation he did not receive any salary from the College at which he gave lectures, and he could not afford to be without the little incomings which his literary labours brought him. Sometimes, whilst he sat, late at night over his work, the thought would occur to him, "Had I remained a Protestant, or a 'Catholic out of visible communion with Rome,' as I considered myself, how differently I should now have been situated! Instead of having literally 'to earn my bread in the sweat of my brow,' an exile, as it were, from my country and my family, looked down upon, because I am a Teacher in a Public School, by the English residents here, and cut off by my constant hard work from the chance of forming the acquaintance of any visitors, I might have been as happy and as free from care, as much surrounded by luxuries and domestic comforts as dear old Ferdinand is at this moment. If it were not for the kindness of my Catholic friends, Mr. Fitzroy, and the Robertses, and one or two others, I don't know what I should do at times, my life here is so lonely, so changed from what it used to be. Yes, it is changed, and changed how infinitely for the better in some respects! When I look back upon that last year of my stay in London, and compare the mental disquietude, the doubts, the uncertainty and the dread of what might be before me, which I then went through, with the perfect peace, the increasing happiness which daily and hourly has been mine, since I entered the Catholic Church, and gave up all that made this world bright and beautiful to me, in order to do so, I feel as if I could never be thankful enough, for the grace which was then bestowed upon me. To live apart from every relation and every friend,—to descend from a life of luxury and independence to one of toil and privation,—to give up, oh, far more than *I* have had to do,—how cheaply at such a price would be purchased the inestimable, priceless boon of the One Saving Faith, the fellowship and communion which a Catholic enjoys with Christ's Holy Church throughout the world, and all the wondrous privileges which are his by virtue of that membership! I cannot,—dare not—repine when I think of these things. I only feel that what I went through in order to become a Catholic, was so little in comparison with numbers of others, that I am ashamed almost to think of it, and must regard it as a proof of my own unworthiness, that I was not called upon to suffer more. How glorious it must be to have to give up any great thing for the sake of the Truth! A large fortune—to be utterly cast off by one's belongings—to be persecuted and really to have to go through *something*, instead of taking all that God can give, and feeling that one offers nothing in return! And yet, only God knows what it cost me to give up Wentmore and Ferdinand—to give up the dream of the future which had I remained an Anglican, appeared so bright a one—to bring such sorrow upon the best of fathers, and the tenderest of mothers,—to wring my darling sister's heart, though, blessed be God, she no longer regrets the step I then took. Oh! yes, I had to suffer—I did not earn all the blessings gained by joining the Church without any cost,—and the loss of worldly goods, even had they been greater than they were in my case, seems as nothing in comparison with such heart pains as those!"

Since Sidney's departure, his engagement as Professor at the College of S. Antoine, and his other occupations, had entirely prevented Gerald from entering into anything like general society. He was satisfied with the friendship of the few English Catholics in the town, to whom he had

been introduced, and by their means he had acquired the *entrée* into one or two of the best Belgian houses, where a convert of good family and
high connections was sure of a welcome, and the
fact that he was obliged to seek literary employment in consequence of his conversion, was only an
additional argument in his favour. But although
gladly availing himself of the recreation which an
hour or so, passed in the company of these kind
friends, afforded him, Gerald was seldom or never
seen at a party of any sort, and often for days and
weeks together, would remain entirely shut up in
his small bachelor quarters, only going out in the
evening for a walk in the Bois de la Cambre, or.
for an hour's stroll in the Zoological Gardens with
Mr. Fitzroy or young Roberts, who would call for
him sometimes when the band was playing, and
almost tear him by force from his work. Some few
of the English Protestant residents, knew there was
a Mr. Lennox living somewhere in the neighbourhood of the Rue de Trône, they "had heard he was
a Roman Catholic, and employed as a teacher at
one of the schools. No one knew him, and it was
supposed he was a person of no family. Lennox
was a good name, but one could never go by
names, especially in a place like Brussels, where
they were so easily assumed by people who perhaps had no right to them whatever, and might
not like their own to be known."

One evening towards the end of August, Gerald

having felt more than usually oppressed by the weather during the whole day, threw down his pen, and set off in the direction of the Boulevard de Waterloo, thinking that a walk as far as the Porte de Hal, would freshen him up a little, and perhaps rid him of the pain in his head, which prevented him from thinking, and almost blinded him at times. He walked slowly, his eyes bent on the ground, and his thoughts far away amongst the home circle at Wentmore, and he sighed involuntarily as he pictured the scene to himself, which no doubt was enacting there at that moment. Blanche, he believed, was still absent from home, but his cousin Margaret was on a visit at the Rectory, and he knew that Cissy Lethbridge was often there too. He imagined his sweet gentle mother, sitting under the trees on the lawn outside the library windows, with her eyes fixed on Ferdinand and Cissy, and her thoughts wandering to her two absent children, both of whom were now associated sadly in her mind, as labouring under what she considered a delusion on the most serious of all subjects, and one which separated them in a certain degree, from that fond heart which had always beat so entirely in unison with theirs till now. He measured the sorrow which Blanche's conversion must be to his mother, by the joy which it gave himself, and he sighed deeply as he did so.

We have before said that Gerald's devotion to

his mother, was something different from the usual affection of a dutiful son for a parent. He loved her with a great unspeakable love—he scarcely knew how great it was himself—and had been sometimes almost frightened by the intensity of his feelings, when dwelling upon the thought of her tenderness and love for him which had been manifested in so many ways, ever since he could first remember her smiling face, when as a little child he would run at her call, and think it a treat indeed to go round the garden or for a short walk into the village, clinging to her hand. His dear mamma—his pretty mamma.   And in after years, the remembrance of her was always the same, only with it blended the reciprocal affection which grew with his growth, and strengthened and deepened each year more and more. What did he not owe that best and dearest of mothers ! If it had not been for her training and the early principles of religion which had been instilled into him by her, would he ever have been led to a knowledge of the Truth, and knowing it, have had the courage to embrace it, even at the cost of grieving that mother's tender loving heart, so sorely ?   She it was who had taught him, always and in everything to make God and His Will the first consideration, and she it was who had suffered most from his unflinching application of the Golden Rule in after years, when it became a question for him, of choosing between his Heavenly Parent and his earthly ones !

How marvellous, how almost bewildering was it to look back and think of these things, and oh ! how earnestly he prayed that the day would come in this world, (he knew it would in the next,) when she might acknowledge herself that he had done right, and receive the Gift of Faith, even in the same measure as it had been bestowed upon him !

Occupied with these reflections as he slowly took his way along the Boulevard, Gerald had not noticed that someone was walking by his side, and was endeavouring to catch his eye without speaking. Suddenly looking up, however, he perceived a smiling face turned towards him, and exclaimed,

"*Bonsoir, mon Père!* I did not see you. You must have thought me very rude."

"*Pas de tout, mon ami,*" answered the Abbé Beaufort, for he it was. "I saw you were meditating, and did not weesh to disturb you. How arre you, my dear sare ? You do not look well. You have been studying too hard, I suspect ?"

"I have not been feeling quite well the last few days," said Gerald, "I am working hard to get a volume through the press before the vacation ends, as after that I shall not have so much time. This evening it is so fine, that I was tempted out for a stroll, otherwise I ought to be writing now."

"*Mon ami,* you write too much, too much,"

said the Abbé, looking anxiously at Gerald as he spoke. "If you do not give yourself a little rest, you will be ill."

Gerald smiled and shook his head, and then changed the conversation by asking the Abbé if he had seen anything of their friend Mr. Fitzroy lately.

The Abbé had seen him, and that reminded him that Mr. Fitzroy, who was always occupied with some good work, was very anxious to dispose of some tickets for a concert in aid of the Society of S. Vincent de Paul, which was to take place soon, nd knowing that he, Gerald, was a friend of Lady Sophia Roberts's, he had, the Abbé understood, . meant to ask him to get her to take some, and distribute them amongst her friends. "Mr. Fitzroy does not go much into society himself, you know," added the Abbé, "and he therefore is not able to do so much in that way as he otherwise might."

"Mr. Fitzroy goes quite as much into what you call ' society,' as I do," replied Gerald, " or rather a great deal more. But I do know Lady Sophia, and I shall be happy to ask her. She will do what she can I am sure."

" Will you come in, and take a prospectus of the concert?" asked the Abbé, as they approached his lodgings, and Gerald assenting, they entered the house together.

The Abbé begged him to take a seat, and hurried off to get the circular. Gerald felt tired, and was glad of the rest. He started up on the Abbé's return, having nearly gone to sleep on the horse-hair sofa of the little room. The Abbé smiled and begged him not to disturb himself, and then proceeding to light his lamp, for it was now getting dark, he read out the programme of the forthcoming concert, and an account of the particular charity for which it was to be held. When he had finished, he glanced at Gerald, whose head was reclining against the head of the sofa, and who did not look up or offer any remark. The other stepped forward, and seeing his eyes closed, smiled, and muttering to himself, " *Il dort*—he is tired—I will not deesturb him," he seated himself quietly in a chair at some little distance, and took up a book to read. After a while, he glanced again at Gerald, and thinking that he breathed very gently for a person in sleep, he approached him softly, and was startled by the extreme pallor of his countenance as he did so. Bending over him, he raised Gerald's head a little, and took one of his hands in his. It was icy cold, and fell lifelessly from his grasp as he let it go. The Abbé started back in consternation; he saw that his young friend was not sleeping, but had fainted.

In another moment, the good priest's housekeeper was in the room, and both were trying hard to bring Gerald back to consciousness, but all their efforts proving ineffectual, the Abbé became seriously alarmed, and despatched the old lady in search of a medical man who lived close by, with directions to bring him back with her, if he was at home, immediately. Monsieur Leblanc was at home, and in two minutes' time stood by Gerald's side, feeling his pulse, and shaking his head. However, under his directions, the restoratives which were applied caused his patient to open his eyes at last, but he did not speak, and soon closed them again.

"Where does he live? We must get him home and put him to bed," said the medical man, addressing the Abbé. "Send for a *vigilante* if you please, at once."

The good little Abbé was sadly distressed, and when the conveyance came to the door, and Gerald, still in a state of insensibility, was placed within it, he got on the box, there being only room for M. Leblanc inside, beside the patient, and directed the driver to the Rue d'Idalie, feeling too anxious to remain behind.

The consternation of Gerald's landlady at seeing him brought back in such a state to the house, was extreme, but she did not waste time in useless lamentations, and hurried off in obedience to the doctor's orders to get his bed warmed, and make herself otherwise useful. She was not surprised, she said, she had told him over and over again he was doing too much, and was overworking himself, and he such a nice gentleman! What would his friend M. Fitzroy say!

M. l'Abbé did not leave the house until he had seen Gerald safely in bed, and had been assured by M. Leblanc in whom he had unbounded confidence, that he was sleeping, and no longer in the half-fainting condition in which he had remained so long. The doctor announced his intention of remaining with his patient during the night, and the Abbé told him he should certainly call the first thing in the morning, to hear how his young friend was going on.

He then hurried to Mr. Fitzroy's residence which was not far off, and informed him of Gerald's sudden seizure that evening when in his house. Mr. Fitzroy betook himself instantly to the sick room, and insisted upon sharing the doctor's vigil with him, which M. Leblanc, who knew him well, after some little demur, allowed him to do.

Gerald had endeared himself to Mr. Fitzroy, during the time he had known him, even more than the latter was aware of until now, when standing by his bedside he gathered from the doctor's expression and from the few words which fell from him, that there was serious cause for anxiety, and at any rate it might be some time before the young man was likely to recover. The next day found him no better, rather worse if anything, and M. Leblanc pronounced it a case of low fever. The brain had been overtaxed, and too close an application to his work during the hot weather had brought on the attack.

The Abbé was in despair, and Mr. Fitzroy seriously uneasy. The latter wished to write to Gerald's family, but Gerald, who although slightly wandering at times, was for the most part conscious of what was going on, assured him that there was no occasion for doing so. "M. Leblanc was frightening them unnecessarily, he should be much better in a day or two and then he would write himself."

And propped up in bed one day, about a week after his seizure, he did write a few lines to Ferdinand, telling him that he had not been very well, and by the advice of his doctor had given up his translating work for the present, but otherwise making light of the matter. Ferdinand, however, suspected from the tone of the letter and from the look of the handwriting, that he was worse than he made out, and wrote a line to M. Leblanc, asking him for his real opinion of his brother's state. The doctor's reply reassured him in some measure, but he made no disguise of the fact that Gerald had been very ill, and was still far from well. Had not Ferdinand been keeping his last term at Oxford, he would have come over himself to see how his brother was going on, but as it was, he had to content himself with Gerald's assurance that he was steadily improving, and

M. Leblanc's promise to inform him if any change for the worse took place.

Gerald's recovery was a very slow one, and it was retarded a good deal by the conviction which stole upon him, that it would be long before he was able to resume his pen, or return to his duties at the College. Indeed, as time went on, and the doctor pronounced it still impossible for him to think of exerting himself in any way, he was obliged to send in his resignation of his appointment, feeling that it was better thus to anticipate what he should otherwise have to regard as his dismissal.

And so it happened, that when the winter season had well set in, and Gerald was able to get about again, having paid his doctor's bill and others incurred during his illness, he found himself deprived of those resources upon which he had hitherto depended, and reduced to a state little short of destitution.

CHAPTER V.

THOSE amongst our readers who have been to Aix la Chapelle and stayed at the Grand Monarque, will remember the two courtyards of that most excellent of hotels. The outer one with its corridors leading to the grand staircases on either side, and the inner communicating with the *Salle à manger* on the right, and the *cuisine* on the left. On a bright summer afternoon of the year 186—, three gentlemen were seated at a small round table, placed in a shady corner of the inner court, drinking coffee and smoking cigars. The *table d'hôte* was over, that is to say, the early one, for during the season, Monsieur Dremel provides two for his visitors. They were English, as might easily be seen from their dress and manner, (we do not mean this satirically, as we have already alluded to the fact of their being *gentlemen*, which all the English one meets abroad are not,) even if their language did not proclaim the fact by itself.

It was too soon to go to the Elisengarten for

the band, and they were whiling away the time by discussing the performance of the Operatic company the night before, voting Aix insupportably dull, and wishing themselves elsewhere.

"I can't think what keeps you here, Bateson," said one. "You don't drink these filthy waters. You have no one belonging to you who does. You say you think it an awfully slow place, and yet here you stop. I know if I was you I should have been off long ago."

"I believe it is the pretty widow, and the impossibility of tearing himself from her side that prevents his departure," laughed the youngest looking of the three. "Bateson is tremendously smitten in that quarter. By the way, she puts me in mind of that lady we met at Bonn the other day, Lucas, whom my wife knew something of. The party with the lightish hair. Don't you remember?"

"Mrs. Vernon, you mean?" returned the first speaker. "Yes. There is a sort of a likeness. But Mrs. Vernon is as you observe, a lady. Now I don't think, (begging Bateson's pardon,) any great shakes of the widow, as she is called, though I was told by a fellow here who knew something about her, that she was nothing of the sort. A *Divorcée*, he said, who found it more convenient to do the respectable, and pass for a widow, and so gave out that she was one."

"Widow or not, she has nothing to do with my

stay here," said the individual at whom these remarks were levelled. "I did not intend to remain for more than a day or two when I came, but as the Sandfords, whom I knew, were at Nuellens, and the Grants here, I found it less dull than Spa where I didn't know a soul. Lots of other people one knows have turned up since, yourselves amongst the number, and I have stayed on from day to day and week to week, more for that reason than any other. If I want to lose a little money, I can always go to Spa and back in the day, and in fine weather this is not such a bad place after all."

"I know I wish to goodness, my wife had not been ordered to try these confounded springs," said he, whom we have described as the younger of the party, although there was not much difference as to age between them. "I shall be off to Spa the moment the doctor gives us leave to stir. Dremel gives one a better dinner than one gets at any of the *table d'hôtes* there, or else I should have bolted ere long."

"I don't agree with you, Graham," rejoined Bateson. "We had a first rate spread at the Orange last week, when we went over for the day. Quite equal to anything one gets here, wasn't it, Lucas?"

"Oh, the food wasn't so bad," was the reply, "but they can't put you up at Spa, as they do here or at Nuellens. This is a stunning hotel. I never was more comfortable in my life."

Does the reader remember a certain Captain Lucas, who together with one of his brother officers, accompanied Mrs. Fraser Smith and her daughters on a visit to Wentmore Rectory one day, as mentioned in the opening chapter of our story? He it was, who now rejoiced in the superior accommodation provided for his visitors by the worthy host of the Grand Monarque, having met a friend of his some short time before, whose wife had been recommended the waters at Aix by her doctor, and who had persuaded him to accompany them thither.

The said friend, was one of the three we have described as seated in the inner court of the hotel at Aix on this particular afternoon. His name was Sidney Graham.

He was but slightly changed since we saw him last. There was much the same careless air and manner about him, though it might be a trifle less so than formerly, and a few hard lines about the mouth, which had not been observable of old, might have been noticed by a close inspector. When Sidney laughed now, which he often did, there was a want of hilarity in the sound which struck painfully on the ear, and he seldom or never smiled. There was a restless, dissatisfied look about the eye at times, which denoted a mind ill at ease, and yet his friends and acquaintance were always telling him what a fortunate fellow he was. Married to a young and handsome wife—possessed of a comfortable independence with nothing to do but to please himself—there were many who envied him his lot, but he was not contented with it nevertheless. Ever since his marriage, nearly a twelvemonth before, he had been travelling with his wife from place to place on the continent, never caring to remain long anywhere, and constantly seeking a change. Their perfect freedom of choice had led them hither and thither, without any particular reason for preferring one spot to another, save the whim or caprice of the moment. Neither of them wished to return for some time to England, although they felt it impossible to settle down anywhere abroad. It was therefore hailed as a relief by her husband, at any rate, when Mrs. Graham who had caught cold from imprudently exposing herself to the night air on one or two occasions during their travels, was ordered by a medical man whom they had consulted in Paris, to try the waters at Aix la Chapelle, those waters being noted for their efficacy in cases of rheumatic affection such as her's had become. Accompanied by Captain Lucas, Mr. and Mrs. Graham had arrived early in the season at the Grand Monarque, and were thankful so far, to have a reason for remaining a certain time anywhere.

Sir Edward Bateson, the same who had been a

guest in former days at Lethbridge Park, was amongst the English at Aix, at the time, and was now seated with Sidney and Captain Lucas on the afternoon in question, discussing the respective merits of the Prussian watering place, and that other favourite resort of a similar kind across the Belgian frontier.

"By the way, Graham, is it true that Charley Lethbridge is going to marry a sister of your wife's? I remember her, a pretty little thing when I was staying down there two years ago. By Jove! how time flies!"

"My wife was an only child," answered Sidney, rising from his seat, and throwing away the end of his cigar as he spoke. "She never had a sister, but as she lived with my uncle, Mr. Lennox of Wentmore, who is her uncle also, for several years, many people supposed that she was his daughter. Whether my cousin Blanche Lennox is engaged to be married to Mr. Lethbridge or anyone else, I don't know, but here comes Mrs. Graham, and perhaps she will be able to tell you."

"It is time to go to the gardens, I suppose," said Captain Lucas. "Shall you come, Bateson?" And he also rose and turned towards a lady, who was seen approaching them from one of the entrances of the hotel. As she draws near, we will likewise take a look at her, and describe her appearance for the benefit of the reader.

Barbara Graham was indeed much altered since

we last beheld her, scarcely a twelvemonth before, on her way from Wentmore Rectory to Leamington. Her large dark eyes looked out upon you with an expression which was unknown to them then, an expression of restless enquiry, as if she would determine at a glance whether you were a friend or a foe. Her face had lost what little colour it ever had, and a look of weariness and of pain would sometimes steal over it which was sad to behold. She was attired in a walking suit of grey, trimmed with blue, and carried a dainty little parasol in her hand.

"Bateson wishes to know if it is true that our cousin Blanche Lennox is going to be married? Have you heard anything about it?" inquired Sidney, as she approached.

"I believe she is," was the answer. "And to your friend Charles Lethbridge, Sir Edward. You know they are very old friends and neighbours in Southshire."

"I heard of it some time ago," observed Sir Edward, "and thinking that you were her sister, I felt sure that Graham would know if it was true. I have not heard from the Lethbridges for ages, but some one told me the other day that the marriage had not taken place, and so I thought it might have been a false report altogether."

"No. I believe not," said Barbara. Then turning to Captain Lucas, she added, "You remember my cousin, do you not? I never had a sister of my own, but she was quite like one to me. When I first married, we used to hear from Wentmore occasionally, but the wandering life we have led has interfered with our correspondence, and I have heard nothing of them for a long time now."

She bent her eyes on the ground, and dug the point of her parasol into it as she spoke. Sir Edward and her husband had gone into the hotel together for a moment, so that she and Captain Lucas were quite alone. He drew near, and said in a low earnest tone,

"I remember her well. It must be a great trial to you to be so cut off from those who were so dear to you. But some people have the power of making friends for themselves wherever they go. I am sure you can never be without them."

"You are mistaken," answered Barbara, looking up at him with a quick earnest glance. "I sometimes think that I am destined to go through the world in a peculiarly friendless condition, for I have not the power you speak of, and it is very seldom that I really make, what I call a friend. When I do, however, I try my best not to lose them."

"How glad I should be if I thought that I was looked upon as a friend by you," rejoined the other, in the same low tone. "Believe me, dear Mrs. Graham, you would have no truer one."

"I do believe you," she said. The words were

scarcely audible, but the smile with which he looked at her and whispered the word, " Thanks," shewed that they had reached him.

At that moment, Sidney Graham reappeared, and offering his arm to his wife, they passed through the outer court of the hotel, into the street beyond, and took their way slowly towards the Elisengarten, Captain Lucas and Sir Edward following them at a short distance.

The gardens were already full, and the music had begun when they entered them.

" I am afraid we shall have some difficulty in getting seats," said Barbara, looking round, " and I cannot remain here in this sun."

" I will go and explore on the bank," said Captain Lucas, overhearing her remark. " I may find some chairs vacant, and you would be in the shade there."

Barbara smiled and thanked him. In another minute he returned, saying, that some German friends of his would give up their chairs to them, as they were going to move, and the seats were in a nice shady corner, so that nothing could be better.

" Come along, then," said Sidney, rather impatiently, " I suppose you will want to stay till it is all over, but I shall very soon have had enough of it. I want to have a game of billiards, and when I am gone Lucas can take my place."

" He deserves a seat, since we should not have

got them ourselves if it had not been for him," observed Barbara.

Captain Lucas had preceded them, and they perceived him standing by two empty chairs in a shady nook, as they ascended the winding path leading to the bank on the left hand side of the garden.

"All right, Lucas. You may have my chair directly, for I shan't stay long," said Sidney. Then placing himself by his wife's side, he took up a programme of the music and scanned it over.

Captain Lucas stationed himself behind Barbara's chair, and declared that he did not mind standing, resolving at the same time to profit by Sidney's departure, and take possession of his chair as soon as it was vacant. From time to time he bent over and addressed a few words to Barbara. He knew most of the people by sight, and was able to tell her who they were. She, on her part, attracted considerable attention from the surrounding groups, and many were the glances directed to the spot where she and her husband sat.

We have said that Barbara was much altered in appearance since we saw her last, although scarcely a twelvemonth had elapsed since then. Many persons who had known her as Miss Barbara Lennox of Wentmore, might have thought her improved in some ways. Her manner and style were doubtless those of one who had seen something of the world, and in the matters of dress and deportment she had acquired an air which stamped her as being a person of taste and high breeding. There was a quiet dignity too about her, which became her well, and at the same time, when she chose, no one could be more pleasing in her demeanour. But one thing would have struck most people who had known her formerly, and that was, that she seemed much older. The young girl who had moved about her uncle's Rectory full of life and energy—whose unflagging spirits had helped to sustain those of her cousin Blanche, when the latter had, from some unexplained cause, become low and desponding—who had taken that ride to Frodsham on that pleasant June day with her cousin Ferdinand,—had become a grave and thoughtful woman. But the change which was discernible by the outward eye, was as nothing compared to that which had taken place within.

Barbara's history during the last twelvemonth had not been a happy one. How was it possible that it should have been, marrying as she had done, a man whom she did not even pretend to love? Up to the very last moment, during the time which elapsed between her departure from Wentmore and her wedding-day at Leamington, she had debated in her mind whether she could make up her mind to carry out her resolution of becoming Sidney Graham's wife or not. Had she not known of his proposal to Blanche, had she not felt convinced from the very first that he cared no more for her than she did for him, she might have persuaded herself that in time she must have loved one who loved her. She divined his motive for asking her to be his wife, she understood perfectly that it was to shew Blanche how little he cared for her refusal, that he had so immediately offered his hand to another. She compared him with herself, and knowing what her own reason for accepting him had been, she owned that they were fitly matched. But there was a bitterness in the admission which augured ill for her future peace of mind.

He came to her at Leamington, and asked her if she was still minded to carry out their engagement. She saw that one word from her would have made him break it off without hesitation, and she felt sure without regret. But she did not speak that word. She told him that she would try and make him a good wife, but her tone was hard and bitter as she said so, and with a smile which almost made her shudder, he replied, that he was glad to hear it. He then informed her that he should write to his uncle, and acquaint him with their intention. She simply bowed her head, and turned away from him, feeling that she could not trust herself to say another word. And as the days passed on, and the one for the marriage drew near, she almost prayed that something would happen to prevent, or at least to postpone it. No word or sign betokened the conflict which she was inwardly enduring, and those about her had no suspicion of the truth. The preparations for the wedding, quiet and unostentatious as they were, went on, and none of those who were concerned in them divined how gladly the bride elect would have put a stop to them altogether, if she could have done so.

Sidney Graham was absent from Leamington for a short time previous to the wedding, and only returned the evening before. Barbara pleaded fatigue, and excusing herself from seeing him, retired to her own room and shut herself up alone. Even then, she felt doubtful of her own resolution, she questioned with herself as to whether she would write to Sidney, and tell him that she could not marry him after all.

Far into the night she sat in the same desponding attitude, her travelling trunks standing open about the room, and the general disorder around her reflecting in some sort the tumultuous tossing of her own soul. She thought of Wentmore and her kind friends there, of Blanche and her tender loving heart. What would she give to be able to throw her arms round Blanche's neck now, and give vent to all her misery and wretchedness! She was truly wretched. In a moment of madness, (she could call it nothing else,) she had consented to become Sidney Graham's wife, in order to avoid the necessity of returning to her uncle's house, when her visit into Warwickshire should have ended. What a reason for linking her fate for ever, with a man like that! During the short period which had passed since her engagement, Barbara had obtained an insight into Sidney's character, which, had not her perceptive faculties been sharpened by suffering and suspicion, she would scarcely have done at any other time. She had never supposed him to be a person of strong or warm affections. She had never given him credit for any deep religious feeling, although she had taken it for granted that he possessed a certain amount of high principle. But, the heartlessness and selfishness which shewed itself in so many little ways, she had not been prepared for.

Would it not be better to go back to Wentmore, to steel her heart and force herself to endure the sight of Cissy Lethbridge's happiness, however hard it might be to do so—would not anything be better than to persevere in this engagement until it was too late to repent, and the irrevocable words had been spoken which would bind her for ever to such a man? She all but determined to send him word that she had changed her mind, and was of opinion that for both their sakes it would be better to bring the matter to an end. She even started up for the purpose of seeking her writing materials in order to begin her letter, but then came the thought of the inevitable return to

Wentmore, of all that would be said and thought, of this person's wonder and that one's remarks, above all, of the every day life that would follow, of Ferdinand's brotherly regard and confidences. She could measure to a nicety the amount of fraternal affection which he would bestow upon her, whilst to another would be given that love which she coveted, and had at one time—oh, fatal delusion—even believed to be hers! And that decided her. Anything rather than the sight of her rival's happiness! There was no fate she would not hail with delight, that would save her from that. No. She would rather die, than go back to witness Cissy Lethbridge's reception at Wentmore, as her cousin Ferdinand's affianced wife. She would marry Sidney Graham were he twenty times the heartless worldling she believed him to be, sooner than do that!

And she did marry him. With a firm voice and collected mien, she pronounced the words which united her to the cousin she did not love. She gave him her hand, but withheld the heart—which was given to the cousin who did not love her!

For some weeks after their marriage, Barbara strove to drown thought by rushing with her husband from place to place on the continent, and giving herself up to the enjoyment of a life which was full of novelty and excitement for her, if indeed, that could be called enjoyment which consisted in a ceaseless endeavour to *forget*. Poor Barbara! When she caught the sound of her own laughter in the box of a German theatre, or overheard the frequent remarks of admiration which were caused by her appearance in the public walks of the places they visited, she tried to persuade herself that she was happy. Yes, happy! As if she did not know in her heart of hearts that that word had now no meaning for her, and probably never would have again.

Neither she nor Sidney, as we have already observed, had any wish to return to England for a time. They must do so some day, they supposed, and that was enough. They had heard of Blanche's engagement to Charles Lethbridge, and of her having become a Roman Catholic. Barbara watched her husband's countenance as he read the letter which contained the double announcement, but he returned it to her without a sign of emotion, or even of surprise. His only remark was, " They don't say when the wedding is to take place. Some time in the winter, I suppose," and she wondered whether he had ever really cared for Blanche after all.

" Gerald will crow over Blanche's conversion," Sidney observed, some time after. " I wonder if he is still at Brussels, slaving away with his pen and his lectures at that d——d college. What a fool the fellow must be to go on like that, when he has ever so much money at his bankers' lying idle, because he doesn't choose to touch it."

"Poor Gerald," said Barbara, musingly, "I should like to see him again."

"Should you? I don't suppose you will then. For my part I don't care if I never see one of the Lennoxes again. I never pretended to have much 'family affection' as it is called. My father hadn't before me. I have often heard him say he hated all his relations, and as a rule I think they are a detestable lot."

"How can you say so?" exclaimed Barbara, indignantly. "I am sure Uncle and Aunt Lennox were always extremely kind to you, and you seemed glad enough to come to Wentmore when they asked you."

"Hey day!" sneered her husband, "we are displeased at any aspersion being cast on our dear Wentmore belongings, are we? I thought some one cared for them as little at one time as I did?"

Barbara bit her lip, but did not reply. She felt the value of the taunt, and only regretted that she had laid herself open to it.

But months passed on, and as nothing more was heard of Blanche's intended marriage, Barbara forgot all about it. The winter found them in Paris again, and for a time she plunged with avidity into the gaieties which that gayest of capitals afforded. Sidney knew a good many people, and they were constantly asked to parties and

entertainments of all kinds. It was after returning late one night from a ball near the Barriere de
l'Etoile, that Barbara caught the cold which re-
sulted in an attack of rheumatic fever, and ulti-
mately caused them to seek the waters of Aix on
her account. The ground was slippery, and one
of the horses had fallen. Sidney sprang out of
the carriage to help in raising it, and Barbara,
frightened and nervous, wished to follow him.
He desired her, however, to remain where she
was, and she was obliged to content herself with
leaning out of the carriage window, eagerly watching the struggles of the fallen horse and the efforts
which were made to raise it. The cloak which
she had over her shoulders fell back, and she forgot in her excitement how unprotected she was
from the night air. The result was that she became feverish during the night, and the next day
was suffering tortures from rheumatism. She was
confined to her bed for some time, and as the
rheumatic affection still remained when otherwise
she had recovered her health, she was, as we have
said, recommended to try the waters at Aix.

The gay scene in the Elisengarten, was not sufficiently attractive in Sidney's eyes to detain him
longer than a few minutes by his wife's side, and
jumping up at the end of the first piece which was
executed by the band after their entrance, he told
Barbara he should leave her under Captain Lucas's
care, and resigned his seat to him. Barbara in-

quired when he would be at the hotel again. He replied, "About six o'clock," and then hurried away.

Captain Lucas instantly took possession of the vacant seat, and remarked in a low tone to Barbara, that he could not understand anyone's being bored by music.

"My husband used to care about it at one time," said Barbara. "I don't think he does now."

As Sidney was leaving the gardens, he turned round and looked back at his wife and her companion for a moment. A dark shade passed over his countenance as he did so.

"Confound that fellow," he muttered to himself. "She can bestow her smiles upon him it seems, though it is seldom *I* get one from her. She never pretended to care for me it is true. What a fool I was!—Well! it's not much use thinking that now!"

CHAPTER VI.

DESTITUTION. It is a serious thing. An ordeal before which the stoutest heart will quail. And yet, it was to this, or to something very like it, that on his recovery after a long and tedious illness, Gerald Lennox, the son of the wealthy Rector of Wentmore—the nephew of the Earl of Norwood, found himself reduced.

He had paid M. Leblanc's bill, and sundry others which lay receipted before him. He had enough money left to meet his quarter's rent which would be due in a few days, and after that, would have about five pounds in the world to call his own. True, there was that money in London, but the more he needed it, the more utterly resolved he was, suspecting as he did the quarter from whence it came, not to touch a farthing of it. There was his father's allowance, which would keep him from actual want if he chose to make use of it. But his father had never written to him, since he had penned that angry letter accusing him of influencing his sister Blanche, and persuading her to change her religion; and Gerald felt too much hurt to avail himself of his assistance in consequence. He did not owe a farthing in the world, that was one comfort, and before the little store remaining to him of his hard won earnings was expended, he might have hit upon some further plan for increasing them by his own exertions. Anyhow, he would face his position manfully, and do the best he could for himself under the circumstances.

The first thing was to quit his present lodgings and seek for cheaper ones elsewhere. This was the second time Gerald had made a descent in the world, in this respect, since his arrival in Brussels. But reasonable as his quarters in the Rue d' Idalie were, he could not afford them now, and he made it his business to find a room which would serve both the purpose of bed-chamber and parlour at a lower rent, at once. In this, after a day's search,  he succeeded, and having secured the services of his landlord's son, he effected the removal of his books and boxes the day following. He assured Madame Lemmens who was in despair at his departure, that he should recommend her apartments whenever he had an opportunity, and might very possibly return to them himself someday, although for the present he was obliged to move.

He mentioned his change of residence in writing to England, in order that his letters might be directed aright in reply, but of any other change, save that his health was in great measure re-established, he said not a word. The Abbé Beaufort, who knew how anxious his young friend was to obtain another engagement in tuition, if possible, exerted himself to the utmost to further his views, but no opening of the kind seemed to present itself. The publisher, M. Poisset, who had been so kind to him before his illness, was in England. His assistant informed Gerald that they had been obliged to get his unfinished work completed by other hands, and it being a slack time with their London correspondent, there was no demand for more translations at present. Truly, if his prospects had seemed unfavourable when he first arrived in the Belgian capital some fifteen months before, they were much more gloomy now. But the Lennox heart was a stout one, and Gerald hoped on even when only a few francs remained in his purse, and starvation almost stared him in the face.

And now, more than ever, he rejoiced in the happiness and comfort which was afforded him by his religion. Constant as his attendance had always been at the services of the Church, he was now, oftener still, to be seen at Mass or Benediction, visiting his Divine Master in one sacred edifice or another. Daily did he frequent the Chapelle Expiatoire in the Rue des Sols. Rarely did Father Anselm say his Mass at the

Carmelites without perceiving Gerald amongst the assistants, but his favourite resort was the Church of St. Gudule, and there both morning and evening was he oftenest to be found.

There were a good many English visitors that winter in Brussels, and most of them, however short might be their stay, made a point of visiting the far-famed Collegiate Church before their departure. It was therefore a common sight, at any time of the day, to see a group of strangers passing from one part of the building to another, often with very little regard for the service which might be proceeding, or the feelings of the worshippers who were engaged in private prayer at other times. One Saturday evening, when the Salut was over, and Gerald was kneeling in one of the side aisles waiting in his turn to approach a confessional, his attention was attracted by the sound of two English voices speaking close to him.

"How beautifully that boy sang! The 'Ave Maria' wasn't it? It was as good as being at the Opera," said one.

"Oh, Julia! What a comparison!"

The hushed tone of reverence, contrasting forcibly with the careless, scarcely subdued voice of the first speaker, caused Gerald involuntarily to look round. Two ladies were standing near him, young and elegantly attired. One had her back turned towards him, but the light of a neighbouring burner fell upon the countenance of the other, who was gazing round the building with a look of awe and admiration which sat well upon her fair young features. Something in the expression of her face put him in mind of his sister Blanche, and he could not remove his eyes from her for a moment.

"Come, Alice, we shall be late," said the other lady, turning round and addressing her companion, "and they will be wondering what has become of us. There is not going to be any more service. I can't think what all these people are waiting here for."

She too was good-looking, but Gerald was not attracted by her in the least. Her manner was brusque, and at that moment, in his eyes, offensive.

"Hush!" was the answer. "Do not speak so loud. They are going to Confession. Do you not see?"

At that moment the speaker's glance fell upon Gerald and met his. He could not help bestowing a smile of approval upon her. By it, he thanked her, as it were, for the reproof which she had given her friend.

She coloured deeply and turned away, and in another moment the two had passed out of sight.

"What a lovely creature!" thought Gerald. "And what a difference in their manner! I wonder who she is."

A quarter of an hour afterwards, as he was

leaving the southern door of the building, a hand was laid upon his shoulder, and a voice accosted him with " Which way are you going ?"

Turning round, he recognized Algernon Roberts, the son of Lady Sophia Roberts, whom he had not seen for some time.

" Home ;" answered Gerald. " How are you ? and how is Lady Sophia ?"

" Quite well, thanks," rejoined the other. "We were only saying to-day what an age it was since we had seen anything of you," and putting his arm within Gerald's, the two walked on together.

At the corner of the Rue du Commerce, Gerald paused, and held out his hand to say goodnight.

" I will come on with you," said young Roberts. " My mother and sisters went off this morning to spend the day with some friends at Tervueren, and they will scarcely have returned yet."

" I am no longer in the Rue d' Idalie," returned Gerald. " I could not afford to stay in my old quarters there, as in consequence of my illness I lost my Professorship at St. Antoine, and I have moved into a humbler *locale*."

" Well, I should have thought the Rue d' Idalie was cheap enough," exclaimed Algernon Roberts. " I forget what you told me you gave for your rooms, but I remember thinking it something wonderfully little."

" Very likely," laughed Gerald, " but all the same, it is beyond my figure now. However, if you will come with me, I will introduce you to my present abode."

It was to a clean-looking house in the new part of the town, beyond the Carmelite Monastery in the Quartier Louise, that Gerald led his companion. But when the latter, after they had ascended to the upper storey of the building, was shown into the little room which constituted Gerald's habitation by day and night, he looked round somewhat surprised.

"My dear fellow!" he exclaimed, "this is a change for you, and I cannot say I think it one for the better!"

"Well, no, I can't say it is," returned Gerald, "but until I can afford something else, it must do, that is all. Won't you sit down? I think I can muster a couple of chairs."

Algernon Roberts sat down, and feeling that it would be indelicate to express further wonderment at his friend's evidently distressed condition, began speaking about the number of conversions which had lately taken place in England. This was a subject which always excited Gerald's interest, and whilst mentioning the names of several families, members of which had recently become Catholics, he alluded incidentally to his sister's reception into the Church, expressing a hope that her example might be followed by some of her friends and acquaintance ere long.

"My mother was so very much interested in

Miss Lennox's conversion," said young Roberts, " she and Lady Frances Lennox were such great friends, I have heard her say, in their early days. Have you any hopes of your brother ?"

" Hopes ! yes," answered Gerald, " I have certainly, but I have no reason to suppose he is in the least likely to change at present."

" He is going to be a clergyman is he not ?"

" Yes.   A priest—he would call it."

" That is the most extraordinary infatuation of all," said Algernon. "How they can read English History, and believe themselves priests of the Catholic Church, whilst remaining members of the Anglican Establishment, I cannot understand !"

Gerald smiled.   " I daresay you people who were born Catholics *do* feel puzzled by that sort of thing, but it is not so long since I believed in the Orders and Catholicity of the English Church myself, you know, and so to me, it is nothing so wonderful."

At that moment a knock came at the door, and in answer to Gerald's permission to " *Entrez*," Mr. Fitzroy entered the room.

Gerald sprang up and advanced to meet him. " This is an unexpected pleasure," he exclaimed, shaking the new-comer warmly by the hand. " I thought you were still out of town ?"

" I came back from Bruges this afternoon, and have been hunting for you for the last half-hour,

Madame Lemmens gave me a wrong number. How are you, my dear Lennox? and what has brought you to this part of the world?" said Mr. Fitzroy.

Gerald explained in a few words that circumstances had obliged him to change his abode, and then Mr. Fitzroy turning to young Roberts, with whom he was slightly acquainted, inquired how some Amateur Performance, in which he had taken part, had gone off. This led to the subject of actors and acting generally, and Gerald remarked that it was long since he had been to a really good play, " And there is scarcely anything I enjoy so much," he added.

" Then come with me to the Theatre du Parc to-morrow evening," said Algernon, "I have a couple of tickets which were given me this morning. My mother and one of my sisters had intended to use them, but they are obliged to go to some party, which they had hoped to get off, instead. I was undecided as to what I should do, but if you have nothing better on hand, we will go together. They have something very good at present there they tell me."

Gerald accepted the offer readily, and soon after his visitors took leave of him together.

" That was kind and thoughtful of you," said Mr. Fitzroy to his companion, as they emerged into the street. " Our friend does not indulge himself often in such pleasures, I suspect, and if you had' asked him to go with you in the usual way, he would most probably have declined, from the simple reason of not being able to afford it. He is very very poor just now, I am certain."

"I am afraid so," was the answer, "and that was one reason why I proposed going, as I could do so without putting him to any expense. What a noble fellow he is to bear his reverse of fortune so well. His people are all immensely wealthy I believe."

"Yes, I fancy so," said Mr. Fitzroy, thoughtfully, "that illness of his was a bad business for him. He lost his employment at the College of S. Antoine because of it, and I am sure his relations do not know how much he has suffered since."

Roberts remarked upon the privilege which converts so generally had of suffering for the Faith, and declared he envied them on account of it. "Those who are born Catholics, like ourselves," he said, "cannot but feel that they have the pull over us in that respect."

"True;" answered Mr. Fitzroy. "But then, we must not forget how much it cost our forefathers to preserve the Faith and hand it down to us, during three centuries of persecution. If we cannot boast of having suffered for it ourselves, we may think with some satisfaction of what they endured."

For a short space the two walked on in silence,

and then as their roads somewhat diverged, they wished each other a cordial good-night, and parted.

The next day Mr. Fitzroy encountered the Abbé Beaufort on the Boulevard, and linking his arm within that of the ecclesiastic, he walked up and down with him for some time. The subject of their discourse was Gerald Lennox, and both agreed that something ought to be done about him.

"He will kill himself—that will be the end of it," said Mr. Fitzroy. "He nearly did so with overwork in the summer, and now he will starve if he cannot get employment, rather than be dependent on his family."

"You arre right," exclaimed the Abbé. "I believe he will indeed. I found out by accident the other day, that he had had no dinner, although it was not a fast day, and I suspect that it was not the first time he had gone without. His landlady told me he never dined *chez lui*, and I knew where he had been all day, so that I was certain he had not done so elsewhere."

"Then, my dear sir, I tell you what it is. If he will not interfere on his own behalf, we must do so for him. I shall write to his brother without saying a word to him, and get him to come over, and he will soon put all that to rights, or else I am much mistaken."

"Right, quite right," repeated the little Abbé. "Ha, ha, Monsieur Gerald, you will not be allowed

to starrve and keel yourselve quite so easily !"
And the good man rubbed his hands with triumph.

The result of this conversation was, that a week
or so after, when Gerald was sitting in his little
room one evening alone, feeling more than usually
depressed and low spirited, the door was opened,
and Ferdinand walked in, having knocked first,
and been told that he might *entrez* by his brother.

For a moment, Gerald stared at him without
speaking. Then jumping up from his chair, he
rushed towards him, exclaiming,

"Ferdinand, my dearest fellow! This is a
surprise. What brought you here? How delighted
I am to see you !"

"Well, I am glad to hear that, at any rate,"
said Ferdinand, after he had examined Gerald
attentively by the light of his solitary lamp. "As
to what brought me here—why—it was the train.
I was tired of waiting for an invitation, and so came
without one. Gerald, how ill you are looking !"

"Nonsense," answered Gerald, trying to laugh
off his brother's scrutiny. "I am all right. And
how are they at home ?"

But it would not do. Ferdinand had received
Mr. Fitzroy's letter, and having determined to
start at once and ascertain for himself how Gerald
was really going on, he had lost no time in doing
so. He had hurried to his brother's lodgings
immediately on his arrival, and was inexpressibly
shocked at the alteration in his appearance.

He did not allow Gerald to perceive how much this was the case, but telling him that he intended taking up his quarters at the Flandre for the present, he carried him off there in his *vigilante* which was waiting at the door, and they were soon comfortably seated in a snug little sitting-room of that hotel, discussing a substantial repast before a bright fire. Far into the night the two brothers sat, talking over many things, and before they parted, Ferdinand had wrung from Gerald a confession of all the miseries and privations with which he had been struggling of late, and extorted from him a promise to accept, at least for the present, some pecuniary aid from himself.

"You may go back to your charming *apartement* for to-night," said Ferdinand, in conclusion, "but to-morrow you will take leave of Madame whatever-her-name-is, and bring your goods and chattels here. You will not get rid of me immediately, and as long as I remain, we must be together if you please. And now, my dearest boy, good-night. I am hideously tired and half asleep already. Come in good time to breakfast. *Au revoir.*"

And as Gerald walked back through the silent streets for the last time to his humble lodging in the Quartier Louise, he knew within himself that his day of actual privation was over. He felt half angry with whoever had written to his brother, (Ferdinand had refused to give the name, but he more than half suspected Mr. Fitzroy,) but at the same time he could not but confess to himself that it was impossible the present state of things should have lasted much longer. Failing engagement of any sort or kind, he must sooner or later have descended from his pedestal, and accepted help from some one, or else have starved—and he was hardly prepared to face the latter alternative with composure.

Ferdinand did not leave Brussels for some time, and when he did so, he had the satisfaction of knowing that his brother was no longer exposed to privations, which it had grieved him to the heart to think he had for a time endured. With Lord Norwood's assistance, he had managed to procure for Gerald an appointment as Foreign Correspondent to a leading London Journal, and he was also engaged to furnish articles for a popular Magazine which paid its contributors liberally, and by this means he was rendered both independent and secure in a great degree from the likelihood of further reverses in the future.

How unfeignedly Mr. Fitzroy and his other Brussels friends rejoiced over this change in Gerald's fortunes may be imagined, and the former often assured him that he owed it entirely to his and the Abbé Beaufort's resolution to put a stop to the state of things which prevailed at the time when he called that evening, and found him with young Roberts in his wretched apartment in the Quartier Louise. Gerald laughed, and declared he would never forgive him for his interference. It was very hard, he maintained, that when he was on the high road to penury and want, he should not have been allowed to pursue so interesting a course, but nevertheless he did not manifest any great desire to return to that enviable condition.

With the return of the summer months, Brussels began to empty itself of its visitors, and the Boulevards and other fashionable districts assumed gradually an air of desertion as the hot weather set in. Gerald's lodgings were in a pleasant and healthy part of the town, but Mr. Fitzroy, who continued to watch over him with fatherly care, had determined in his own mind that he should not remain in the capital during the extreme heat again, and as the season advanced, he proposed that he should accompany him on a visit to Spa, which at that time of the year was a favourite resort of his.

"I shall not allow you to go too often to the Rooms though," said Mr. Fitzroy, smiling. "If you were to acquire a taste for play, that would be a nice thing for me to feel I had led you into!"

"Never fear," answered Gerald. "I am not quite such a fool as that, though I confess that *roulette* has a kind of fascination for me. I have never been to Spa, but some few years ago, when I first came of age, I went to Homburg amongst other places, and I managed to lose a little money there with great satisfaction to the *croupiers* at any rate !"

And to Spa they went. The little watering place was full, and as they drove from the station into the town, the numbers of English and other foreigners they saw, all of them well dressed and with apparently no object in life but their own amusement, impressed Gerald with the notion that there must be a great many rich people with nothing to do in the world. True, Spa was a place of resort to some on account of the salubrity of its chalybeate springs, but there was no doubt that by far the greater part of these fashionable loungers had been attracted thither, not because the waters of the *Geronstere* were famed throughout the civilized world for their efficacy to sufferers under certain complaints, or because the family doctor had prescribed a course of matutinal visits to the *Pouhon*, but in consequence of the brilliant programme set forth by the Proprietors of the Redoute for the entertainment of its patrons, and the irresistible fascination which *rouge et noir* and the *roulette* table possess for certain minds.

Having taken up their quarters at the Pays Bas and dined at the *table-d'hôte*, Mr. Fitzroy and Gerald strolled down to the Promenade de Sept Heures, where the gay world assembled every evening about sunset to listen to the band, and when that was over, they took their way to the Rooms.

So well known are these "Rooms" in the present day, that a description of them and of the assemblage which for twelve hours throngs them daily, from the beginning of May till the end of October, is unnecessary on our part. Suffice it, that when Gerald Lennox entered them on this particular evening of the summer of 186—, they presented very much the same appearance as they had done at that time of year, (Spa being at the height of its season and unusually full) for a long time past, and are likely to do for some short while longer still. Both the card-room and the one devoted to the mysteries of *roulette* were crowded with visitors. The reading-room with its rich *fauteuils* and plentiful supply of Belgian and foreign journals was also filled, and from the large ball room in the distance the sound of dance music was borne upon the air.

Mr. Fitzroy was contented with one turn of the rooms, and then betook himself to a corner of the *Salle de Lecture*, having obtained possession of the "Times" newspaper, and there he remained comfortably ensconced for the space of an hour or more. Gerald stayed in the card-room, watching the progress of the game, every now and then taking a look at the *roulette* table to see how matters were going on there. The scene was an exciting one, and it was long since he had witnessed anything of the kind. The sums of money so carelessly lost, so easily won, the look of utter indifference on some faces, and of keen, eager, almost terrible anxiety on others, made him regard both the *croupiers* and the company with wonderment at first, but that feeling soon wore off, and he found himself after a while taking no more notice of a *coup* which some lucky gamester had made, or of some equally startling loss on the part of a less fortunate individual, than if it had been his daily habit to frequent a Redoute for the last twelvemonth.

But at length he began to tire of simply watching others win and lose, and staking a napoleon on *Rouge* at the card table, he took up in addition, which he placed on the green cloth in the *roulette* room. There also he won, and smiling at the successful issue of his small ventures, he strolled into the reading-room in quest of Mr. Fitzroy.

"I have been playing tremendously, and winning," he said, as that gentleman seeing him approach, laid down his newspaper and looked up. "See here;" and he drew a handful of gold coins from his pocket.

"Very bad, very bad," said Mr. Fitzroy, shaking his head. "It is always a fatal sign when people begin by winning. They invariably go on and lose frightfully at last. If we stay here long I shall have to write home and warn your friends, and what they will say to your turning out a gambler, I don't know!"

"It will be all your fault for having brought me here," answered Gerald, laughingly. "But it is so hot in these rooms, won't you come and have a turn in the open air? or are you too tired?"

"I am too comfortable where I am," said Mr. Fitzroy. "But do you go, and you will find me here when you come back."

"All right," returned Gerald. And with one more glance at the tables, he turned and left the Rooms.

On his way down the broad staircase, he encountered several persons who were ascending in the opposite direction. A lady and gentleman met him on the landing, half way down, and without looking up, he drew a little on one side to let them pass. As he did so, the lady said to her companion,

"I hope you are not going to play much to-night, Sidney. You lost so often this afternoon I am sure your luck has turned, and you ought to wait till it comes back again."

"Nonsense. You needn't frighten yourself," was the reply. "If I find that I am losing, I shall leave off."

Both voices were familiar to Gerald. With an exclamation of astonishment he turned round, and beheld his cousins Sidney and Barbara Graham.

CHAPTER VII.

Sidney was two or three steps ahead of his wife, and he did not see Gerald, but Barbara's eye met his, and she gave a little scream of delight and surprise as she recognized him. Gerald put out his hand, and she grasped it warmly.

"Gerald! Is it really you?" she exclaimed. "I never dreamed of meeting you here! Although we are in Belgium, of course, and it is a place everyone seems to come to!"

Hearing Barbara's exclamation, Sidney stopped and looked round. He stared at Gerald for a moment, and then called out,

"Why, Gerald, old boy, where do you spring from? From Brussels, eh? Well, no one stays there who can get away just now, I imagine. And how are you?"

Hardly waiting for an answer, he caught hold of Gerald's outstretched hand, shook it, and hurried on into the Rooms. Gerald turned to Barbara.

"Does Sidney play?" he asked.

"Yes. It amuses him," she answered in a low tone. "He is generally fortunate, but it excites him, and I wish—I cannot bear his coming here as often as he does." As she spoke she looked up into her cousin's face, and he saw that her eyes were filled with tears.

"I will speak to him about it," said Gerald, pressing her hand affectionately. "I am sure he would not do it, if he knew it vexed you."

"No, don't say anything to him," she exclaimed hurriedly. "Pray don't. He would only be annoyed, and it would do no good."

They had now entered the Rooms, and Gerald took Barbara at once up to Mr. Fitzroy, who was nodding behind his newspaper, and stared in astonishment on being roused by a tap on his shoulder, at seeing his young friend returned so soon accompanied by a lady.

"I declare you were asleep," said Gerald. "But you will forgive me for disturbing you as I want to introduce you to my cousin, Mrs. Graham, of whom you have often heard me speak, and who, by the way, is, I daresay, an old friend of yours, as I know you were acquainted with my Uncle Geoffrey in former days?"

Mr. Fitzroy jumped up and took Barbara's hand in his.

"My dear young lady, I am indeed pleased to make your acquaintance. I remember you a very

tiny individual in your mother's arms, and I have
often wished to see you since.   Ah, yes! you have
your mother's smile and your father's eyes.   He
and I were brother-officers for a time in the same
regiment, but that was before you were born.
And is your husband here?"

Whilst he was speaking, Mr. Fitzroy led Barbara to a seat, and placed himself by her side.
She had heard of him at Wentmore as a friend of
Gerald's, and as having known her father in former
years.

"This is a second unexpected pleasure," she
exclaimed, after informing him that she and her
husband had arrived at Spa from Aix la Chapelle
some ten days before.   "I shall have agreeable
reminiscences of the Redoute from this time
forth."

"I shall leave you two to discuss all the various
things which have happened to both since 'last
you met,'" said Gerald, laughing, "and go and
look after Sidney.   I will bring him back with me
if I can."

"Ah, you will not be able to do that, I suspect," murmured Barbara to herself, as she
watched her cousin's form disappear through the
doorway.   Then turning to Mr. Fitzroy she began
an animated conversation with him which lasted
for half an hour or more, when Gerald returned
accompanied, not by Sidney, but by someone else,
at sight of whom Barbara coloured and exclaimed,

"Good evening, Captain Lucas, I thought you were dining at the Bretannique with a large party? I am surprised you should have got away so soon." Then without waiting for an answer, she added, "You and Gerald are old friends, I suppose? I know you were often at Wentmore like most of the Hillsborough officers."

"I never had the pleasure of meeting Mr. Gerald Lennox before," replied Captain Lucas, taking possession of a vacant seat next to Barbara, "but Graham introduced me to him, and as I have so lively a recollection of my visits to Wentmore Rectory, and of the kindness which Mr. Lennox and Lady Frances always shewed us poor subs at Hillsborough, I was delighted to make his acquaintance as you may suppose."

"Sidney is trying a *système*, as he calls it," said Gerald, who was leaning with his back against a chair opposite his cousin, "and is certain to win, he says, if he continues it long enough. He wished to speak to you if you would go to him presently."

"Let us go at once," cried Barbara, starting up. "It amuses me to watch the *roulette*, and the people here look cross at our chattering, which is quite against the rule in this room, I believe."

Taking Mr. Fitzroy's arm, and followed by Gerald and Captain Lucas, she passed out of the Salle de Lecture, and in another minute was standing by her husband's side at the *roulette* table. He turned his head for a moment, and nodded to her, but did not speak. The oft repeated "*Rien de plus*" had just been pronounced, and every eye was fixed with anxiety on the little white ball which was spinning round so swiftly. It stopped.

"*Zero Rouge!*" was the cry.

Sidney Graham won, and turned round to Captain Lucas. "I had given up the '*Douzes*' for a turn, and just placed my money upon *Zero à cheval*. That is what I call luck," he said.

Lucas smiled, and pressed forward to place a five franc piece down on his own account. At that moment a slight movement took place at their end of the table, and Gerald stood aside to allow one or two people who had been standing in the inner circle to pass out. One of these was a young man whose ghastly features stamped with an expression of despair, arrested his attention, and he involuntarily turned to watch him as he left the room. One or two others did the same, and shrugged their shoulders with the remark. "*Le pauvre gamin! Il à perdu!*" and then turned to the tables again with the usual indifference to the fortune of others which is so notable a feature in the *salons* of a Redoute. But Gerald could not so easily forget the look of misery which had struck him in the stranger's face, and momentary as had been the sight of it, he felt as if in some way which he could not account for, that the features were familiar to him, or at least that he had seen them somewhere before.

"Poor fellow," he thought, "I wonder who he is."

"Confound this *roulette!* I shall go and have a try at the cards. Go home, Barbara, and don't sit up for me. Lucas or Gerald will see you across the street, I daresay."

Sidney had lost, and was leaving the *roulette* table in disgust. He touched his wife on the arm as he spoke, and then hurried off into the next room. Captain Lucas heard the words, and came forward to offer his services to Mrs. Graham.

"Thanks, I daresay my cousin will take care of me," said Barbara, looking round for Gerald as she spoke. "Oh, there he is," she added, perceiving him at a little distance, speaking to Mr. Fitzroy. "Will you kindly tell him that I am not going to wait for Sidney, and ask him if he will escort me home?"

Captain Lucas bit his lip and departed with his message. He had been in the habit of escorting Barbara to her lodgings regularly each night. She did not like remaining in the rooms the whole evening, and Sidney seldom left till the last. Henry Lucas was always within reach, and never seemed so happy as when performing any little friendly office for the young wife, who accepted his attentions as a matter of course, and was hardly aware herself of how dependent upon them she had become. She believed in the young man's friendship, and was glad that he should have followed them from Aix to Spa, as without some other companionship than that of her husband, knowing so few of the visitors at the little watering place as she did, she must often have found it dull.

"I am tired," she said, as Gerald came up to her in obedience to Captain Lucas's summons. "Sidney is not going home yet. Will you take me across the way? It is only two minutes walk, and you can come back again directly."

"Oh, Fitzroy and I were just going," answered Gerald. "We have had quite enough of it for to-night, I shall be delighted to go with you."

"Good-night, Captain Lucas," said Barbara. "We shall see you to-morrow, I daresay."

Captain Lucas bowed, and murmured something about "looking forward to that happiness." Then nodding to Gerald, whom he did not regard with very friendly feelings at the moment, and whose stay at Spa he hoped would be short, he sauntered into the further room, and took up his position behind Sidney Graham's chair, to watch the upshot of the game.

Mr. Fitzroy quitted the rooms with Barbara and Gerald, and parted with them at the foot of the stairs, telling the latter that he would find him at their hotel on his return. The Grahams had an "*Apartement*" not far from the Redoute, and as they crossed the quiet street in the bright moonlight, Barbara looked up into Gerald's face, and said,

"How little I thought when I last saw you, that this would be our next place of meeting!"

"True," answered Gerald. "Tell me, Barbara, how are you? I heard that you were ordered to Aix for your health. Have the waters there done you good?"

"Yes. I am a different creature to what I was when we got to Aix first of all. Come in, Gerald, for a few minutes, will you?" Barbara said as they reached the door of the house where she and Sidney were lodging, "I have so many questions to ask you about Wentmore and them all."

Gerald followed her up the stairs in silence. This meeting with Barbara moved him strangely. He, too, felt as if there were many things he should like to ask her, above all, why she had married Sidney, and whether she was happy. But those were the very questions which it was most difficult to put, and he contented himself for the present with answering her enquiries respecting the dear ones at home, hoping that she would voluntarily furnish him with the information he wished for concerning herself.

They had much to speak of, but Barbara kept aloof from anything purely personal. And when she had exhausted Gerald's stock of information respecting Blanche's engagement, (Ferdinand's she touched very lightly upon,) and other news from England, and he in his turn began to put a few questions to her about her travels and so forth, she cut him short by remarking that it was getting dreadfully late, and she was sure he must be very tired, so that she would not let him stop another minute.

"Good-night, Bibi, I shall see you to-morrow," said Gerald, stooping to kiss her on the forehead in his old brotherly fashion.

"Yes," she answered, and her voice slightly trembled as she spoke. "Come as early as you like. Good-night."

From the window of the *salon* Barbara watched her cousin cross the street and go towards his hotel. She followed his form with her eyes until it vanished in the distance, and then she threw herself back in a chair, and covered her face with her hands.

"Oh, those old days! those old days! Gone—never to return," she cried, and choking sobs stayed her further utterance.

The next day was Sunday. Gerald and Mr. Fitzroy went to Communion at the Parish Church before breakfast, and to the High Mass afterwards. As they came down the steps which lead into the town from the north entrance of the church at the conclusion of the service, Gerald glanced up at the balcony of the house where his cousins were lodging, and perceived Barbara standing at the open window. She saw him, and beckoned him to come up.

"I shall take a turn on the Marteau," said Mr. Fitzroy, "but don't think of me. If you don't appear at the two o'clock *table-d'hôte* I shall conclude that you are spending the day with Mr. and Mrs. Graham. Remember me very kindly to her."

"I was watching for you, as I thought you would be coming out of church about this time," exclaimed Barbara, turning to receive her cousin as he appeared in the doorway of the *salon*. "Why did you not bring Mr. Fitzroy up with you? By the way, I did not know he was a Roman Catholic?"

"He has always been one," answered Gerald, quietly, "I am sure he would have been delighted to come and pay his respects to you, but did not like to intrude. Shall I go and fetch him? He has only gone down the Marteau, and I can soon overtake him."

"No, no, I would rather have you to myself, so it is just as well. I hope you intend to give your whole day to us, Gerald, Sunday is so intolerably stupid here. I think it is worse than at Aix la Chapelle, and that is saying a good deal, and it is a mercy to have some one to speak to. Sidney and Captain Lucas have gone out to smoke, and I have been amusing myself with watching the people from the window for the last half hour, and waiting for you to come out of church."

"I was surprised to see you when I looked up," said Gerald, "I thought you would be in church yourself. At the English Chapel I mean. Do you never go?"

"Well, not often," answered Barbara, looking somewhat confused. "Sidney won't go, he never goes anywhere, and it is so disagreeable going alone. Sometimes I get Captain Lucas to go with me. But I would much rather go to your church, Gerald. Will you take me this evening?"

"Yes, with pleasure," replied her cousin. "I suppose Sidney would not mind your going?"

"Oh, I should not care if he did, and as to that, it is about the last thing he would trouble himself about. He goes his way, and leaves me to go mine. We don't interfere with each other much."

"I am sorry to hear that," said Gerald, gravely. Then feeling that the conversation had taken an awkward turn, he added, "You seem very intimate with this Captain Lucas. Is he a nice person? I remember hearing Blanche speak of him as a friend of the Fraser Smiths, but I don't think they admired him particularly at Wentmore."

"Sidney has known him for a long time," answered Barbara, carelessly. "We met him on our way to Aix, and he was there all the time we were, and at the same hotel, so that we necessarily saw a good deal of him. I like him very much, and do not know what I should do without him sometimes, he is so very useful and good-natured. I think we will go out and have a turn as it is so fine." She continued, starting up from her seat, "I will go and put on my bonnet and be back in a moment. We shall meet all the English coming out of church, and they will be so scandalized at my walking about with a young man, instead of having toiled up that hill to sit in a hot room listening to a long sermon. It will be great fun."

She ran off with a little laugh to get ready, and Gerald stood at the open window awaiting her return, an expression of deep thought upon his countenance.

It was a lovely evening, and the promenade was thronged with visitors. The bells were ringing for service, and the people ascending the steps of the church in groups of three or four at a time. Barbara Graham, escorted by Mr. Fitzroy and Gerald, had been listening to the band, but as the sound of the bells reached them, they rose and proceeded slowly towards the church.

"If any of my Protestant friends were to see me, they would think I was going to become a Roman Catholic," said Barbara to Gerald as they walked along.

"I wish you were," answered he, smiling. "But so many of the English go to our churches to hear the music, that there is nothing remarkable in that."

"Gerald," said Barbara, in a low tone, "Blanche's conversion must have made you very happy!"

"God only knows how happy," was the reply.

They had reached the church, and there was no time to say more. Gerald offered Barbara some holy water as they entered, but she declined it with a smile and shake of the head. She was not the least inclined towards Catholic forms or observances, nor did she understand much about them, although before her marriage she had been what is called High Church, and had sympathized to a certain extent in the Wentmore view of such matters as embodied by Ferdinand and Blanche. But she liked the feeling of being again in church with one of her Wentmore cousins, and as she knelt by Gerald's side, she almost fancied herself back in the old church where they had worshipped together so often in former days, and the tears filled her eyes at the remembrance.

The service commenced. On this particular evening it consisted of that most beautiful and touching of Catholic devotions, The Way of the Cross. Barbara had never been present at it before, and was much struck by the fervour and earnestness with which the large congregation joined in the different prayers, as the priest and acolytes proceeded round the church on their way from one station to another. When it was over, and they were slowly descending the steps outside, Barbara whispered to Gerald,

"I liked it very much. Do you know that old Curé ? What a dear old man he seems."

"He is a dear old man," answered Gerald. "I have heard a good deal of him, although I do not know him personally myself as yet. I intend, however, to call and make his acquaintance to-morrow."

During the next few days, Gerald spent most of his time with his cousin Barbara. Of Sidney he saw but little, and that little was unsatisfactory. The old pleasant familiar footing between them seemed to have come to an end. Sidney was civil and friendly when they met, but that was all. His time was chiefly spent in the gaming rooms, or wandering up and down the Avenue of Limes with a cigar in his mouth. His wife he knew was looked after by Lucas and Gerald, and he did not trouble himself in any way about her.

Mr. Fitzroy and Barbara became great friends, but his stay at Spa was cut short in consequence of some letters he received, compelling his return to Brussels about ten days after he and Gerald had arrived. He had been appointed trustee under the will of a Belgian friend, and had been left guardian to some young children as well, and his presence was required in the capital on their account.

"I shall come back as soon as I can," he said to Gerald, as they parted at the railway station, "and shall expect to find you here when I do. The change has done you a world of good already, and you must stay another six weeks at the least."

Gerald laughed, and assured him that he was quite contented to remain where he was. "And if I am cleaned out at the tables," he added, "I shall telegraph to you for fresh supplies, as it will be your fault for leaving me here."

Mr. Fitzroy shook his head smilingly, and said something inaudible in reply as the train moved off.

Gerald walked slowly back into the town, and meeting Captain Lucas at the entrance of the Redoute, he went up the stairs with him to take a look at the players. It was early in the afternoon, but the Rooms were already full, and the seats round each table were occupied by those who meant "business." A number of persons stood on each side of the card table watching the progress of the game, and Gerald took up his position amongst them, whilst Captain Lucas who espied Sidney in the adjoining apartment, strolled off to see what was going on there.

The *Trente et Quarante* room was the most crowded of the two, and large sums of money were frequently gathered up by the players, or swept off by the unsparing rake of the *croupier*. In addition to those who were seated round the table, several persons standing in the crowd were playing, and amongst these Gerald noticed the young man whose face of despair had haunted him on the occasion of his first visit to the Rooms, on the night of his arrival. He stood a little withdrawn from the front row of lookers on, and it was only now and then that he made a push forward to take up his money, or place some down as the case might be. On one of these occasions as he remained rather longer than usual bending over the player who was seated in front of him, hesitating, as it seemed, whether to try his luck on *Couleur* or not, Gerald felt convinced that he had seen him before, but could not in the least remember where or when. Having decided on which part of the table to place his money, the young man drew back and resumed his former position amongst the bystanders. As he did so he raised his eyes for a moment, and they met Gerald's earnest gaze fixed upon him from the other side of the table. It was only for a moment, but Gerald was certain that he too had been recognized, and his wonderment and perplexity increased. He called to mind the faces of all his London friends and acquaintances, at least those whom he had known at all intimately, repeating their names over to himself in succession, but to none of them did those finely cut and rather delicate looking features belong.

More and more puzzled as he thought upon the matter, Gerald resolved to go round the room and see if a closer examination would enable him to determine as to whether he was mistaken in supposing he knew this young man, who interested him so strangely, or not. But when he did so, and reached the spot where just before the object of his curiosity had been standing, he looked for him in vain. He had disappeared, and must have moved away in the contrary direction, Gerald fancied, as he himself came round from the other side. He went into the next room and looked about that, but he was nowhere to be seen, and feeling sure that he should meet him again at one or other of the tables before long, Gerald betook himself to his hotel where he had several letters to answer which the post had brought him that morning both from Brussels and England.

That evening he spent with Barbara, who had invited a few friends to tea in her small "*aparte-ment.*" Captain Lucas was there, of course, and equally of course, Mr. Sidney Graham was not. When the little party broke up, Gerald and the Captain walked down the street of the town together, and ascended the stairs of a large corner house, the upper storey of which was brilliantly lighted, and was known by the *habitués* of the place as the " English Club." They entered the reading room, which at that hour was filled with loungers, and after turning over one or two of the papers which had newly arrived, the two young men strolled into the billiard room adjoining, and amused themselves with knocking about the balls for an hour or more. Both were fair players, and Henry Lucas who preferred an inexperienced hand for an antagonist as a rule, proposed at the end of three or four games that they should adjourn to the Redoute.

Gerald descended with him into the street, and then as the night was extremely fine, said he should take a walk down the Marteau before going into the Rooms. So nodding a farewell, the captain left him, and betook himself without further loss of time to the *locale* consecrated to the mysteries of *Trente et Quarante*.

Left alone, Gerald lighted a cigar and turned his steps towards the Marteau. Arrived at the Hotel du Midi, however, he changed his mind and returned slowly in the direction of the town. The air was warm, and through the open windows of the Redoute he could distinctly hear the "*Faites votre jeu Messieurs*" as he passed below. Beneath the archway of the building stood a number of chairs, which, during the day, were generally filled by those frequenters of the place who had exhausted their luck above stairs for a time, and were ruminating on the fact, or by such as meditated a venture at *roulette* or the cards bye-and-bye, and were indulging in a little calculation as to the chances in their favour beforehand. Only two or three of these seats were occupied at this time by sleepy looking individuals, and Gerald flung himself on to one and amused himself with watching the groups of people who sometimes noisy and excited, and at others gloomy and despondent, descended the stairs at intervals, and passed out of the building.

He was getting drowsy, and oppressed by the heaviness of the atmosphere was half asleep and half awake, when he was startled by the sudden appearance of a young man who rushed past him, and whose features as he caught sight of them by the light of the lamps at the corner, he recognized as those of the person who had attracted his attention that afternoon in the rooms above. His face was ghastly pale, his head was uncovered, and there was something in his whole appearance which impressed Gerald with a vague feeling of alarm and uneasiness. He felt a strong inclination to follow him, he scarcely knew why, and only hesitated from a doubt as to whether he had any right to do so; but the more he thought of it, the more convinced he felt that something was wrong, and that the poor fellow was almost beside himself for some reason or other. He could still hear his footsteps hurrying down the street in the direction of the Avenue of Limes, and feeling that if he wished to overtake him, not a moment was to be lost, he set off in pursuit.

The young man had been running when he

passed Gerald, and he was running still. His pace however had slackened, and as Gerald quickened his, he gained upon him sensibly. Gerald had resolved on coming up with him to ask if anything was the matter, and to notice, as an excuse for his following him, that he had lost his hat. Presently, however, the object of his pursuit increased his speed, and Gerald, in order to keep him within sight, was obliged to do the same. He could see the uncovered figure by the light of the lamps on the Place, disappearing in the shade of the lime trees, and he feared that if once involved in the obscurity of the avenue, he should lose him altogether. The chase now became exciting, and Gerald forgetful of all other considerations, and bent only upon coming up with the fugitive, hastened after him at the top of his speed. The Place was deserted at that time of night, and the echo of his own footsteps as he ran was the only sound which fell on his ear.

The avenue was lighted at long intervals by lamps fastened against the trees, and Gerald who could hear nothing now of the other's receding footsteps, felt that the chances were greatly against his overtaking him. A momentary glimpse of him, however, as he passed at full speed under the light of a lamp at the further end of the avenue, shewed Gerald which direction he had taken, and more bent than ever upon coming up with him, he continued the pursuit. Another

minute and he had gained the end of the shady
walk. It was lighter here, and he paused, for
only a few yards in front, at the foot of a roughly
hewn flight of steps which led up on to the wooded
height above, stood the man he was following,
who did not see him however, and was evidently
debating as to which way he should go.

An involuntary exclamation on Gerald's part
caused him to look round. He uttered a cry of
terror and dismay, and rushing up the steps, disappeared in the windings of the path above.

. If Gerald had determined to overtake him before, he was still more resolved to do so now, for
he was certain that either the poor fellow was
out of his mind, or that he was possessed with
one of those fits of despair which he knew sometimes seized upon the gambler, and hurried him
too often to self destruction.

Urged by his fears of, he knew not what, Gerald
tore up the ascent with lightning speed, and
guided by the sound of the other's flying steps
which rang out on the harder surface of the moun-
tain path with distinctness, he felt sure at length
of overtaking him. The path wound higher and
higher up the side of the hill. Far below, the
lights in the little town appeared at intervals
through some opening in the trees and bushes
which skirted the way. The moon shone brightly
overhead. Nothing disturbed the solitude and
stillness of the place save the headlong race which

these two were having, a race which to the excited
mind of the pursuer seemed to be one of life and
death.

At length, on reaching an eminence on which a
seat had been placed, fronted by a small stone
balustrade, the fugitive paused. He was only a
few yards ahead of Gerald, and the latter felt sure
that he had given in. He heaved a sigh of relief,
which was quickly changed into a cry of horror as
the other turning his head for a moment, and perceiving Gerald so near, sprang forward and disappeared over the parapet.

Gerald had often stood and looked down upon
the valley below from that spot. The seat had
been placed there because of the extensive view
which its great height commanded. Just below
was the deep cutting of a chalk quarry, and Gerald
shuddered as he thought of the fate from which
nothing but a miracle could save the other
now. He did not pause to reflect then, but it
often occurred to him afterwards that his own
thoughtless pursuit, acting upon the over-heated
imagination of the fugitive, had been doubtless
the cause which had driven him to so desperate
an act as to leap as it were, upon certain death, in
order to avoid capture—and he reproached himself accordingly.

Scarcely had the form of the young man vanished over the side of the precipice, than Gerald
gained the summit of the path. To swing himself

over the parapet, to which he clung with one arm, and search with agonizing gaze for any trace of the other which might be seen below, was the work of a moment. The ground sloped gently down a certain distance, and was thickly covered with shrubs and bushes, which concealed the yawning abyss below from observation, but Gerald could see its gleaming sides by the light of the moon, and he knew that if the other's descent had not been arrested, all hope, humanly speaking, of saving him, was at an end. At first, he could see nothing but the waving boughs and short branches of the shrubs and thickets which covered the slope, but on turning his gaze a little to one side, he perceived a dark mass, cowering down within two feet of the precipice, and supported by a projecting piece of earth which threatened every moment to slip from its place.

"In God's Name, do not stir," cried Gerald, "until I come to you. Now—take my hand and hold fast for very life's sake."

As he spoke, he lowered himself to within a yard of where the other lay, still holding fast as he did so with one arm to the lower part of the balustrade, and then reaching forth the other, he seized the stranger's outstretched hand with a grasp of iron.

Luckily, Gerald's arm was a strong one, and additional strength seemed lent him for the moment. Almost before he was aware of it, the unhappy man had himself caught hold, with his other hand, of a projecting branch above, by the aid of which he steadied himself sufficiently to enable Gerald, with one more vigorous pull, to place him within reach of the balustrade, and in another moment both were once more standing in safety on the other side.

The young man turned towards Gerald. His pale face became paler still, as the light fell upon Gerald's features.

"Is it you!" he cried, and fell forward in a swoon at his feet.

* * * *

"I should have known you, I am sure, if it had not been for that beard and moustache. I had never seen you before save with a smooth face and chin, and it was that which puzzled me."

"I recognized you at once. You are but little altered since I saw you last."

The speakers were Gerald Lennox and the young man whose life he had saved. The latter was lying on Gerald's bed in his room at the hotel. For three days he had watched· beside him, and now the medical man who had been called in to attend him, and who had shaken his head on first seeing the state of his patient, had given leave for him to sit up and speak to Mr. Lennox for a few minutes.

"But only for a few minutes," he had said.

" We are not out of the wood yet, and the least thing might bring on a brain fever."

And who was this young man? Gerald evidently knew him now.

And the reader would have known him too, had it not been for the disguise which had puzzled Gerald. He was altered in other ways as well, since we saw him last, but he had suffered much since then.

His name was Arthur Woods.

CHAPTER VIII.

"My dear Hester, will you answer me one question? How long has Blanche Lennox been engaged to young Lethbridge?"

"About a year, aunt."

"And how long has Miss Lethbridge been engaged to Ferdinand?"

"Oh, that was talked of a little before Blanche's engagement, but it was not announced in any way. I suppose they have been formally engaged about the same length of time."

"And is any date fixed for either marriage?"

"Not that I know of."

"Then I say, it is ridiculous. If people don't know their own minds they should not talk about marrying at all, and if it is settled that they are to marry, they *should* marry and not go on dilly dallying in that fashion!"

Mrs. Gregory was in a querulous mood. The butcher had not brought the piece of meat she had ordered that morning, and her culinary arrangements for the day had been upset. She had had a quarrel with the cook, and was now relieving her mind by taking her niece to task on the subject of the pending alliances, which notwithstanding the lapse of time, were still only pending, between her neighbours at the Rectory and Lethbridge Park.

Hester was well known to be in the confidence of both the brides elect, and her aunt felt sure that if there was any reason why the marriages did not take place, she was aware of it. She therefore continued,—

"I can understand both Mr. Lennox and Colonel Lethbridge thinking Cissy and Ferdinand have plenty of time before them, and till he is ordained it is no doubt just as well that they should wait, but with the other two it is different. And there it seems to me that the young lady hangs back. I am very fond of Blanche Lennox as you know, Hester, but to my mind a young woman has no right to play fast and loose with anyone in that fashion."

"And I am sure Blanche is the last person to play fast and loose with anybody," exclaimed Hester, indignantly. "She and Charles Lethbridge were to have been married three or four months ago. It was quite settled to take place in the spring, but——"

"But what, my dear?"

"Well, aunt," said Hester, looking up from her work into the old lady's face, and speaking very gravely. "If I tell you what made them put it off, you must promise not to mention it again, as Blanche would be vexed with me for having repeated it."

"What does the child take me for?" cried Mrs. Gregory, sharply. "Mention it? Of course I shan't mention it. The idea of such a thing!"

"You know Blanche is a Roman Catholic—" said Hester.

"Yes, I know it, and more's the pity," interrupted Mrs. Gregory. "But what of that?"

"She does not think it right to marry a Prot —— one who belongs to our Church," continued Hester, "unless he will hold out some hopes of his becoming a convert to what she considers the only True Faith, and Charles Lethbridge will not do anything of the sort. He says he does not care what she believes, or what Church she belongs to, as he told her from the beginning, but he is quite satisfied to remain as he is, and declares he will not change his religion to please anybody."

"And quite right too!" exclaimed Mrs. Gregory. "I admire Charles Lethbridge for that more than I can say."

"He reproaches Blanche for having allowed these scruples to take possession of her, and says that he knows they have been put into her head by the priests. No difficulty of the sort was made at first, and he does not understand why any should be made now. But Blanche says she was wrong ever to engage herself to a Protestant, (as *she* considers Charles,) and—"

"Do you mean he is *not* a Protestant?" asked Mrs. Gregory in astonishment. "I declare, my dear, I don't understand what you are talking about. What else can Blanche consider him, if she won't marry him on that very account?"

"Oh, aunt, you know that we do not call ourselves Protestants, and that we consider ourselves more truly Catholic, (Ferdinand and Cissy say so at least,) than Romanists are in this country. It is one of those things you never will understand, and so it is of no use trying to make you."

"I know that you talk a great deal of nonsense, child. If we are not Protestants, I should like to know what Cranmer and Ridley died at the stake for? and what all the Reformation was about? When I was a girl we believed what we were told in our History books, but now-a-days you young people have changed all that, and one would think that there was no difference between the pure, scriptural, Reformed Church of England, and the corrupt, idolatrous, Virgin-worshipping Church of Rome! But you will never convince me of that, my dear Hester, as long as you live!"

"And I don't want to convince you of anything of the sort," replied Hester, energetically. "Of course there is a difference. But both Churches are branches of the One Holy Catholic Church, to which we all profess to belong, and as to Roman

Catholics worshipping idols and all that sort of thing, you know, aunt, that is all stuff as well as I do !"

" I don't want to discuss the question, Hester," said the old lady, who knew that in a theological dispute with her High Church niece, she was generally in the habit of coming worst off. " You say that Blanche Lennox won't marry Charles Lethbridge because he won't become a Papist. If I was him, I should have nothing more to say to her. But young men have no spirit now-a-days !"

" You forget, aunt, that they are very much attached to each other. Blanche is quite miserable about it, for she sees the delay is making him wretched, and yet she says she cannot act against her conscience. Mr. Findlay told me he was very uneasy about her, and it is on her account that they are going away next week. He says she must have change of air."

The windows of Mrs. Gregory's drawing-room looked upon her garden, which just then was in its full bloom. The centre one was open, and the ladies had placed themselves near it in order to enjoy the soft breeze which blew gently in upon them as they sat at work. Mrs. Gregory was about to make some rejoinder to her niece's observation about Blanche's health, when Hester looking up suddenly, exclaimed,

" Why, here is Blanche herself, coming across the garden ! She said she should call on her way back from the school. It must be later than I thought."

"How she can go toiling up to that school such weather as this, I can't think," said Mrs. Gregory. "Bring her in, my dear, and make her sit down. She looks tired to death, poor child!"

Hester ran out, and in another moment returned in company with Blanche Lennox who looked pale, and confessed to being tired. She had been forbidden to teach her class or have anything to do with the school for some time, but lately the mistress's entreaties with the Rector had prevailed so far, that since she declared the girls made no progress now in comparison with what they did "in Miss Lennox's time," he had consented to her going to look after the work, and superintend generally once or twice a week. But the old class-taking days were over, and to Blanche, who was very fond of the children, and delighted in teaching them, this was a real sorrow. Her patient, pleasant way with the little ones had always made them feel that with Miss Blanche lessons were no task at all; and it was quite as great a grievance to them to be deprived of her teaching, as it was to her to be prevented from instructing them. Lady Frances had begged Mr. Lennox to allow her to give her old pupils their lessons in reading and secular matters as before, but he was firm in his refusal.

"Everyone knew that his daughter had forsaken the Church of her fathers, and adopted the pernicious errors of Rome, and if she was permitted to teach in the school, it would be assumed that she was inoculating the children with her Popish notions, under his sanction. It would be impossible to prevent people from thinking this, and so he would not allow it."

Lady Frances repeated his words to her daughter, and Blanche had ventured gently to hint that in leaving the Anglican communion for that of Rome, she had "returned" to the Church of her fathers instead of forsaking it. Lady Frances shook her head, and sighed as she pressed a kiss on her child's forehead. Papist or Protestant, she was the same precious darling to her, but as to those controversial points, she never entered upon them, and did not pretend to understand them. "You and your father are both much more clever than I am, and know about these things, but of course whatever he says I must think most of. He believes in the Church of England, and so I believe in it too. If he gave it up, I daresay I should do the same."

Blanche never attempted to argue with her mother, but she could not help saying with a smile that "If dear papa was infallible, it would be very well to abide unquestioningly by his decision, but supposing he was mistaken, what then?"

Lady Frances put her fingers to her ears, and said she could not listen to such dreadful heresy,

and Blanche kissed her and changed the subject.
She knew enough of Protestants to be aware that
whilst rejecting the Infallibility of the Church and
of the Pope, they invariably leant upon the infallibility of some self-chosen teacher or guide, unless
they preferred the light of their own Private Judg-
ment, and were utterly blind to the inconsistency
of their conduct.

"I knew you would be expecting me," she said,
as she sat down on the sofa by Hester's side,
"and so I came round this way, but I cannot stay
a minute, as all our plans have been changed, and
I am going off in a hurry to-morrow. Papa and
mamma can't leave home for another fortnight,
and Mr. Findlay says I must go at once, so Mrs.
Vernon who has some friends at Kingstanton, and
is leaving Lethbridge on her way there, takes me
with her. I don't like the arrangement a bit, as
without mamma I shan't enjoy being anywhere,
but she is so certain the change will do me good,
and is so anxious for me to go that I am obliged
to acquiesce with the best grace I can."

"Kingstanton is in Norfolk, isn't it?" asked
Mrs. Gregory. "What makes you go there?"

"Mr. Findlay says it is a nice sea-side place.
It is quiet and out of the way, which is what I
shall like, and Mrs. Vernon is going and takes me,
which settles the matter," answered Blanche.

"And why can't Mr. Lennox and Lady Frances
go?" enquired Hester.

"Papa must attend a meeting of the clergy at Westling as Rural Dean, which the bishop has begged him to call for some purpose or other, and he says it will take him quite a fortnight to arrange it," said Blanche, "and mamma will not leave him, as she thinks he does not take care of himself when she is away, and she is always so afraid of his knocking himself up as you know, so it can't be helped, and I must just make the best of it !"

As Hester Spencer said, Mr. Findlay was uneasy about Blanche Lennox's health, and he and Lady Frances, after a lengthened consultation on the subject, had decided that she must have a change, and that without further loss of time. The doctor knew what ailed his patient. It was not medicine she wanted. She had got a religious crotchet in her mind, which was interposing between her and happiness, and till she got rid of that, nothing he could prescribe would do her any good. "Give her a change. Get her away from this place," he said to her mother. "She doesn't like London ? then don't take her there. A quiet sea-side village if she fancy it, by all means. And if she cannot have those priests and fellows about her, all the better !"

Who the "fellows" were that in company with Mr. Findlay's favourite bugbear the "priests" Blanche was supposed to like to have about her, did not seem quite clear; but Lady Frances smiled in acquiescence, only remarking that she was sure her daughter would not like any place where she was not within reach of a Catholic church of some sort.

"She can get to one from Kingstanton by rail, easily enough," answered Mr. Findlay. "There are some nice people about there who will just give her the sort of amusement she wants. It will do her good to see a few fresh faces, and when she comes back she will be in a healthier frame of mind altogether. I expect we shall have a wedding in the old Church before long, although our friend Charley does continue a heretic!"

Lady Frances smiled sadly. "You forget that there will be no wedding *here*, now," she said.

The journey from Wentmore to Kingstanton was a long day's work. Blanche had to be up early in the morning in order to be ready for Mrs. Vernon, when she called for her on her way to the station, and that lady was sure not to be a moment too soon. Mr. Lennox stood at the hall door with Blanche's cloak on his arm. He knew she would forget it, he said, and was ready to throw it over her at the last moment. The young lady herself was taking leave of her mother upstairs.

"Here is the carriage!" cried Mr. Lennox, at the foot of the stairs. And at the same moment the Lethbridge equipage dashed up to the door.

Blanche came flying down the stairs. The

tears stood in her eyes. She could not bear part-
ing from her mother, even for a short time.

" I am quite ready," she said.

" We have not a moment to lose, dear," said
Mrs. Vernon, as Blanche after exchanging a fervent
embrace with her father stepped into the carriage.
" The train is horridly punctual, and we are rather
late, I believe, as it is."

The drive to Milsom Station was soon over. As
they drew up at the entrance to the booking office,
a porter led a saddle horse away from the door, at
sight of which Mrs. Vernon exclaimed,

" Why, surely that is Charles Lethbridge's
horse? It is exactly like it."

" Yes ma'am," said the footman who was let-
ting down the steps, "it is Mr. Lethbridge's mare.
He has just ridden over."

Madeline Vernon glanced at Blanche, who
coloured up and busied herself in collecting the
shawls and packages belonging to herself and her
companion, with which the carriage was strewed.
Poor Blanche! Her heart with all its strong
power of affection, its deep true devotion, was
given to the man she had accepted as her future
husband, and she was torn in pieces between her
love for him, and the fear of doing. wrong which
her newly imbibed religious principles had in-
spired, by marrying one who was an alien from
the Faith.

Charles Lethbridge had started on horseback

immediately after the carriage containing Mrs. Vernon and her luggage had driven from his father's door, and having taken a shorter *route,* had arrived at Milsom Station before the travellers made their appearance. He had seen Blanche the day before, and said good-bye, promising her that wherever she went, as he had obtained an extension of leave, he should follow her in the course of a few days. She had assured him that he would find Kingstanton very dull, as she knew that it was a very quiet place, and he had replied as a matter of course, that away from her the liveliest scene on earth would be dull for him, and where she was, the sunshine of her presence would make a Paradise of the dreariest spot in creation. Not that with Charles Lethbridge such assertions were a mere *façon de parler* by any means. His love for Blanche had deepened with the lapse of time, and the very difficulties which her religious scruples now threw in their way, served to increase his admiration of her character, although they drove him at times almost to the verge of distraction.

He came forward to hand her from the carriage, Mrs. Vernon having already alighted.

"You are only just in time," he said. "The train is in sight."

She looked up in his face with a smile.

"You are not going too?" she asked.

"No. I have only come to see you off. But I

have a piece of news to tell you. My mother has taken it into her head that a few sea breezes would do Cissy good, and I am to bring her down to Kingstanton at the end of the week, if you will kindly secure rooms for us somewhere, against our arrival. It is curious that we should be likely to meet again so soon, isn't it?" added Charles with a mischievous smile. "As of course, if it hadn't been for this sudden idea of my mother's about Ciss, I should never have thought of coming down on my own account!"

"It will be delightful to have dear Cissy," said Blanche, "and as she could hardly travel all that way alone, I suppose we must put up with her chaperon as a necessary evil!" And she heaved a plaintive little sigh as she spoke.

Mrs. Vernon had taken the tickets, and the train coming up at that moment, there was no time for further *badinage* on either side.

"God bless you, dearest. Take care of your-self," whispered Charles, holding Blanche's hand as the train moved off.

"We shall expect you on Friday," she answered. And judging from her looks, the brother's advent was at any rate, as eagerly looked forward to as the sister's, notwithstanding the speaker's assumed indifference on the subject a moment before.

"Now, confess I was very good and con-siderate," said Mrs. Vernon, turning to Blanche, and giving her hand an affectionate little squeeze, when they had fairly started. "I did not take the least notice of you, and busied myself at the further end of the carriage as long as he stood at the window. But, my dear Blanche—I may call you Blanche?—you must not make a stranger of me, and let me tell you, you are a fortunate girl in having secured the affections of such a man as that. Charles Lethbridge is one in a thousand, and if I were you, I should not let anything, however strongly I might feel on certain subjects, stand between me and my happiness. You will forgive me for having said so much as this, won't you ?"

Blanche had seen a good deal of Mrs. Vernon lately, and she liked her better than she had done at first. But she was shy and reserved, and although she did not resent the way in which Mrs. Vernon had touched upon the subject of her engagement, she did not feel disposed to encourage any further remarks about what was so entirely her own affair. So returning the kindly pressure of that lady's hand, she smiled and thanked her for the interest she had expressed, and then asked some questions about Kingstanton, and the sort of people they were likely to see there, as a hint that she wished to change the conversation.

"We shall be there for the week of the Volunteer Review," said Mrs. Vernon, "and that is the gayest time. My friend Mrs. Stanley has been looking out for rooms for me, and so I am quite easy on that score, but you have no idea what a rush there is, just for that one week. Every lodging in the place is engaged, and the one hotel (at least to which anyone could go,) is always full to suffocation. They have Amateur Theatricals, and there is a Camp Fire on one of the nights, and altogether the little place is quite gay whilst the encampment lasts."

" Indeed !" cried Blanche, rather in alarm. "I had no idea such would be the case. I would much rather not have gone till the Review week was over, I thought it was sure to be so very quiet and out of the way of all that sort of thing !"

" Oh, you will find it quiet enough, you need not distress yourself about that," returned Mrs. Vernon, "I shall have had quite enough of it, I know, very soon. The short season, whilst it lasts, is the only endurable time at Kingstanton. There are some pretty rides and drives, and when Cissy and Charles arrive, you will be able to go about with them, and I am sure will enjoy yourself very much. And when you are tired of it, why, you can leave—that's all."

But Blanche declared it was too bad of Mr. Findlay to have said nothing about this Review business when he recommended Kingstanton as a place to go to. She believed he had urged her to go just then, on purpose that she might come in for it. However there was no help for it now, and so with a shrug of her pretty little shoulders she said she supposed she must make the best of it.

Mrs. Vernon supposed so too, and laughed at the notion of a little gaiety of the kind being anything to object to.

The train from Shoreditch started at eleven o'clock, and there was scarcely time to make the transit from one terminus to another on their arrival in town. Mrs. Vernon was a very dependent person, and never went anywhere without a maid. The one she now had, had been with her only a short time, and was evidently not experienced as a traveller. She had to look after her own boxes and Miss Lennox's as well as her mistress's at the station, and a good deal of time was lost owing to a mistake she had made in the number of things, and having to go back for a box of Blanche's which had been left behind, after they had started on their way to Bishopsgate St. Mrs. Vernon scolded Burt, (that was the maid's name,) for her stupidity, and Mrs. Burt did not admire being scolded. Blanche was divided between her consternation at losing her box and her fear of their missing the train, so that the equanimity of the whole party was a good deal disturbed as they rattled over the streets towards the Eastern Counties Station.

"I will help Burt to look after the luggage, if you will get the tickets," said Blanche to Mrs. Vernon when they arrived at Shoreditch.

"Very well, dear," answered Mrs. Vernon. "Then you will see that she does not forget anything."

In a few minutes more they were puffing slowly out of the station. The weather was fine, and Blanche let down the window of the carriage, and gave a sigh of relief as she felt the pure country air blowing against her cheek once more.

"How people can stay in London at this season of the year, I can't imagine!" she exclaimed. "Even just that rush through it, was enough for me. And I am so delighted to think we shall be at the sea-side in so short a time. It is so long since I have been to a really enjoyable sea-side place, for Brighton I don't look upon as anything."

"For my part, I would much rather be in town," said Mrs. Vernon, who had not yet entirely recovered her good humour. "I am disgusted at my cousin for not having asked me to stay with her this year, but she has her house full of some Indian relations, and so could not make room for me. I can't think how anyone can prefer the country to London in the season."

Blanche only laughed, and said, that it would not do if all tastes were alike, and then opening a book, she began to read.

"I wonder you can read in a train," observed Mrs. Vernon, presently, "I never can. You have often been on this line before, haven't you?"

Blanche laid down her book.

"Yes," she said, "I have been down to stay with our cousins, the Derehams, once or twice in Norfolk, and we have often been to pay visits in Essex and Suffolk by this line. We shall escape the worst part of it by branching off at Ely to-day. It always used to shake dreadfully between Ely and Wymondham, I remember."

At Cambridge they stopped for a few minutes, and as the carriage door stood open, a young lady who was walking up and down the platform with a tall, distinguished-looking man, saw Blanche, and ran up to her with an exclamation of surprise and delight.

"Why, Blanche, is that you!" she cried. "Where are you going?"

"My dear Charlotte," answered Blanche, springing forward and kissing her affectionately. "This is an unexpected pleasure! I am on my way to Kingstanton for a blow by the sea-side. I thought you were all in town now?"

"So we are," returned the other, laughing, "but papa and I have just been home for two days, as there is some building going on he wanted to look at. We are going back now!"

"How-do-you-do, my dear young lady?" said the gentleman alluded to, coming up to the carriage door, and taking Blanche by the hand. "I thought Charlotte had gone mad, she rushed off from me in such a way. I hope they are all well at Wentmore ?"

Blanche had only time to nod her head and say good-bye, as the train moved off again. "Give my love to the others," she cried, as her young friend waved her hand to her.

"Who is that highbred-looking girl?" asked. Mrs. Vernon, when they were again fairly on their way. "It struck me that I had seen her somewhere before."

"A very great friend of mine," answered Blanche, "Lady Charlotte Aston. Her father, Lord Cheshire, lives near here, and I have been to stay with them at Aston Castle several times. They are all charming, but Charlotte is my particular favourite."

"I think I must have seen her at the Chandos's in Eaton Place," said Mrs. Vernon. "I have heard Mrs. Chandos speak of the Lady Astons as if she knew them, and Lady Charlotte's face seemed quite familiar to me."

The train sped on, and as the hours went by, Blanche began to feel tired and to wish she was at her journey's end.

"I suppose we are not far from Kingstanton now," she said, as at length they approached the coast, and she caught sight of the sea in the distance.

"It is the next station, I think," said Mrs.

Vernon, "and as it is nearly five by my watch, I am sure we are due now."

"Then I shall begin collecting my things," said Blanche, and seizing a large travelling-bag which was lying by her side, she stuffed a book and smelling-bottle and several other *et cæteras* into it, after which she put on her hat which she had tossed off during the journey, and securing her parasol in her hand, announced the fact that "she was quite ready, and the sooner they stopped, the better she should be pleased."

"I am dreadfully tired, and am dying for a cup of tea," said Mrs. Vernon. "I shall leave Burt to look after the boxes, and we will go at once to the Terrace, where Mrs. Stanley has engaged rooms for us. Where did I put the address? for I am sure I forget the number. Oh! here it is. I see. No. 5, that's all right."

In a few minutes the train stopped, and their tickets were demanded. Of course Mrs. Vernon had put them carefully away somewhere, and of course she could not find them anywhere, so the collector was kept waiting for some minutes at their carriage window, which was a trial to his temper, as well as to the patience of the other travellers. At length they were discovered and delivered up, and the train after moving on a few yards further, again stopped, and they had arrived.

"Now, Burt, mind you collect all the things, and then follow us as fast as you can. Miss Len-

nox and I are going to walk to our lodgings which
are close by," said Mrs. Vernon, as she alighted
on the platform, and Mrs. Burt advanced towards
her from a second class carriage.

"Yes, ma'am," answered Burt, looking somewhat dismayed. "But how shall I find my way?
I don't know it at all."

"Oh, anyone will tell you. A porter will bring
up the luggage. No. 5, The Terrace; he will
know where it is, and you will have nothing to do
but to follow him."

"I think I shall like this place," said Blanche
to herself, as they emerged from the station, and
took their way across a green towards a row of
cheerful-looking houses on one side of it, immediately fronting the sea. "I suppose they are
expecting us?" she asked, turning to Mrs. Vernon.

"Of course," replied that lady, "and here we
are. The house looks clean outside, I hope it is
comfortable in."

The landlady of No. 5 came forward smiling,
and curtseying as soon as the bell rang. "Mrs.
Stanley had been that afternoon to see that everything was ready for the ladies, and she hoped they
would approve of the apartments."

"Oh, how nice, and how pretty!" exclaimed
Blanche, as they entered a bright little room on
the first floor, the windows of which opened on to
a balcony facing the sea. "What charming
flowers! and how well arranged! Have you a

garden at the back of the house?" she added, turning to the landlady who was following them in.

"No, Miss," answered the woman. "Mrs. Stanley brought the flowers over and placed them in the vases. She thought they would make the room look more homelike, she said."

"How very kind and nice of her!" said Blanche.

"Yes. It was just like Mrs. Stanley to think of that. And now, Mrs. Fairlight, let me have a cup of tea, and get the dinner ready as fast as you can. I hope Burt will be here soon. Do you see anything of her?" said Mrs. Vernon, throwing herself on a sofa, and turning to Blanche who stood at the window.

"Yes," answered Blanche, "I see her coming up the road with a porter and the luggage. She looks hot and tired, poor thing. I daresay she will be glad of some tea."

"She is a stupid woman, and I daresay will have left something I shall want the first thing behind her," said Mrs. Vernon. "Now, my dear Blanche, you may go out and have a walk with her when she has opened my boxes, or you can wait till after dinner, whichever you like. I shall lie here for the next hour, for I feel like a dead creature, but in the evening I will take a little turn on the green with you."

"Thank you," returned Blanche, "I shall not go out before dinner, as I feel tired too, and I

want to get some of my things unpacked. Bye
and bye I should like to have a walk very much."

The next morning, as Blanche stood for a moment at the open window, having just come in
from a walk on the cliff which she had ventured
upon on her own account, Burt being occupied
with her mistress who had sent word that she
should breakfast in bed, she saw a pony car drive
up to the door in which a lady was seated, who
looked up with a pleasant sunny smile at the window, and then addressing the landlady who came
bustling forward, inquired if Mrs, Vernon had
arrived.

"That is Mrs. Stanley, I suppose," said Blanche
to herself. And she withdrew a step or two into
the room.

In another moment the door was thrown open,
and the lady appeared.

"Mrs. Stanley, ma'am," announced the landlady.

"Mrs. Vernon is rather knocked up by her
journey, and has not made her appearance yet,"
said Blanche, coming forward. "I will go and
tell her you are here, but I must thank you first
of all, for bringing us over these charming flowers
which made the place look so very nice, when we
arrived."

"Oh, pray do not mention that," said Mrs.
Stanley, taking Blanche's proffered hand and giving it a kindly little squeeze. "I am so fond of

flowers myself, I always think other people must like them too. I only wish I had been able to do better for you in the way of rooms, but the place is so full just now, that it was difficult to find anything. However, Mrs. Fairlight is a person I have known for years, and I am sure she will do her best to make you comfortable."

"I have no doubt of that," answered Blanche, and she ran upstairs to tell Mrs. Vernon that Mrs. Stanley had come.

Mrs. Vernon was just dressed, and made her appearance almost immediately. The little lady was attired in an elaborate morning dress, and had got her hat on ready to go out.

"My dear Madeline, how glad I am to see you!" cried Mrs. Stanley, coming out to meet her on the landing, and giving her an affectionate embrace. "But how altered you are! I should scarcely have known you. Why, your hair is a different colour to what it was when I saw you last! Surely it is much lighter than it used to be?"

"Do you think so?" said Mrs. Vernon, hastily. "And how are you, dear Mrs. Stanley? I am so much obliged to you for getting us these rooms. They are just exactly in the right situation. And now sit down and tell me who is here, and what is going on."

Mrs. Stanley sat down as she was told, and

began a full account of the various arrangements at Kingstanton for the week following.

"You know it is our 'one week' in the year here, Miss Lennox," she said, turning to Blanche, when she had told them of all she could remember, "and we are all in a state of wild excitement as long as it lasts."

"For my part I wish your 'one week' was over," returned Blanche, laughing. "I came here hoping to find it a very quiet place, and am quite disappointed at being let in for so much gaiety."

"And where is Cecil?" inquired Mrs. Stanley. "Is he upstairs? I suppose he has grown quite a big boy by this time. I have not seen you, you know, since Major Vernon left England."

"He is not here," answered Mrs. Vernon, "I left him at Lethbridge, where they are so fond of him, and he is quite happy. People say he is grown. Blanche, dear, shew Mrs. Stanley that photograph book. There is one of him in it, taken a little while ago."

Blanche handed Mrs. Stanley the book, and Cecil's likeness was duly commented upon and admired. Mrs. Stanley at the same time expressing much regret at his mamma's not having brought him to Kingstanton, as she had reckoned so much upon seeing him, and making him known to her boys, one of whom was just his own age.

"Now, my dear Blanche, if Mrs. Stanley does

not mind we will go out and take a little turn," said Mrs. Vernon, rising and taking a general survey of herself in the glass. "It is such a lovely morning, it is a shame to waste it indoors."

Mrs. Vernon's "get up" on this occasion, was entirely light blue with white lace about it, and she was impatient to shew herself off to the benighted people at Kingstanton.

Blanche jumped up, and said she was quite ready, and they all descended the stairs. Mrs. Stanley told the little boy who was holding her pony at the gate that she would be back in a quarter of an hour, and he must wait there till she came.

If Mrs. Vernon desired to attract attention, as she slowly promenaded backwards and forwards with Mrs. Stanley and Blanche on the green, she certainly attained her object, and her companions felt rather uncomfortable as they walked by her side. Almost everyone they passed turned round to look at them, and some of the gentlemen put up their glasses and eyed the trio in what Mrs. Stanley thought a very impertinent manner.

"People do not dress very much here, do they?" asked Blanche, in an aside to Mrs. Stanley, as after taking one or two turns they sat down on a bench facing the sea.

"Oh, dear no," replied that lady. "No one cares what they wear. I always go about the greatest figure myself, but then my husband says

I never am dressed properly. But it is one of the advantages of a place like this, that you need not dress much, and if people do, they only get stared at, which is not pleasant."

" Decidedly the reverse, I think," said Blanche. " I shall persuade Mrs. Vernon to put on something else when I go in, and I daresay she will, for she likes changing her dress, I know."

That evening as Mrs. Vernon and Blanche were sitting on the balcony after tea, they noticed a man making his way towards the house from the direction of the railway station.

" Do you think that man is coming here, Blanche ?" said Mrs. Vernon. " He looks as if he had a telegram, or something, in his hand."

Blanche started violently.

" A telegram! Oh, I hope not," she exclaimed, turning pale.

" Do not be frightened, dear," said Mrs. Vernon, " I daresay it is nothing of the kind."

At that moment, the object of their discussion rang the door bell below, and two minutes after, Mrs. Fairlight made her appearance with the unmistakable large envelope in her hand.

" A message, if you please, ma'am," said she, presenting it to Mrs. Vernon.

Mrs. Vernon tore it open.

" From Charles," she said, handing it to Blanche, " to say they will be here to-morrow, which reminds me that we have done nothing

about getting rooms for them yet.   But I daresay
Mrs. Fairlight will be able to tell us of something
that will do, near at hand."

Blanche took the telegram, and read it with a
feeling of relief.   She was always frightened by
these short and sudden messages, but there was
nothing alarming in this one, certainly.

CHAPTER IX.

THE evening train had just come in, and Blanche, attended by Mrs. Burt, had gone down to the station to welcome Cissy and Charles on their arrival.

Mrs. Vernon sat on a low chair which she had drawn out upon the balcony. She had an opera glass in her hand, and was amusing herself by reconnoitering the various groups which passed to and fro in the distance. The arrival of a train always caused an excitement at Kingstanton, and it was something for the promenaders to do, to go and watch the new comers as they emerged from the station.

From time to time, Mrs. Vernon turned her glance in that direction, and presently she exclaimed, " There they are ! I knew Cissy would have on that frightful drab suit of hers, and that unbecoming hat she is so fond of ! She is a dear girl, but never had the least idea of dressing herself. Charles is in good looks at any rate, and

Blanche does not appear sorry to see him again. But whom have they got with them? That old woman with a shawl over her arm and a huge umbrella! Oh, it is Campbell. I did not know they were going to bring her. Where she is to sleep, I don't know. And who is that running up behind, and taking Charles by the arm? Good gracious! No, it can't be? Yes—it is actually! Cecil! What can have induced them to bring him in all the world!"

And in her excitement Mrs. Vernon arose and stood leaning over the balcony. As the others approached, they caught sight of her, and Charles Lethbridge pointed her out to her son who waved his hat and kissed his hand to her, and she could hear his clear young voice calling out, "Halloa, mother! I see you!"

When they reached the house, Mrs. Vernon was awaiting them in the passage below, and whilst her boy was clinging round her neck and smothering her with kisses, she asked what on earth could have made them think that she wanted to have him there!

"Well, the fact is," said Charles, shaking hands with her, "when the young gentleman found that Ciss and I were coming, nothing would persuade him to remain behind, and so *faute de mieux* we brought him, and here he is! And so this is Kingstanton?" he added, turning round and taking a survey of the green from the door steps.

"Where on earth do all these people come from?
for there don't seem enough houses for them to
live in!"

"Oh, Kingstanton extends further than you
imagine," said Blanche, as they ascended the
stairs. "There is Old Kingstanton, and several
places round about from which people come. This
is the fashionable *rendezvous* and the time of day
when everyone is to be seen walking about, but
generally speaking, the green is not so crowded."

After dinner the whole party turned out, and
wandered about the sands. Cecil Vernon was
in high glee, and his mamma was in constant
alarm on his account.

"I know he will be over the cliff, if he tears
about like that. Do, Charles, look after him,"
she would say, and Charles would call out to the
youngster and shake his fist at him, threatening
all sorts of condign punishments if he did not
come back and conduct himself properly, whereat
Master Cecil would laugh defiantly, and betake
himself to some more exciting and fear-inspiring
pastime than before.

After a time, Mrs. Vernon and Cissy sat down
under the rocks, and chatted quietly together,
whilst Charles strolled with Blanche along the
sands. Kingstanton had suddenly become to
Blanche one of the most charming places in the
world, and as Charles looked down upon her sweet
face and listened to the music of her voice, he felt

as though he should not mind if that evening stroll were prolonged *ad infinitum*. For a time both forgot the clouds which seemed of late to overhang their horizon, and gave themselves up to the full enjoyment of that peaceful hour.

During the Review week, as Mrs. Stanley had led them to expect, Kingstanton abandoned itself to gaiety and dissipation. The omnibus which dragged itself along the dusty road from Old Kingstanton to Kingstanton St. John's, (as the group of houses adjoining the green was called,) without so much as an outside passenger, as a general rule once in the four-and-twenty hours, was now filled both outside and in, and obliged to run two or three times backwards and forwards in the course of the day, besides an extra conveyance in the shape of a large waggonette and pair of horses, being started to convey the unusual number of passengers who desired to be transported to the spot where the valiant defenders of their country had pitched their tents. This, by the kindness of its owner, they had been permitted to do in a fine well-wooded park, adjoining the old town, or village of Kingstanton. Mrs. Vernon and her party were always going over, either to indulge Cecil with a perambulating expedition among the tents, or to spend the afternoon with Mrs. Stanley, whose pretty place was within a few minutes walk of the spot where the encampment was held.

But the grand event of the week was the inspection of the Volunteer force by a neighbouring Magnate who had retired from the army on half pay, and was to appear "For this time only," in all the resuscitated splendour of his military habiliments, attended by a brilliant staff, and to put the assembled troops through no end of manœuvres in presence of all the rank, fashion, and beauty of the district. In the evening an Amateur Performance was to take place in a large marquee erected in the park; and, in short, Kingstanton was to excel itself on the occasion.

The morning proved fine, and the open carriage which Charles had secured some days in advance, to convey the fair Mrs. Vernon and Blanche to the ground, was early at the door of their lodgings. Mrs. Vernon had attired herself most becomingly in anticipation of many conquests during the day, and there is no doubt but that the equipage containing herself and her fair young companion, (Cissy rode on horseback with her brother,) attracted a good deal of admiration, not unmixed with envy, from some of the ladies present, as it drove into the park and took up its position among the others which were drawn up in a row fronting the scene of operation.

"Where is Cecil, I wonder?" said Mrs. Vernon, looking round in quest of that young gentleman who had gone off with Charles's soldier servant, (who had come down with the horses the night before,) leaving word that they would find him on the ground when they arrived.

"I daresay he will see the carriage and make his way towards us presently," said Blanche. "It is impossible to distinguish anyone in this crowd."

Cissy and Charles had preceded the carriage, and came cantering up from some distant part of the field a few minutes after it appeared. They had seen Cecil, and relieved Mrs. Vernon's mind on his account. He was with Mrs. Stanley's party, and making himself quite at home with them.

"Oh, I have no doubt of that," said his mamma. "There is Mrs. Stanley, I think? Who is that lady with her, do you know? They are coming this way."

The question was addressed to Charles, who turned his head, and saw Mrs. Stanley approaching at a little distance accompanied by another lady, and her second son, a lad of fourteen, beside whom marched Master Cecil. He looked at them a moment. "I don't know," he said.

"How do you do, Mrs. Vernon?" exclaimed Mrs. Stanley, coming up to the side of the carriage. "Is Miss Lennox with you? Ah! there she is. I am so glad. My friend Mrs. Courtenay of Sett Whisson, has driven over from Hunslynn where she is staying for a few days. Hearing me mention Miss Lennox's name, she asked if I knew to what family she belonged, and when I said that

her father was Rector of Wentmore, she exclaimed
that she was a relation of hers, and so I set off at
once to find you out."

"Louie Courtenay!" cried Blanche, eagerly.
"Did you say she was here? Of course!" she
continued, as Mrs. Stanley's companion came forward. "I should have known you again directly,
although I daresay I have changed a good deal
since you saw me last?"

"Indeed you have, my dear Blanche," said
Mrs. Courtenay, taking her outstretched hand.
"Considering you were just fourteen the last time
I was at Wentmore before my marriage. I am so
delighted to see you, and looking so well. How
are they all at Wentmore? Are you all alone?
or who is here with you?"

"Mrs. Vernon,—to whom let me introduce you.
My cousin Mrs. Courtenay—Mrs. Vernon has
kindly taken charge of me for a while, as papa and
mamma were not able to leave home just now, and
the doctor thought I needed change of air. But
you see there is not much the matter with me."

"And do you stay here long?" inquired Mrs.
Courtenay.

"I do not think we shall," replied Blanche.
"Did not Mrs. Stanley say you were at Huu-
slynn? If so, I shall come and pay you a visit
before I go. Is there not a Catholic church
there?" she added in a lower tone, as she leant
forward.

"Yes, I believe so," was the answer. "Ah! I know why you ask me. I have heard all about it. I cannot help being sorry, you know, but it is no affair of mine. I thought when Gerald went over how it would be. Have you heard from him lately? Where is he now?"

"He is at Spa, where curiously enough he has just met the Grahams. You remember Barbara, do you not? I daresay you were as much astonished at her marriage with Sidney as we were. They have been travelling abroad ever since, and happened to be at Spa when Gerald got there."

Mrs. Courtenay had been a Miss Lennox. Her father was the head of the family, and first cousin to Mr. Lennox of Wentmore. She was consequently related to Barbara and Sidney Graham in the same degree as to Blanche and her brothers.

"Yes, we were all rather surprised," she said. "But talking of marriages, Mrs. Stanley tells me that Mr. Lethbridge is here. Am I right in thinking that is he.? Will you introduce me to my future cousin?"

Blushing and laughing, Blanche complied with Mrs. Courtenay's request, and Charles, dismounting from his horse, came round to the side of the carriage where she stood, and began talking to her. Cissy Lethbridge expressed a wish to walk about a little, and Blanche said if Charles would pilot them she should like to do so too.

The young guardsman assisted his sister from

her saddle, and his servant approaching, led off the two horses to walk them about until they were again wanted. Then opening the carriage door, Charles handed Blanche out.

"I will go with you, Blanche, and play *chaperone*," said Mrs. Courtenay. "I have so much to say to you. How pleased they will be at Bentley to hear of our meeting."

Bentley was the name of the family seat where Mrs. Courtenay's father lived.

"I shall take your place, Miss Lennox," said Mrs. Stanley, "and stay with Mrs. Vernon till you return. That is to say, if you will let me?" she added, turning to that lady.

Mrs. Vernon expressed herself delighted, and Mrs. Stanley got into the carriage and sat down beside her.

"Do look after Cecil," cried Mrs. Vernon, as the others moved off, saying they should not be gone long. "I am always uneasy when he is out of my sight, and afraid he will get into some mischief."

"Oh, you need not be anxious about him," said Mrs. Stanley, "my Charles will look after him. They are great friends, and my boy knows exactly where to go, and will take care of him, I promise you."

Mrs. Courtenay was to sleep at Mrs. Stanley's, and it was arranged that they should all meet at the theatrical performance in the evening. When the evening came, Mrs. Vernon was tired, and said she should not go, and sent Blanche and Cissy under Charles's escort, with strict injunctions to place themselves under Mrs. Stanley's wing as soon as they arrived at the theatre. This they promised to do, and set off in high spirits as soon as their tea-dinner was over. Cecil had remained with the Stanley party, and was to join them at the theatre.

Blanche arranged an expedition to Hunslynn with Mrs. Courtenay during the evening. She told her cousin of Cissy's engagement to Ferdinand, and Mrs. Courtenay could not help saying in a whisper that it was evident he was not marrying for beauty. But she did not doubt that Miss Lethbridge was a very nice person, indeed, she was quite sure of it, and offered her congratulations accordingly.

"When papa hears of it, he will say that it is not extending the family connection !" she added, laughingly.

With the departure of the volunteers, Kingstanton resumed its wonted quiet, and Mrs. Vernon declared she should very soon have had enough of it. The weather was fair without being too hot, and the whole party were out of doors as much as possible. Blanche and Charles seemed perfectly contented, and the latter told Cissy he should remain there as long as his leave lasted. Cissy laughed, and said she had no doubt but that he would like to stay on for ever if Blanche could be there too ; there was no fear of his finding it dull in that case; but for her part she rather inclined to agree with Mrs. Vernon, and to wish for a change.

One afternoon, or rather evening, as it was getting late, Blanche and Charles were strolling along the sands and beginning to think it was time to go in, Cissy had been spending the day with Mrs. Stanley, and Mrs. Vernon who had come out with Charles and Blanche was sitting under the cliffs near the steps which led down to the beach.

"May I speak to you, sir, one moment," said a voice behind him, and Charles turning round saw his man Gooch standing there as white as death, and looking the picture of dismay.

"Something has happened;" cried Blanche. "You have had a telegram—some one is ill at home?"

"No, Miss," said Gooch, "there has been no telegrams, but we are frightened about Master Cecil. No one has seen him since dinner time. I thought he had gone with Miss Lethbridge to Mr. Stanley's, and Mrs. Campbell she thought he had been with me out along the cliffs, and it was not till just this minute, when young Master Stanley came down for him to go up there immediate, that we found he was missing."

"Well, Gooch," said Charles, "I do not see why you need be in such a fright. The young rascal deserves a sound thrashing for going off without leave, but of course he is about somewhere. Most likely at the lighthouse. He has made friends with one of the keepers, and says he means to apply for the next vacancy."

"He is not at the lighthouse, sir," said Gooch, solemnly. "No, nor yet down at the *cameray*, nor nowhere else where it is safe and proper for him to be. He is out on the sea all alone by himself in a boat."

"Good heavens!" cried Charles. "Why did you not tell us so at once? When did he go? Are you sure of what you say?"

"I was looking for the young gentleman everywhere, and one of them fishermen a very decent sort of man————"

"Oh, confound the fellow's decency," interrupted Charles, "tell us at once where the boy is."

"All I can say, sir," said Gooch, "is, that the little green boat that he and Master Stanley and I went out in yesterday, is missing, and one of the preventive men has been in to say that they could make it out with their glasses between two and three mile out at sea, and just one little figure in it with a scarlet and white cap like Master Cecil's on its head."

A scream behind them made them all turn hastily round, and they saw that Mrs. Vernon had come up unperceived, and had heard without any preparation the terrible news the man had brought.

"My boy! my boy!" she shrieked. "My darling Cecil! Oh how shall I ever face his father again if I have lost him! Gooch, I trusted him to you," she went on, turning fiercely round to the poor soldier who stood trembling, the tears filling his eyes.

"God knows, ma'am," he replied, "I would rather be at the bottom of yon sea myself, than to think of that dear child being in such peril on it. I shall never have a moment's comfort again in my life if we cannot bring him back safe. They are bringing down a boat now, and four of the best rowers in Kingstanton are going out after him."

"Dearest Mrs. Vernon," said Blanche, earnestly, "they may be wrong after all. The boat was so far off they could only tell by the cap, and there are plenty like it in the place."

"Not one;" said Mrs. Vernon, even in this moment of agony, clear and accurate in her recollections of dress. "That was just what I was so proud of—there was not another boy here looked so well."

"But Charlie Stanley has one not very different," persisted Blanche, "and they could not see to distinguish really at that distance."

"Master Charles has a deal more sense than to go as near the current as that boat were seen to be a going. Why a man would have hard work to keep himself out of it, let alone a child," said a fisherman, who had heard their concluding remarks.

"The current!" said Blanche with a shiver. She and Charles in their conversations with the fishermen, had heard much of the dreaded current that extended in a long winding track outside the bay, and from the highest point of the cliff they had seen it looking on a calm day like a band of seething oil, in the midst of the ever changing dancing ripple of the sea around, but changing into one white mass of foam and tossing breakers when even a moderate breeze was blowing.

"He was seen not far from the current," said the man with a shake of the head. "And it is a providential thing for him as the tide is still a coming in, and a good strong flood tide too, that may keep him off for a while, but when the turn comes, the Lord have mercy on him if we ha'nt a reached him by then. Come lads, what are you about there together, shove off, can't ye?"

"I shall go with them," said Mrs. Vernon, and before any opposition could be made, she had got into the boat which was now lying half in the water ready to be pushed off.

"I will go with you too," exclaimed Blanche, then turning to Charles, she added, "It is not fit she should go alone, it looks dreadfully stormy, and the men will have enough to do without looking after her if you cannot———"

She paused, unwilling to give her forebodings substance and reality by expressing them.

"Well, you would be only frightening and worrying yourself to death, if you stayed here alone," said Charles, "and there is no danger for us. That storm will not break yet awhile, so come along."

He lifted Blanche into the boat, and placed her by the side of Mrs. Vernon who was standing up in the bow, gazing with a wild haggard look out to sea. Blanche put her arm round her, and in her soft coaxing way persuaded her to sit down, whispering to her all the hopeful things she could, while her own heart was sinking and dying within her, in terror at the thought of the young boy alone, and in such frightful danger.

"Come, men, what are you waiting for?" shouted Charles, as the men lingered on the beach.

"We're awaiting for Lanky Jim," said the oldest man of the party, who seemed to direct everything. "He's a wonder to pull, he is, and this here's a job where minutes is precious."

"So it seems by the way you're wasting them. Here, tumble in, and I'll take Lanky Jim's place."

The old beachman scratched his head, and looked doubtfully at Charles's figure, which though firm and well knit, looked very slight against the large massive frames of the fishermen.

Charles caught his puzzled expression and

laughed. "So you think I can't hold my own with you fellows? Make your minds easy, I learnt to row at Oxford if I did nothing else!"

"River rowing aint altogether the same as rowing in the sea," growled the old man, but he obeyed Charles's soldier-like tone of command as if by instinct, and tumbling into the boat took his place at the helm.

The tide was running strong against them, and though the day had been calm, a considerable ground swell had risen, and long heavy rollers were coming into the bay from the open sea beyond. The sun was sinking in a dark threatening bank of cloud, and a chill breeze was rising and ruffling with long sudden sweeps the heaving glassy surface of the sea. Mrs. Vernon shivered and drew her shawl up round her, and moaned piteously as she hid her face in her hands.

"Dear Mrs. Vernon, God will take care of him," said Blanche, trying to soothe her.

"Oh, I have been so selfish, so wicked," was the reply, in a heart-broken voice. "I never looked after him, never cared for him as I ought; and now he is being taken away from me; and oh, what will George do! He was so wrapped up in the boy, he will never forgive me." And the thought of her husband's anger seemed almost as terrible to her, as that of losing her child.

"But what could I do, Blanche?" she went on, after a pause. "I could not keep him always with me, a great boy like that. It was all Gooch's fault for not looking after him, or Charles's"— with a sudden flash of anger—"for bringing him here at all. I am sure I did not want him, and now I shall never see him again, my darling, handsome, affectionate boy !" And she burst into a flood of tears.

Blanche was almost glad to see her cry. Her conflicting feelings of remorse, anger and affection would find their easiest vent that way, so she only gave her hand a long warm pressure, and then set herself to look out over the water for the little green boat and the lonely boyish figure in it, which she longed so intensely to see.

There was silence over the whole party. The men pulled resolutely, and each individual in the boat seemed too much occupied by the all engrossing subject of what progress they were making, to think of aught else. But Blanche, although she could not speak, could pray, and most earnestly she did so. As her lips moved, she made the sign of the cross. One of the men who was nearest to her, observed it, and bent his head forward for a moment.

" Be you a Catholic, Miss ?" he asked in a low tone.

" I am ;" said Blanche, and struck by the man's look of interest, she added, " Are you ?"

" Yes, thank God," was the reply, " and glad I

be to think there's two of us here together. Pray
for him, Miss."

"I am doing so," gently answered Blanche,
"and do you ask our Blessed Lady to help us."

"I will, Miss, and be assured she will. I said
a 'Hail Mary' for the little chap before we started,
and I have never had no fear but what we find
him."

They had come some way already, Blanche was
surprised to see how far. Kingstanton looked
quite a small cluster of houses in the distance,
and the sea no longer confined between the arms
of the bay, was stretching out wider before them.

Charles's style of rowing and the strength with
which he handled the long heavy oar, had won
upon the men. "'Taint the first time, Cap'en,
as you have pulled a boat in salt water," observed
one.

"Not by a good many," was the reply. "An
uncle of mine has a place on the Hampshire coast,
and when I was staying there as a boy, my cousin
and I were never off the water when we could
help it. We had some narrow escapes too, but
boys have as many lives as cats, and that's my
best hope for the youngster we are after to-day."

"Ay, ay, Cap'en, but then there's yon current,"
said another of the men, with a backward jerk of
his thumb. "We may chance find the boat bottom upwards, but the poor little chap will ha'
been washed out of her long ere this I reckon.

'Tis a pity, for he was a free spoken, handsome little gentleman as ever I see."

"Hush," said Charles, "you forget his mother is close to you. Blanche," he added, in a low tone, "can you see nothing?"

She was standing up, looking out over the tossing waste of waters, now dyed blood red with the stormy sunset light. It was a difficult matter to see one little speck of a boat, when the whole surface was broken into deep hollows of densest shadow, interspersed with vivid gleams of crimson and orange light.

"There goes the preventive service boat," she said, as the light well-manned boat shot across their path some distance ahead.

"Pearson said he would warn them," said another of the men. "They had need be of some use, the prying meddling chaps, for once in a way."

"We are coming near the current, I think," said Blanche, as a sudden violent lurch nearly made her lose her balance, and she was obliged to kneel on the seat and hold by the edge of the boat. "How slowly we are going now!"

Their speed had slackened certainly considerably, and yet Blanche could see by the way they lay on their oars, they were pulling even more strenuously than before, and a sick dread came over her as she realized what the absorbing and entrancing force of the current was, and how little chance a mere boy like Cecil had of contending with it.

Mrs. Vernon had risen from her crouching posture, and was looking out with wild dilated eyes and haggard face over the gloomy sea.

"Blanche," she said, in a hoarse whisper, not in the least like her natural voice, "I can see nothing. Have those awful angry waves swallowed him up? What do they mean by the current I hear them whispering about?"

"The revenue boat is out," said Blanche, evading her question, "and more boats are sure to come out from Old Kingstanton when they hear what has happened, the men say. We must have patience, we are hardly out of the bay yet."

No word was spoken for some minutes more. The rowers pulled in silence, the old steersman standing up and searching in every direction with his glass, now and then giving a direction as to their course. They had crossed the dreaded current more than once, with not more difficulty than some minutes of extra hard work and a good deal of tossing could surmount, but one could see how little chance a small boat with one weak childish pair of arms to guide it would have, if once involved in its boiling circling waves. Suddenly the revenue boat darted in sight again, and the mate sang out, "What luck, boys?"

"None," was the melancholy answer, and a chill fell on the hearts of all the crew as if they had, in owning the misfortune, made it a confirmed and hopeless fact.

"Come, my men, we won't give in yet," said Charles, cheerily; "the boat may have drifted a long way from where it was first seen, and there is still some light left."

"If the boat has drifted, Captain," said the old steersman, "we know pretty well where she has drifted to. Howsoever we'll do your bidding. It shall never be said as we did not do all we could for the poor little lad."

They pulled on again for more than a quarter of an hour longer. The sun had set in the dark bank of clouds, the red glow had gone from the waters and was succeeded by something of the ghastly green grey light that follows, on the high Alps, the glorious rose and purple of sunset. It was getting too dark to see more than a few yards ahead, the men had begun to rest on their oars, and talk of the rising storm, and the necessity of getting the ladies safely back before it broke. Suddenly Mrs. Vernon appeared to catch their meaning, and stood up in the boat.

"You shall not go back!" she said, her voice rising with every word till it became almost a shriek. "I will never go back without my boy. Have you no hearts, you lazy cowards?" she went on in her passion. "Have you no children at home, that you can think of leaving my poor darling to perish alone in this dreadful sea?"

"It is no good throwing away more lives," began one of the men, sullenly, when a cry from Blanche stopped him.

"Pull, pull!" she cried, "I see something out there on a line with that white foam. Pull, and shout that he may hear you!"

Her words were like an electric shock. A loud shout went up from the boat, and the men began to try wildly at their oars, but no one knew exactly what course to take, and even Blanche grew bewildered in the medley of tumbling waves, and could no longer distinguish the little speck of a boat.

"I am afeard the young lady was mistook," said the old sailor. "'Twere a porpoise or one of them things. 'Tis almost too dark to see an Ingyman, let alone a mite like that ere boat."

"No, she's right!" cried Charles, who had been gazing in the direction Blanche pointed to. "Here, give me the tiller lines and pull lads as you never pulled in your lives before."

Two minutes of breathless suspense—two hours it seemed to the mother and Blanche—and they had come up with, or rather as it seemed, stumbled on, (so dark had it grown,) the little boat, and Cecil drenched through and through by the waves that had gone over him, with his boat half full of water, but brave still, and pulling away with all the small strength of his weak exhausted arms. In an instant he was pulled into the large boat and given over to his mother, who kissed and embraced and cried over him convulsively, till poor Cecil, worn out with fatigue and terror, burst out crying too, and she had to check herself to soothe him. They had not found him a minute too soon. The poor boy had given himself up for lost, when he heard them cheer.

"I knew all about the current," he said, "and felt my boat was getting drawn into it, so I said my prayers as well as I could, but I knew papa would say a soldier's son must be game to the last, and I thought I would row as long as I could, but I was very tired," and in a whisper, "I was very much afraid too."

The poor child was quite exhausted, and they had nothing on board to give him. They had started in such a hurry.

"If ever I go without my hunting flask again—" said Charles. But the hunting flask was on *terra firma*, and the only thing to do was to get there as soon as possible.

Blanche took off her shawl quietly, and wrapped it round the boy. His mother gathered him closely up to her, and in a few minutes he was fast asleep, while she sat, quiet tears falling down her face, her heart full of joy and thankfulness, watching him. Blanche sat at the side of the boat, looking out upon the sea in a dreamy sort of way, very different from the anxious straining glance of a few minutes before. It was quite dark, and the wind was rising rapidly and the sea with it. The tide had turned and was running out fast. The wind too was against them, and the wearied men had some difficulty in making any progress at all.

They were coasting along a bank of sand, never entirely covered except at unusually high tides, and separated from the main land by a shallow channel about a quarter of a mile wide, dry at low water. The plash of the waves as they fell off from the steep bank had something in it very melancholy, and altogether it was a dreary scene that the moon showed at intervals, as it cast an uncertain gleam from between the hurrying masses of cloud. The black outline of a large wrecked vessel, the bare ribs and broken spars of which stood up dark against the sky, did not contribute to the cheerfulness of the scene.

"Is it long since that vessel was lost?" said Blanche to one of the men near her.

"Nigh upon three year, Miss," was the answer. "She got blown out of her course one special bad winter's night, and got aground here, and for all as the land is so near, there was not a soul could be saved though the folks tried hard. It's rather a fatal sort of a spot this," he continued. "A poor fellow was lost here from them houses yonder only this spring, in quite a curious kind of way."

"How was that?" asked Blanche, whose curiosity was excited.

" Well, you see, Miss, he had been a soldier and been to the Ingies and there he got struck with a queer kind of blindness that they catches in them parts. I've heerd that he could see right enough by day, but the moment it was twilight or moonlight he were as blind as a mole—couldn't see his hand afore his face. Well, some of the boys jeered at him, and he being a bit hot-tempered, got mad with them, and made a bet with one young fellow that he would go across the channel there, and bring a bit of wood from the wreck by moonlight, as easy as one of them could. So he started one bright night, and the queer thing was that he came across the sands and struck up the bank very nigh the wreck, and got up to her with very little difficulty. There were lots of us watching him. He got the wood, and then somehow in turning back again he seemed to get confused, and went round to the wrong side. We shouted to him, but he never seemed to hear, and went wandering and stumbling on till he got to the water's edge. He must have thought the tide had risen in the channel, and that he could run through, for he ran on till the water was breast high. We got out the boat as quick as we could, but he were dead, poor chap! I aint over fond since then of coming by here, for you see, Miss, that bank aint all regular sand, but mud and clay like, and footmarks on it sink deeper and deeper in it, till they take two or three storms like to wash the marks out, and it's only about a month ago that I could still see the prints of that poor fellow's feet where he wandered backwards and forwards. But these last tides have washed it all smooth and straight."

"There is some one there now!" cried Blanche, suddenly, as a bright gleam of moonlight made the dripping wreck clearly visible. "And he is coming towards us. Oh stop! stop!"

"Not possible;" said the man. "There has been four feet of water over the whole of that bank to-day. The wind lay so strong that way."

"The young Miss has good eyes," said the old steersman, "she saw the boat when none of us could. Can you see him still, my lady?"

"Yes," said Blanche, "I think I can, but a shadow has come over; yes, now I do—how fast he is coming! Charles, Charles, can you see nothing?"

He sprang to her side, for she looked greatly excited as she stood, the wind blowing her light dress and long fair hair which had escaped from some of its fastenings. It had come over very dark again, but Blanche continued to gaze into the gloom, with a sort of fascinated horror-struck look that thrilled through them all. She was half drawing back as if longing to turn away, and yet compelled to look and almost to follow.

The idea seized Charles Lethbridge that she would spring over the side of the boat.

"Blanche!" he cried, seizing her arm, "what is the matter? what do you see?"

She gave a shuddering sort of sob, and hiding her face against his shoulder, pointed in the direction in which she had been gazing.

"Look!" she said. "Can you not see? can you not see?"

A rush of mist and rain went by, driven by the cold wind, and he almost fancied he saw amidst it the outlines of a dim retreating figure, but the storm was on them in earnest, and his one thought was to get Blanche home safely again.

"You are cold and shivering," he said, as he replaced her on the seat, and wrapped her in his coat that he had taken off. "What have you done with your shawl? Now men, row with a will. We must get the ladies home out of this as fast as we can."

Few words were spoken on that long way home, it was all they could do to make any head against wind and tide. Charles leant forward several times and spoke to Blanche, but she remained cowering down on the seat, almost in the same attitude Mrs. Vernon had done when they went out, and only shook her head or answered in monosyllables.

At length to their infinite joy the lights of Kingstanton began to glimmer through the misty rain. Boats came out to meet them, and learn how they had sped; and when wearied out and aching in every limb, they reached the shore at last, a score of brawny arms were stretched out to drag the boat up high and dry, and such a ringing hearty English cheer broke forth as the cliffs of Kingstanton had not echoed to for many a long day.

Charles was one of the first to spring to land, and lifting Blanche out of the boat, almost carried her up to their lodgings.—Mrs. Burt met them at the door, and an exclamation of horror at the sight of Blanche's drenched soiled dress was the first greeting they received.

"La, Miss Lennox! and such a pretty dress! New on to-day and quite entirely ruined, I never did!"

"Confound the woman!" said Charles, in high wrath. "Where's my sister or her maid? Is there no one here with a grain of common sense?"

"Miss Lethbridge and Mrs. Stanley and all of them are down on the shore," said the staid Mrs. Campbell, coming forward. "But I was to stay and see everything was in readiness."

"Then take this poor child and put her to bed at once, and I think she ought to have a doctor to see her. Where is one to be found?" Charles said in a low voice. to Campbell. But Blanche overheard, and roused herself to smile and decline any such unnecessary precautions.

"I shall be all right," she said, "when I have changed my dress and had some tea. Now, own Charles, that you think me slightly delirious and wandering in my mind?" And she ran up stairs laughing, to Charles's infinite relief, for he had thought the strain and anxiety of that evening had made her really ill.

CHAPTER X.

Mrs. Vernon and Cecil, accompanied by Mrs. Stanley and Cissy, were not long in making their appearance from the beach. Mr. Stanley was also with them. He had come down when he heard, on his return from a long day spent in magistrate's work, of the alarming disappearance of Cecil. But neither he nor his wife would remain, although pressed by Mrs. Vernon to do so, thinking, and not without reason, that Master Cecil's escapade had caused quite commotion enough, and that the sooner everybody could be in peace and quietness, the better.

Poor Cecil was so worn out, that he submitted very quietly to having his supper brought upstairs, and being consigned to bed immediately after ; but Cissy in vain persuaded Blanche to follow his virtuous and submissive example. "I cannot rest," she said, "I must go down." And go down accordingly she did, and took her place at the table with crimson cheeks and strangely bril-

liant eyes. But Charles, who could not help feeling
uneasy about her, saw her shiver, and on touching
her hand found that it was as cold as ice.

He brought her a shawl and placed her in an
arm chair by the fire, saying all he could think of
to tempt her to eat, but she only crumbled her
toast to bits on her plate, and answered with one
of her bright wonderful smiles when he remonstrated.

" I will bring you no more tea," he said, "till
you have eaten something. You have had nothing
since the middle of the day."

" Oh, Cissy, do speak to him," said Blanche,
" and tell him how wicked and cruel he is. How
can I eat when I am dying of thirst ? and what
are three tiny cups of tea ?"

" You must settle it between you," replied
Cissy, philosophically, " but I must say I think
for once Charles is in the right."

The contest continued, however, with very little
success on either side, till Mrs. Vernon went off to
look after Cecil; and Cissy, with a benevolent
feeling of doing as she would be done by, followed
her from the room. Then Blanche desired Charles
to leave off being silly, and come and sit down by
her for she had a great deal to tell him.

But the 'great deal' seemed difficult of com-
mencement, for she sat a long time gazing into
the fire, with her head resting on his shoulder
without saying a word.

"Well, dearest," he said at last, stroking her hair back from the fair pure forehead, and kissing it fondly. "What were you going to say? Cissy and Campbell will make a descent presently, and carry you off to get the rest you must need so much, my brave little heroine."

"Oh, Charles!" she cried, "I am not a heroine at all—only a foolish frightened girl—I want to tell you what I saw to-night, and yet I do not feel as if I could. Did you see nothing?"

"Nothing distinctly," said Charles. "There might have been some one prowling about the wreck, to see if there were a few rusty chains or bolts to be got out of her still, but it was too dark and misty to distinguish anything."

"I saw him distinctly," said Blanche, hiding her face against Charles as she spoke, till he was obliged to bend down low to catch what she said. "He seemed to come quite close, and held out his hands as if to draw me towards him. His eyes were open wide, but with a fixed glassy look, and though it seemed to me that I heard my name called, the sound did not seem to come from his lips but from all the air round—I am sure he is dead," she went on, after a pause.

"Whom do you mean? I do not understand;" broke in Charles, much perplexed.

"Arthur Woods;" whispered Blanche, in the lowest tone possible, but Charles's quick ear caught it, and a sharp pang of jealousy darted through his heart.

"You mean that curate of your father's?" he said, in a cold displeased tone, "who I once heard had the cool impudence to admire you. What has he to do with you, Blanche, that his living or dying need affect you in this manner? Good heavens!" he went on, as she made no answer, only lifted her head from his shoulder, and hid her face in her hands. "You do not mean to tell me you cared for that fellow? Speak to me. Look at me." And he knelt down on the rug at her feet, and took her hands from her face. "Tell me you are ill—over excited—anything but that!"

"Charles," answered Blanche, with that simple childlike dignity, which was at once so honest and so modest and maidenly. "You know perfectly well that I never have loved anyone but you, but poor Arthur Woods one day told me that he loved me very much, and when I said I could not care about him, he went away and was very ill, nearly dying, afterwards. He recovered, but Minnie Smith told me he had not gone on well since. He was the last person in my thoughts at that moment," she added simply, "but the instant I saw the dim figure in the distance, I felt it was he, and then on a sudden he seemed to come quite close and to call me. And oh, Charles, I have heard so many stories of people appearing at the moment of their deaths to those who have influenced their lives for good or ill, and he may have come back to reproach and curse me for all the harm I had done him!" And a convulsive shudder shook her slight frame from head to foot.

"Nay, my darling," replied Charles, reassured by Blanche's straightforward candour, as to the degree of interest with which the poor young curate had been able to inspire her. " It was not your fault that you could not like him well enough to marry him, and if a man has no more pith in him than to go to the bad because a girl won't have him, why he can't be worth much. Particularly a . parson," he added, as a twinge of conscience reminded him that it would have gone hard enough with him had Blanche refused him.

'He was the only son of his mother, and she was a widow,' murmured Blanche. "How his mother will hate and loathe me when she hears of his death!"

"Now really it is too absurd our taking it for granted in this way that the poor fellow's a dead man. Look here, Blanche, you heard what those fellows said last night about the way that footmarks remain in that sand or rather mud? Now if I go out there to-morrow morning before the tide is up again, and find great hob-nailed shoe marks all over the place, will you promise to believe that you had been dreaming, and that it was only some fisherman coming to set lines or get a bit of the wreck to light his grandmother's fire that you saw, and translated into this miserable curate's ghost?"

"When we are married, darling," he went on, "we will have him hunted up and a snug berth found for him in Devonshire or the Land's End or John o' Groats House—somewhere handy and comfortable. And Blanche, my own dearest one, you must not keep me in suspense much longer, I cannot bear it. You must let me speak to Lady Frances about our wedding as soon as we get home?"

He had both his arms round her, and tried to draw her close to him, but she laid her little hands on his shoulders and held him back, gazing earnestly into the kindly handsome face that was looking at her, with such love and devotion shining in the dark grey eyes.

All the life of love and happiness which lay before her, rose in vivid distinctness while she felt at the same time, in the depths of her soul, she should have by her own act and deed to give it up. Yes, to turn her back upon it all, to wring with pain the honest and noble heart which had showered all its wealth of love upon her, to renounce the protector who would have guarded her through life with the courage, devotion and tenderness he had shown to-day, and go on alone and desolate, weary and heart-broken. And all for what? Were they not one in so much that was

essential ?   Did they not worship the same God ?
trust in the same Redeemer ? say almost the same
prayers ?   At that moment of agony and excitement she could not think of one point of difference
that need make their separation necessary, and yet,
with that strange duality of our nature, she knew
with the morrow would come back the old difficulties which had seemed so great before.   She would
feel that there was a wide and deep gulf between
Charles and herself, and that unless he would
cross it, (of which she had no hope,) their paths
in life must be far apart: at this terrible, over-
whelming thought the poor girl's courage gave .
way, and she burst into violent hysterical sobs.

Luckily for both of them, Cissy and Campbell
came to the rescue.   The former scolding her
brother soundly for allowing Blanche to agitate
and distress herself after such a trying day, and
the latter quietly walking her off to her room,
undressing her and putting her to bed like a
child.

The night was a long and dreary one.   The
howling of the wind and plashing of the rain, would
have made sleep almost impossible had Blanche
been inclined for it, but she was feverish and
wakeful, and tossed about till morning, when she
fell into unrefreshing sleep oppressed with terrible
dreams.   It was from one of these she started to
hear Charles's voice below.   Hastily ringing her
bell, she gave the little maid of the lodgings who

answered it, a note for Mr. Lethbridge with a pencilled enquiry whether he had been to the sand bank and if he had found any marks.

The answer was an evasive one. The whole place was washed clean with the rain. Daniel Lambert himself might have walked over it for hours, and left no traces that such rain could not wash out. Now this was only partially true. The rain and spray had washed over the bank with great force throughout the night, still Charles could perceive a little way below high water mark the furrow cut by the keel of their boat, where they had rested partially aground last night when Blanche exclaimed she saw a figure, and the sight gave him an uncomfortable sensation.

Blanche asked him no questions on the subject, however. She did not leave her bed till the evening of the following day; not that she felt ill, she said, exactly, but her head ached so, and when she tried to stand she was dizzy and faint. Master Cecil had been pronounced to be suffering from a "bad chill," and was doomed to a day's imprisonment in bed, but he made his gaolers' lives such a burden to them, that Burt's indiscretion in allowing him to get up to dinner, was strongly suspected to have been winked at by Mrs. Campbell, who revenged herself upon the unoffending Blanche, and was with difficulty persuaded to allow her to come down on the evening of the second day.

She found Mrs. Vernon very anxious to get away from Kingstanton as soon as possible. She should never have a moment's peace, she said, as long as they were there, whenever Cecil was out of her sight; and as to having him always with her, that was only one degree less of misery. So it was settled they were to go on the day but one following, and Lady Frances, who was in London at her brother's house, was warned she might expect the whole party by dinner-time on the next Tuesday.

The day before their departure, as they were strolling along the cliffs, Charles begged Blanche to come out with him to the sand bank, and see under its usual aspect the place which had caused her so much terror.

" It will be the best way, believe me, of removing your gloomy impressions, otherwise you will always be haunted by them whenever you are ill or depressed ;" he said.

Blanche assented, and leaving word where they had gone, they started in a boat with a couple of rowers for the dreaded sand bank. She was in unusually good spirits. One of the vague hopes that sometimes cheered her that, after all, Charles would become a Catholic, had taken form and substance from his having declared the evening before, after hearing a bitter controversial sermon directed against Papists, that " three more such sermons would send him straight over to the Church of

Rome." And he had gone on enumerating the
Saints and Martyrs, the noble works of charity to
the suffering, of zeal, and success in converting the
heathen, to be found in that contemned and abused
Church until Cissy roused herself from a letter of
Ferdinand's, received only the evening before, and
which she was reading over for the sixth time, to
remark that he was almost as bad as Blanche.

It was a passing fit of enthusiasm, almost of
contradiction, but poor Blanche dwelt upon it and
clung to it, as a dawning hope that her terrible
sacrifice might yet be averted, and joy and happiness be hers even in this life.

So it was with a joyous heart that she started
on their little expedition, and found herself in
what seemed an incredibly short time, remember-
ing the weary length of their return on that sad
evening, close to the long sand bank.

Certainly she would not have recognized the
scene again. The tide was much further out, so
that a long expanse of sand stretched gleaming in
the sun. The wreck some distance off, instead of
looking the ghastly skeleton it had done in the
fitful stormy light, made simply a good foreground
for the bit of distant coast with its picturesque
group of cottages nestled under the low cliff.
Boats were passing and repassing in the narrow
channel, and the sea-gulls sailing hither and
thither flashed their broad white wings in the
sunshine.

"Well," said Charles, smiling, "the place does not look so very ghastly and eerie now does it? Are you not glad you came?"

"Yes, very;" owned Blanche. "I think you are right, and that I must have been dreaming. The whole scene looks quite cheerful to-day." Yet even as she spoke, the recollection of the tragedy, she had been told had occurred at that very spot, fell like a shadow on her.

Before leaving Kingstanton, Blanche found out her Catholic sailor, and had a long talk with him. The man was a convert. He had been shipwrecked once off the coast of Spain, and had been nursed by an English Sister of Charity during a long illness brought on by distress and want. What he saw then of the religion he had never heard of except as something to hate and despise, convinced him that it must be the True one, and as soon as he was well, he put himself under instruction and was received into the Church. He had come back to England, and been many long voyages since then, but his Faith was as firm as ever.

"A hard time I've had of it, Miss, I can tell ye," said the man, "but they all know it is of no use trying to laugh me out of it now, and I tell them, poor fellows, there's not one but would be the same, if they only knew the peace and comfort of it. Not one!"

He was married, and lived at Kingstanton with his wife and children. He earned a livelihood with his boat, and his wife kept a small shop in the village.

"And every Sunday morning, we goes to Huns-lynn, and we have to start often before it's light, to do it;" he said in conclusion.

In taking leave of him, Blanche gave him a trifle, and begged him to remember her in his prayers.

"Aye, that I will, Miss," was the answer. "And the young Cap'n too! God bless ye both."

Their journey to town the next day, was not at all an unpleasant one, in spite of the slowness incidental to a Great Eastern train. Mrs. Vernon always liked change, and was much pleased at the idea of a fortnight she was going to spend with some friends in town. Cissy was elated at the thoughts of seeing Ferdinand who was to be in London to meet them. Blanche was in the serene, hopeful spirits of the day before. The most melancholy of the party was poor Cecil, who considered that his stay at the sea had been cut short in a most unjustifiable manner, and who had nothing more pleasant in view than a speedy return to school.

Lady Frances received them with open arms in Grosvenor Square on their arrival, and thanked Mrs. Vernon in her sweet cordial way for the care she had taken of her child. Mrs. Vernon was in a hurry to depart, now that she had deposited Blanche safely under her uncle's roof, and turned

to take leave of her after exchanging a few words
with Lady Margaret.

"Goodbye, dear," she said.   Then with a sudden burst of feeling she threw her arms round
Blanche's neck, and whispered, "God bless you,
dearest Blanche.   I shall always feel that you
saved my boy's life.   If it had not been for you
we should not have seen him, and I shall never
forget it."

Blanche kissed her tenderly, and then bidding
farewell to Cissy Lethbridge and Charles who had
accompanied them to Grosvenor Square, Mrs. Vernon hurried down the stairs as if half ashamed of
the emotion she had shown, and getting into the
cab which was waiting at the door, drove off to
her friend's house in Belgravia, whither Cecil and
the luggage had proceeded direct from the station.

"And now, my darling child," said Lady
Frances, drawing Blanche towards her and regarding her with fond scrutiny, "Let me see what
good Kingstanton has done you."

"You must not judge of that to-night, dearest,"
said Blanche, laughingly.   "I am tired and good
for nothing, and it would not be at all fair.   I
have enjoyed my trip immensely.   Kingstanton is
a very nice place, and I never liked the Norfolk
people so much before.   As for Mrs. Stanley, I
never shall forget her kindness, and everyone was
so nice.   The only drawback—"

"Was having a certain young gentleman there,"

said Lady Margaret, mischievously, kissing Blanche
as she spoke. "Yes, that must have been a
dreadful bore certainly !"

"Don't be silly, Margaret," said Blanche, returning her cousin's embrace. "The only drawback was not having this dear little mother of
mine, with us. If she had been there it would
have been quite perfect."

"Ah, but I could not leave papa you see," said
Lady Frances. "It was very reluctantly that he
spared me for a couple of days now. He has been
so much taken up with this Ruri-decanal meeting
of his, and all the questions they had to discuss at
it. I did not think him looking well when I came
away, and shall be glad to be home again and able
to look after him."

"Now ladies," exclaimed Lord Norwood, entering the room, "it is time to be dressing for dinner; and my dear Margaret," he continued, addressing his daughter, "I have ordered the carriage
punctually at ten o'clock this evening, so mind
you do not keep me waiting. I shall want you to
put me down at the House; and Dereham will
escort you to your ball, as he is coming to dine
here, and will go with us."

"I am glad of that," said Lady Margaret,
laughing, "as now I shall have someone to speak
to, and I don't suppose I should have met with
much attention from either of the other gentlemen
present."

" How can you say that, Margaret ?" cried Ferdinand, who had been enjoying a quiet *tête-à-tête* with Miss Cissy at the further end of the room, and now came forward. " When you know how exemplary my conduct is on all occasions, and how equally I bestow my attentions."

" Oh, yes, we are quite aware of that," rejoined his cousin, " and I suppose Mr. Lethbridge would say the same thing, but somehow or other you neither of you seem to have a very clear notion of what is required of you in that respect. I believe you think it quite sufficient if in a general sort of way, you recognize the existence of us nobodies, whilst the 'world' to you is summed up in the person of one young lady in particular !"

Both Ferdinand and Charles exclaimed loudly at this, but Lady Margaret shook her head and ran upstairs followed by the other ladies, two of whom were rather inclined to scold her for her remarks.

After dinner, the gentlemen soon followed the fairer portion of the community to the drawing-room. Lady Margaret was looking over some new music with Blanche and Cissy in the front room as they came in, and Ferdinand, taking Charles Lethbridge by the arm, led him into a small recess in the back drawing-room, saying,

" Come here a minute, Charles, I want to read you a letter I have just had from Gerald. He has been dreadfully upset by the death of a poor fellow, who was once my father's curate. Arthur Woods—do you remember the name?—whom he came across the other day at Spa, under peculiar circumstances. It is a singular story altogether, and I have not said anything about it to my mother or Blanche as yet. Just listen."

And he drew a letter from his pocket as he spoke, and began to read it aloud, but in too low a tone for anyone to hear in the adjoining apartment. He did not look up in Charles's face, or he must have seen the expression of startled astonishment which came over it, at the mention of Arthur Woods's name.

The letter was as follows:

"I have not answered your last letter, my dearest fellow, so soon as I should otherwise have done, as my time has been greatly taken up in attending, what proved to be, the deathbed of our old friend, Arthur Woods. I told you in my last despatch, that a curious incident had occurred, which I had not time to enter upon then as I wrote in haste. He was at that time very ill, but not, I imagined, in danger, and I was not alarmed about him. Poor fellow. I can hardly believe it is all over now. It seems only yesterday that I first saw him in the gaming rooms here, and felt puzzled by his likeness to someone, I could not think to whom, for he had grown a beard and moustache, and was otherwise altered so that I did not recognize him at once. It seems that he never really recovered his strength after that serious illness, which he had in town upon leaving Wentmore. His unfortunate attachment to our darling Blanche, which he could not overcome, prevented him from settling to any work again in England, and he came abroad by the advice of his friends and medical attendant, with the idea of finding amid foreign scenes and travel, the distraction he needed to prevent him from continually brooding over his disappointment. But all his efforts to this end seem to have been unavailing, and finally, on coming to Spa, he took to play, (although, as you may suppose, he had not much money to lose,) in the hope of drowning thought by the excitement gaming produces. At first he won, and the pastime became a passion which, as so often happens, carried him away, and very soon reduced him to the greatest straits; for in one desperate *coup* after a long day's run of varied luck, he staked and lost all, and more than all, he had about him or could call his own. It was at this time that I, by accident, (as we say,) came to Spa, and first encountered him, without knowing or even guessing his identity. In a fit of despondency he shut himself up in his room for some days, refusing to see anyone, or go anywhere, and could hardly be induced to take sufficient nourishment to support life. But after a while he, obtained a loan from some acquaintance in the town, and returned to the tables to try his fortune

anew. For a time he succeeded, but at length
he lost, and then he gave himself up entirely to
despair. I happened to be sitting outside the
entrance of the Redoute that night, and saw him
come out. He was running, his head uncovered,
evidently almost beside himself. Impelled by
a powerful feeling of mingled curiosity and compassion, I followed him; and in a few minutes
found myself engaged in a pursuit which became
exciting. It seems, that the poor fellow, when
he became aware that he was followed, took it
into his head that it was by someone to whom he
owed money, who had watched his losses at the
table, and was pursuing him to demand payment.
The end of it was, that he took a frightful leap to
avoid me, and I gave him up for lost, but by the
mercy of God, was able to save his life. The
details I will give you another time. I then had
him carried to my own hotel where for some time
he lay very ill, but the doctor I called in did not
seem uneasy about him, and by degrees he appeared to mend. It was then I found out whom
he was, and heard his story up to this point from
his own lips.

"He had recognized me, when we first met,
and had purposely avoided me, hoping that I did
not remember him, which was indeed the case.
I never saw anyone so utterly wretched and cast
down as he was. He would sometimes sit for
hours without speaking, in a chair by the open

window, looking out into vacancy, and nothing I
could do would rouse him. Instead of getting
better, he seemed gradually to get weaker, and
when I privately asked the doctor who was attending him, his opinion, he shook his head, and said,
he thought if the young man had any friends or
relations in England they should be written to.
As gently as I could I told poor Woods what Mr.
Fowler had said, and he begged me to write to his
mother and tell her that he was very ill. 'And
ask her to come to me, if she can,' he said, 'but
do not alarm her, if you can help it.' I did as he
wished, and when the letter was gone, he turned
to me and asked me to let him know the truth.
'Mr. Fowler thinks I shall not recover?' he said.
I was obliged to admit that the doctor did not
give much hope, but said all I could to keep up
his spirits, and expressed my wish to send to
Brussels for further advice. He shook his head.
'No,' he said, 'I am dying. I know that. I
only wanted to know if Mr. Fowler thought so
too.' Then seizing me by the hand, he cried
convulsively, 'But I am not fit to die. I cannot
die as I am. What am I to do? I, who have so
often preached to others and prepared them for
death, now that it has come to me, am unable to
face it.' I knew that the poor fellow had been
leading a careless life of late, in fact that his dis-
sipated habits had accelerated his end, but knowing what I did also of his previous history, I felt

all the greater pity and sorrow for him. I tried to raise his thoughts to Heaven, and spoke to him of Repentance, and the Forgiveness there is for the greatest sinner. 'I know, I know all that,' he said, 'but such comfort is not enough for me now. I have stood by the dying and spoken to them myself often enough, and bitterly I have felt too, my inability to help them as they needed. Cannot *you* do something more for me than speak to me of Repentance and Forgiveness *beyond the grave...?* I thought that your Church had Sacraments especially to help and strengthen the dying? I want Help and Strength. Such Help and such Strength as I have never been able myself to impart to others. Can you not procure me what I need?' And his imploring earnestness I can never forget. I know, my dear Ferdinand, that you will not be angry with me for acting as I did, after such an appeal. Happily there was an Irish priest in the town, whose address I knew, and although he had no faculty for hearing confessions in this diocese, he could receive that of a dying man. I asked Arthur Woods if he desired to be received into the Church, and explained to him, that only as a Catholic, could he be admitted to the privileges and sacraments of the Catholic Church. He said that he had long been persuaded of the truth of the Roman Catholic Church, (some books of mine which accidentally found their way into his keeping, seem to have first led him to

think that the Truth might be with us,) and now
he desired nothing so much as to become a Catholic and to die in the right Faith. I flew to my
friend the Curé, and told him the whole story.
He returned with me to the hotel. Woods could
speak French well enough to make himself understood. Father O'Donnell heard his confession,
and gave him Absolution. The Curé administered
conditional baptism, and afterwards gave him the
Viaticum and Extreme Unction. The peace and
happiness which seemed to fill his soul when he
had received the Sacraments, shewed plainly that
he had found the Help and Strength he needed.
With what a full heart I thanked God and our
Blessed Lady, no words can say.'

"In a few days an answer came to my letter,
from his sister. The poor girl wrote in great distress at hearing of her brother's illness, and said
that Mrs. Woods could not come to him, as she
was herself confined to her bed ; and she implored
me to let her know how he really was. I read
him the letter, and he was much moved at the
thought of not seeing his mother again. 'But I
am not dying amongst *strangers*,' he said, taking
my hand and looking up in my face. 'I have you
with me, and I am in the arms of my Holy
Mother, the Church. Tell them I was happy,
very happy.' He lived only a few days after the
letter came from his sister. I wrote again to say
he was dying, and the poor girl came out herself,

accompanied by a female friend. She had left her mother at her own earnest entreaty, but when she arrived he was no more. His last moments were rather disturbed. Before he died he told me some things which surprised and moved me greatly, but of these I will say more another time. Just before the end, a singular change came over him. He became suddenly very much excited, and started up in his bed, crying, 'I must see her again! I cannot die without seeing her once more!' I tried to soothe him, and asked of whom he spoke? 'Blanche!' he cried, 'your sister, my love—my only love!—Oh, God, that I should die without seeing her again!' I spoke to him of the meeting hereafter, and told him of the happiness it would give her to hear he had become a Catholic before his death, but he did not seem to heed me. He stretched out his arms and gazed earnestly before him without speaking, and then sinking slowly back he looked at me and murmured, '*I have seen her!* Tell her my last thought was of her.' I seized the Crucifix and placed it to his lips. I saw a change coming over his face. Father O'Donnell began the prayers for the agonizing, and before he had finished, Arthur's spirit had fled."

Ferdinand paused. He had been much moved on first reading his brother's letter, but whilst doing so aloud, he could scarcely steady his voice towards the end, and Charles who had listened with mingled feelings to the narrative, now laid a hand on his shoulder and whispered hoarsely,

"For God's sake, don't let Blanche see that letter."

Ferdinand was about to reply when the sound of a heavy fall behind them caused both to turn hastily round.

" Good heavens ! She has overheard it;" cried Charles, springing towards Blanche's senseless form which lay stretched upon the ground.

It was true. She had come into the room whilst the letter was being read. Arthur Woods's name had caught her ear, and she had remained · rooted to the spot, listening to every word, and when it was ended she had staggered towards a chair, failed to reach it, and losing all consciousness had fallen in a heavy swoon upon the floor.

CHAPTER XI.

"Mamma, how could you go and make such a mistake about that Mr. Lennox! It was all your fault that we did not know him last winter. You would have it he was an adventurer and all sorts of things, and when Madame Le Grand wanted to introduce him to us, you would not let her. And now, he turns out to belong to one of the best families in England, and is in a much better set here than we are ourselves. It is so very provoking, and you are always doing that sort of thing!"

"My dear Harriet, that is not the way to speak to me. How could I tell that Mr. Lennox was different from the general run of good looking young Englishmen one knows nothing about, who come over here every winter, and try and get into society if they can? One cannot be too careful, and when you hear of anyone being employed as teacher or professor, or whatever they call it, at one of these colleges, you naturally assume that he is no one really worth knowing. I am as sorry as you can be about it, but the mistake was a very natural one, and there is no reason why you should not become acquainted with him now if an opportunity offers."

"But no opportunity is likely to offer. Edith and I were walking on the Boulevard with the Richardsons this morning when he passed, walking arm in arm with the Prince de L—— on one side, and a good looking man, who was evidently English, on the other. Kate Richardson asked us if we knew who that was, and thinking she meant Mr. Lennox, I said yes, that he was a master or something in one of the colleges, quite a person that you would not let us know, but she meant the other one. She knew Mr. Lennox by sight, and said we were quite wrong in thinking he was not a person to know, for he was very intimate with some of the best Belgian families, and who should the other person be, he was walking with, but Lord Dereham. So, there you see, mamma, what a nice mess you have made of it, turning up your nose at a person who is on intimate terms with lords and princes."

The speakers were a Mrs. and Miss Bolton. Mrs. Bolton was a widow lady who came every winter to Brussels with her two daughters, and lived *en pension* in one of the hotels whilst there. The Miss Boltons were fine, showy looking girls, and they, as well as their mamma, were anxious to impress upon their friends and acquaintance the notion that in England they mixed in the very "best society." They gave out their determination to become acquainted with none but the *elite* of the Belgian capital, and were very particular as to whom they were introduced to, and what houses they frequented. But somehow or other it was remarked that the Boltons were not seen at the really good houses, and moved in rather a second rate set altogether. They had been to one of the Court Balls it is true, but their entrance to the Palace had been easily effected, owing to the simple fact that on one never to be forgotten occasion, they had been presented at a Drawing-Room at St. James's, and this they made the most of. Their grand ambition, however, was to be invited to the Embassy, and in spite of all their endeavours they had not been able to get there as yet.

Gerald Lennox, as we know, had gone very little into society when he first arrived in Brussels, and subsequently had not done so at all. But it is impossible for an English person to live long in Brussels without being known by sight, and by name as well, to most of the English there. A distinguished looking, handsome young man, like Gerald, was sure to attract attention, and many were the enquiries and surmises his appearance gave rise to. But after a time it was noticed that Mr. Lennox (his name had very soon transpired,) was never seen at either of the English chapels, and one day the Miss Boltons came home brimfull of the discovery that he was a Roman Catholic, for they had actually seen him on his knees in the street as the Host went by! Our readers will perhaps remember, that on a certain occasion Gerald did kneel down when the Blessed Sacrament was being carried from the Eglise St. Jacques to a sick person's house, and that some English ladies present had regarded him with considerable amazement for so doing. The Miss Boltons were the ladies in question, and from that moment they had felt doubtful as to the propriety of making such a strange person's acquaintance, however prepossessing his appearance might be. Then came the report that he was poor, earning his living by giving lessons in English or something of that sort, and when during a party given by an English lady, who had married a Belgian, at which Gerald had happened accidentally to be present, the hostess offered to introduce him to the Miss Boltons, their mamma declined the honour with thanks.

But now, they were beginning to find out their mistake, and great was their tribulation in consequence.

"And it was very nice to have those Richardson girls laughing at us for thinking Mr. Lennox was not good enough for us to know," exclaimed the younger Miss Bolton, who had hitherto not joined in the conversation. "*They* would give their heads and ears to become acquainted with him; they saw him one night at Lady Sophia Roberts's, and you know *we* have never been able to get there!"

"As if it signified what the Richardsons said;" retorted Mrs. Bolton, who was not a little put out, at being thus attacked by both her daughters. "They are as jealous as they can be, because they are not asked out as much as we are, and don't really know so many people. As to that Lady Sophia Roberts they are always talking about, she is a Roman Catholic, and that is quite reason enough for my not caring to be introduced to her. They have never been presented at Court, and they can't say they have been invited to the Palace. You have always that advantage over them. Did they pretend they knew Lord Dereham?"

"No, not personally, but he had been pointed out to them as one of the swell English visitors here this winter," answered Miss Edith. "Somehow or other they always contrive to know who people are and all about them, and they have a detestable way of saying, 'I suppose you know Lord So and So; or have met Sir Somebody Something, in London?' One is obliged to say, No, and although I always say it with an air of supreme indifference, and as if it was a mere accident our *not* being acquainted with that particular Lord or Baronet, I don't believe they are

taken in about it a bit.   I am sure I wish we did
know somebody worth knowing, for I am tired to
death of only knowing snobs."

"I declare, that is Katey Richardson crossing
the Square at this moment, all by herself;" cried
the eldest sister, who was standing at the open
window. "And she is coming here. What can
she want, I wonder?"

"Goodness knows.   They are always boring in
about something or other.   I daresay it is to ask
us to go somewhere with them this afternoon,"
said Edith, "but I am sure I wont."

"Now, girls, I insist upon your being civil to
Kate, if she does come in.   You know I can't
afford to quarrel with them.   I must go and
change my cap, for I am not fit to be seen."

Mrs. Bolton had only just time to leave the
room by a side door communicating with her
sleeping apartment, when the other door opened
and admitted a young lady who rushed up to the
youngest Miss Bolton, and putting her arms round
her neck, embraced her affectionately, exclaiming,
"Here I am again, you see!"

"Yes, dear," returned Miss Edith, hardly concealing her impatience.   "And what is it you
want?"

"To tell you something;" said the other, seating herself on a sofa, and crossing her hands
before her. "But if you don't care to hear it,
I can go away again."

Harriet Bolton, who had hitherto taken no notice of her visitor, now turned round, and said coolly,

" Since you have taken the trouble to come over on purpose, you may as well tell us what it is. So don't be stupid, Kate."

" Well," replied Miss Richardson, " I don't think you deserve to hear it. But I won't teaze you any longer, dears, and if you must know, why —I've made another discovery about that Mr. Lennox of yours !"

The sisters tried hard to look unconcerned, and Edith said with an assumption of dignity,

" I don't know what you mean by calling him *our* Mr. Lennox. He is nothing of the sort I am sure."

" No, no ;" returned her friend. " We are quite aware that a person who may be good enough to associate with the tip-top Belgian families here in Brussels, and all that sort of thing, may at the same time not be sufficiently—you know what I mean—to be introduced to *you*. But, I do think, my dear children, you have been rather mistaken in this particular instance. I told you that was Lord Dereham he was walking with this morning ?"

" Well ?"

" Well. No wonder this 'Nobody of a Teacher,' or whatever you called him, seemed on intimate terms with his Lordship, for it turns out he is his own first cousin."

"How do you know that?" asked both the listeners in a breath.

"Gertrude Roberts (whom you don't know, by the way,) came to lunch with us to-day. I told her we had seen Lord Dereham walking on the Boulevard this morning, and asked her if she knew him at all. She said she did not, but she believed he was a very nice person, as she had heard a good deal of him from his cousin Mr. Lennox, with whom they are very intimate."

"Ah, yes. But if she only said 'cousin' he may be a very distant relation;" said Harriet Bolton. "Third, or fourth, or something of that kind."

"Not at all," returned Miss Richardson, "for I asked her, and she said Mr. Lennox's mother, Lady Frances Lennox, was Lord Dereham's aunt, and a very old friend of Lady Sophia's. So there you see! And now I think you will allow that Mrs. Bolton was slightly in error about Mr. Lennox's being such a Nobody? He is the grandson of an Earl at any rate."

"Yes, and the nephew of the present Earl," said Edith Bolton, who had opened the 'Peerage,' and was studying it attentively. "Here it is. *Lady Frances Catherine, married to the Rev. Reginald Lennox, Rector of Wentmore, Co. South-shire, and Rural Dean.*'—And oh!—I declare!"

"What?" cried her sister and Miss Richardson, as she paused, evidently in amazement.

"Why, he is actually related, or at least connected, with the Duke of Horningtoft, in whose honour the grand ball at the Embassy is to be given to-morrow night! The present Earl of Norwood married a daughter of Richard, second Duke of Horningtoft. She is dead, I see, but that makes him uncle to this young Duke, and he is Mr. Lennox's uncle as well! So they are very nearly connected!"

The Duke of Horningtoft's recent arrival in Brussels, charged, as it was understood, with some mission of special importance to the Belgian Court, had created no small stir amongst the British residents in that capital. The young ladies were all anxious to see him, as the Duke was reported to be very good looking, besides being young and unmarried. But as it was only such as were on the visiting list at the Embassy, who were likely to be brought into personal contact with his Grace, those who had not that honour, did not take so keen an interest in the matter. The Boltons had seen the Duke's arrival announced in the papers, and they talked as glibly on the subject as anyone else, but they were not going to the Embassy ball, and were not likely to meet him, excepting by accident, anywhere else.

"Well! that is too disgusting," exclaimed Harriet. "Of course Mr. Lennox will be at the

Embassy, and if mamma had only not been such a goose, he might have got us invited. Who knows ?"

"The ball is to be on a scale of unprecedented magnificence, I believe," said Miss Richardson, quietly. "Madame Bertrand has promised to send us our dresses home to-night. They will be lovely."

"Are *you* going?" cried Edith Bolton, almost starting from her seat. "How on earth is that? You never told us a word about it, and you have never been to the Embassy before !"

"No, but Lady Sophia has asked leave to bring us," answered Miss Richardson. "It was very kind of her, wasn't it? We did not say anything about it, because it was not worth while. Of course we should have gone there often before, if mamma's health had been stronger, and she had been able to take us. But you know how seldom she goes anywhere."

"I think it is rather a distinction *not* to be asked to the Embassy parties," said Harriet with a toss of the head. "Anyone can go who likes to fish for an invitation. If they were to draw a line somewhere, and make it a rule, for instance, to invite none but those who had been presented at Court in England, *that* would make a difference, and then one would be sure of meeting only ladies and gentlemen."

"Well, yes, it would be a good plan perhaps,"

returned Miss Richardson, laughing. "But I suspect the Drawing Rooms in London are easier to go to than Ambassadors' houses abroad, as a rule; and in these days everybody is presented, so it is really no longer any distinction. But now, my dears, I must be going," she added, rising from her seat, "I shall see you again bye and bye, I daresay, and I will come on Thursday and tell you all about the ball, I promise you. Give my love to your mamma."

With a hurried embrace to each of the sisters, which was not returned with much warmth in either case, the young lady then took her departure. Scarcely had she closed the door when Harriet exclaimed,

"Nasty spiteful thing! She came over on purpose to tell us about Mr. Lennox's grand connections, and that they were going to the ball. I don't believe they had an idea of going till yesterday at the furthest. And it is only by tacking themselves on to the Robertses that they can manage it after all. As to Mr. Lennox they don't know him any more than we do, and the Miss Robertses will take care not to introduce him, I daresay."

"I should like to have boxed her ears," said Miss Edith. "And oh, Harriet! To think of our having given them the crow over us, all through that stupid mistake about Mr. Lennox! If we had known the Robertses even! But Mrs. Richardson always took care to keep them out of our way. They were in the room once, if you remember, when we called, but we were not introduced. As to mamma's not liking to know them because they are Roman Catholics, that is all nonsense. The great thing when you come abroad, I think, is to know as many Catholics as possible, for, of course, the best society is always made up of them. But do come and tell mamma about the Richardsons going to the Embassy. *That* is the most enraging part of it all!"

And thereupon the Miss Boltons repaired to their mother's room, and spent the next hour in abusing their friends and acquaintances in general. Mrs. Bolton who was suffering from headache, begged them not to make such a noise or get out of temper, as doing so did not improve their beauty. But they only talked the louder, and got more angry with her and everybody else, in which amiable state of mind we must take leave of them for the present.

The winter season had again set in in Brussels, but long before the fashionable arrivals began, Gerald Lennox had returned from Spa. Mr. Fitzroy had gone back there as soon as his business affairs would allow him to do so, and had remained a short time with Gerald to enjoy the last of the fine weather.

His unremitting attentions to Arthur Woods during his illness, and the shock he experienced at his death, had somewhat affected Gerald's health, and for a short time he was on the sick list himself. Barbara Graham, who, from her former acquaintance with Arthur Woods, naturally felt interested in him, had done all she could to alleviate his sufferings, and had frequently visited him at his own request. Before the arrival of Mabel Woods at Spa, she had secured rooms for her and her companion, close to Gerald's hotel, and when the poor girl came, she met her at the station, and broke the sad intelligence of her brother's death to her as gently as she could.

Gerald had been much struck by the quiet, thoughtful way in which his cousin had come forward to help in nursing Arthur Woods. When all was over, and the sorrowing sister, who together with Gerald, had followed the remains to the quiet resting-place in the cemetery on the hill, had taken leave of him and Mrs. Graham, and again set out with her friend, Mrs. Wilson, for England, he told Barbara how much he appreciated the kind way in which she had acted, and thanked her warmly for all she had done.

Barbara's eyes filled with tears, and she pressed both Gerald's hands in hers, but she turned away without speaking, and never again referred to the subject save one day when Gerald took her to the cemetery, and shewed her the simple cross which had been placed at the head of the grave. Then she said in a low tone,

"It was very singular our being here with him when he died, having both of us known him in the happy days gone by at Wentmore. It was a great pleasure to me to do what I could for him. He had been so fond of Blanche, and I often thought when I was with him, of the sick beds I had stood by with them both, in old times."

There was something in the way in which she said this, and in the sigh which followed, that went to Gerald's heart. So much of regretful sorrow, of present weariness and unavailing regret seemed compressed into those few words.

The Grahams remained at Spa, when Gerald took his departure with Mr. Fitzroy and returned to Brussels. Sidney had been winning lately, and appeared unable to tear himself from the tables. "But we shall follow you soon, I hope," wrote Barbara to her cousin, a day or two after he had left. "And very glad I shall be to do so, as I am heartily tired of this place now."

Gerald's holiday, notwithstanding the melancholy episode which had attended his visit to Spa, had recruited both his health and spirits, and it was with renewed zest that he returned to his literary labours in Brussels. He was no longer in pecuniary difficulties, owing to the satisfactory nature of his relations with the firm in London to whom he sent his contributions, although at the same time he was far from rich. Mr. Fitzroy prevailed upon him to go out a little more into society, and Gerald, whose taste for pleasant and congenial companionship, had always made it a hard struggle for him to give up the chance of forming agreeable acquaintances, was nothing loth to do so. At Lady Sophia Roberts's he had first met the young Prince de L——, whose father was one of the leading members of the Belgian Cabinet, and this winter he saw a good deal of him both at her's and other friends' houses, and having many tastes and pursuits in common, the two young men soon became fast friends.

An unexpected pleasure also awaited Gerald, in the arrival of his cousins Lord and Lady Dereham at Brussels for the winter; or at least, as they said, for the greater part of it. They had always been great allies of his, and after they had taken up their abode in the Rue Belliard, he was with them as often as his occupations would permit. Lady Dereham was delighted to have him for an escort to the various picture galleries and places of interest, which she could not get her lord to take her to. "He gets so dreadfully bored by all that sort of thing," she said to Gerald one day, when they were about to start on a starring expedition through the town, "and it is such a comfort to have someone with one, who knows what is worth seeing, and enjoys it all as much as one does oneself." Her husband fully coincided in her remark, and expressed himself deeply grateful to Gerald for taking her off his hands on these occasions, but he bargained at the same time for his share of his cousin's society, and when Gerald was not driving or lionizing with the Viscountess, he was generally to be seen walking or riding with the Viscount.

One morning, when Gerald rang the bell of the house in the Rue Belliard, having promised to be there soon after breakfast, in order to accompany Lady Dereham to Malines, where they were to spend a long day, and return in the evening, he was informed that "Milor and Miladi" were in the breakfast-room still, and accordingly he was. shewn in there.

They were not alone. A young man, whom Gerald did not recognise, was sitting with them. He laughingly reproved them for being so late, and Lord Dereham exclaimed,

"It is not our fault. Horningtoft (whom you remember, Gerald, don't you?) arrived last night after you were gone, and kept us up till goodness knows what time, talking about everything under the sun, and consequently we were none of us able to get up this morning. So you must blame him, not us."

Gerald had met the young Duke at the house of their mutual relative, Lord Norwood, on one or two occasions, but it was some time now since he had seen him, and for the moment he did not remember him. He had heard, however, like everyone else, of the Duke's expected arrival, and so he was not surprised at seeing him.

"How do you do, Mr. Lennox?" said the Duke, rising, and holding out his hand to Gerald. "As we are both nephews of the same uncle, I can't understand how it is we are not first cousins, but if we are not related, at any rate we should be very good friends."

"Your Grace is very good," returned Gerald, smiling. "Before Dereham mentioned your name I thought I knew your face, but could not feel quite certain. It is some time since I last saw you in Grosvenor Square."

"It is indeed," replied the Duke. "I take it we are both altered since then, and I doubt if I should have remembered you again had not Dereham told me you were expected."

"But now, Selina," said Lord Dereham, turning to his wife, "if you intend to go to Malines to-day, you had better be putting your bonnet on. We have been an unconscionable time over breakfast, and it is getting late."

Lady Dereham rose immediately and left the room, saying she should not be a minute getting ready, and her husband who had some letters to read, retired to one of the windows, leaving his two cousins to entertain each other and become better acquainted.

The Duke of Horningtoft had heard all about Gerald's conversion to the Roman Catholic Faith,

and of his having had to give up his property and
independence in consequence. The story had interested him greatly, and he was glad to have this
opportunity of discussing various subjects with
which he knew Gerald was conversant, and of
hearing his opinion upon points which were just
then of special interest to him and the party in
the State to which he belonged. The tone of
foreign literature, the influence of the Church and
her hold upon the masses in that part of the world,
the spread of Rationalism and other like topics
the Duke enlarged upon in turn, and Gerald delighted him with the frankness and originality of
his remarks, as well as by the intelligence which
he evinced upon each subject.

"We were having a most interesting talk,"
said the Duke to Lady Dereham, when she reappeared, ready to start with Gerald. "And I
am only sorry that you are going to carry Mr.
Lennox off with you."

"Oh, this has been a long talked of expedition,"
answered Lady Dereham, "and I cannot let you
monopolize Gerald any longer, Duke. I daresay
you will have plenty of opportunities for discussing
politics and religion, which I know you are both so
fond of doing, before you go, and we really must
be off now."

"I hope we shall meet again before long," said
the Duke, turning to Gerald, "but my time I am
afraid will be much taken up during my stay. I

suppose you will be at the ball the Embassy people are going to give me on Wednesday ?"

Gerald had only time to answer hurriedly that as the Ambassadress had been good enough to send him a card for the occasion, he hoped to be there, although he seldom went to balls, when Lady Dereham called to him from the door to say she was waiting, and he hastened out to hand her into the carriage which was in readiness.to take them to the station.

It was the night of the ball, and Gerald who had arranged to accompany his cousins, was to go first to their house, and then proceed with them to the Embassy. He had dressed early, and was waiting in the sitting-room of his bachelor lodgings in the Boulevard, for the *vigilante* which was to convey him to the Rue Belliard. He was lost in deep thought, and once or twice as he stood leaning against the chimney-piece and gazing into the fire, he exclaimed, "How wonderful ! How extraordinary that it should have been so !" whilst a look of grateful happiness pervaded his countenance.

Of what was he thinking ? In the letter which Ferdinand had received from his brother, containing the account of Arthur Woods's death, it will be remembered that Gerald referred to some things which that poor fellow had told him before he died, which had surprised and moved him greatly, but of which he did not say further at the time. It was one of these communications on the part of the dying youth, over which he now pondered, and as he did so he wondered more and more at the mysterious and marvellous way in which an apparently insignificant act, it might be, almost an accident at the time, would in the end sometimes entail the most momentous consequences.

"And to think," he went on, in a kind of reverie to himself, " that that journey of mine from Calais to England, should have led to such blessed, and, at the time, such utterly unforeseen results !"   .

His sister Blanche's conversion, and that of poor Arthur Woods himself! Both, as he thought it over, seemed plainly owing to the determination he had formed that morning at Calais, to return to London, and look for that pocket-book, which after all he had with him, as it afterwards turned out,—and when he had arrived that night in London, his having given another name at the hotel instead of that of Lennox. Upon these two things, as it were, all that followed seemed to turn. If Arthur Woods had caught him up that night and given him the parcel of books with which he had been entrusted, he would have carried them abroad with him, and neither Blanche nor Woods himself would have benefited by their perusal. If he had not come over to England at all, the parcel would never have been given even to Arthur's friend Mr. Storey, because, as he,

Gerald, had subsequently ascertained from Father Clifford himself, it was only in consequence of Mr. Hayward's having met Storey, a few hours after his encounter with him in the train, and having spoken of it to him, that the fact of his return to England had transpired. "Do you think, then, that Mr. Gerald Lennox is in London?" Father Clifford had asked, and Storey had replied, that he was not sure of that, but that if not in London he was doubtless at Wentmore, where a friend of his, Arthur Woods, was going early the next morning, and would convey any message to Gerald, Father Clifford might wish to send. "I want to send him these books," said Father Clifford, handing him the parcel. "If your friend will take charge of them and deliver them himself to Mr. Lennox, I shall be much obliged." Storey had accordingly taken the books with him to the London Bridge Station where he knew he should meet Woods that night, but, as our readers already know, although Gerald was in England, he did not receive the parcel: Woods took it down to Wentmore, thinking he should find him there; but before it came into his hands, which it did not do until after some time had elapsed, both Woods himself and Blanche had studied the books, and by 'God's Infinite Mercy, they had been the means of opening their eyes to the Truth!

And as Gerald thought on these things, his eyes filled with tears, and his breast heaved with emotion, but the tears were those of joy and thank-fulness, and the feelings which filled his heart were those of devout and adoring wonder.

He was roused from his reverie by the announce-ment that his *vigilante* was at the door, and in a few minutes more he found himself in his cousin's drawing-room in the Rue Belliard, where Lady Dereham was awaiting him in a most becoming and elegant *costume de bal*, and as he declined the offer of tea which she pressed upon him, they were soon on their way to the scene of festivity.

"Dereham has been dining there, you know," said Lady Dereham, as the carriage drove through the streets. "I was invited to the dinner, where all the 'big wigs' were to meet the Duke, but sent an excuse as I wished to be at the ball, and should certainly have been knocked up, and unable to enjoy myself in the least, if I had gone through a long heavy dinner first of all."

The extensive suite of reception rooms at the English Embassy had been thrown open on this occasion, and when Lady Dereham and Gerald entered, the brilliant arrangement of the lights and flowers, the beautiful dresses of the ladies, many of which glittered with diamonds, the gentlemen with their decorations and not a few in uniform, produced a most dazzling effect. Gerald had been introduced to his noble hostess on a former occa-sion. She knew all about him, and albeit a stern Protestant herself, in virtue of his position, and his near connection with the principal guest of the evening, she accorded him a very gracious recep-tion. He soon espied the Robertses and other friends of his in the room, both English and Belgian, and being asked by Algernon Roberts to be his *vis-à-vis* in a quadrille which was just coming off, he secured a partner and followed him into the ball room.

The dance was half over, and Gerald was standing by himself for a moment, in one of the figures, his eye wandering round the room, when suddenly it fell upon a face which he had seen once before, and only once, but the recollection of which had dwelt with him ever since, and he uttered an involuntary exclamation of delighted surprise as he recognized it. There was the same elegant form, the finely shaped head, the soft blue eyes, the exquisitely chiselled features, and he was just near enough to hear the sweet accents of the voice which he remembered so well, as she made some remark to her partner at a moment when the movements of the dance brought her within hearing. As Gerald fixed his gaze earnestly upon her, she looked up. Their eyes met, and she gave a little start, colouring deeply as she did so. She turned away immediately, and Gerald lost sight of her for a minute or more, but it was quite enough. She had seen him and remembered him too! What ecstasy was there in that thought! And yet from that night in the Church of St. Gudule, now nearly a year ago, to this, he was sure they had never met. That he should have forgotten her would have been simply impossible. Once seen, that face was not one to forget easily, but that she should have known *him* again—there was something in that reflection which made his heart beat, and every nerve in his body thrill with delighted excitement. As soon as the young lady he was dancing with was again by his side, he turned to her, exclaiming,

"Do you know who that is, Miss Somerville? That young lady in white, with rosebuds all over her dress, and rosebuds in her hair. Don't you see which I mean? There she is dancing in that set next to ours."

His manner was so excited and his tone so eager, that Miss Somerville looked at him in some amazement. She put up her glass to her eye, and turned her head slowly in the direction indicated.

"Which do you mean?" she said. "Oh,—that one. No, I do not know who she is, but I can easily find out as she is dancing with my brother. I will ask him presently and tell you, if you are so anxious to know. Do you think she is nice looking?"

"Nice looking! I think she is lovely," returned Gerald. Then with an assumption of indifference, for he saw that Miss Somerville was rather astonished at his enthusiasm, he made some remark about the excellency of the music, and asked her if she had been to the Opera yet, the season having just commenced at the Monnaie.

As soon as the dance was over, however, he took care to lead Miss Somerville in the direction her brother was taking, intending when they were near enough to remind her in an off-hand way of her promise to ascertain the name of the fair unknown. Miss Somerville was the daughter of a General Officer of high standing, who rejoiced in the prefix of "Honourable" to his name, and amongst the English young ladies at Brussels she took rather a high stand. Every moment as they passed slowly through the crowd, she was stopped by some white-gloved hand and forced to exchange "How d'ye do's" with a dozen dear and intimate friends at once. Her impatient companion chafed considerably at these continual interruptions to their progress, but he could not hurry her along, nor could he desert her until he had restored her to the side of her *chaperone*, who, of course, as he looked round in search of her, was nowhere to be seen. In the meantime the brother and his partner had vanished out of sight, and Gerald gave up the pursuit in despair.

"If you will leave me here, Mr. Lennox, that will do," at length said Miss Somerville, as she passed a lady friend who was sitting on a couch at one end of the room. "I haven't seen Mrs.

Prideaux for a long time, and want to speak to her. Thank you."

With a bow, and inward sigh of relief, Gerald consigned her to the care of Mrs. Prideaux, and departed at once in search of the couple he had lost sight of, and was so anxious to meet again. By dint of perseverance and a little of the *savoir faire* in a crowded ball room, which his old London season days had taught him, he passed through the brilliant, high-bred throng, and gained the next room into which many of the dancers had found their way. It was quite full, and at the further end of it, the Ambassadress was still receiving her guests as they continued to arrive.

Gerald looked round, and almost immediately perceived young Mr. Somerville standing at a little distance, but he was no longer accompanied by the real object of his search. He was talking to some other men, and had no young lady with him. Nor was she to be seen anywhere near.

"Are you going to dance this waltz?" asked Lord Dereham, passing him in the direction of the ball room, with a partner on his arm.

"I don't know;" answered Gerald, and he proceeded to walk slowly round the rooms, his gaze penetrating into every corner in search of the graceful form and sweet face of her he longed to behold again.

Suddenly, he saw her. She was sitting in the recess of a window, talking to an old lady, a Belgian Countess, who was a friend of Gerald's, and he resolved at once what to do. Slowly approaching the spot, he pretended to be very much struck by a small painting of great beauty which hung upon the wall close by the recess in which Madame de St. Lys and her fair companion sat. He then looked up, as if quite by accident in their direction, and catching the old lady's eye, bowed low with a smile of recognition. As he hoped and expected would be the case, she immediately beckoned him to approach.

"How arre you?" she said in her broken English. "Ees thees not a charming ball? Arre you dancing much?"

Gerald, who felt as if he could have embraced her for speaking to him, made some incoherent reply, and then bending down his head, he begged her in a whisper to introduce him to her companion.

"*Ah, oui certainement,*" exclaimed the Countess, smiling. "You arre boath Engleesh,—Let me introduce you."

And then she pronounced their names, but so curiously, that Gerald who heard himself called Monsieur Leen' something, gave up the attempt to make out the other, and not caring so much about the name, now that he was introduced to her in person, begged to know if she was engaged for this dance, and being answered with a smile and a blush in the negative, he held out his arm, and they moved towards the ball room together.

What a waltz that was! Surely never before was music so inspiriting, or a floor so exactly the right thing. Gerald had always been fond of dancing, and he had met with many good partners in his day, but never did he remember one like this. He scarcely felt her. She seemed to float on the air, so lightly and gracefully did she lean upon his arm. And when they paused at length, she looked up in his face with such an enchanting smile, and said,

" What a delicious waltz this is. Do you know the name of it ?"

Gerald did not know what it was called, but he agreed with her it was a most delightful waltz. He felt in the seventh heaven of delight. How often had he thought of her since that winter night, so many months ago; how often had her form appeared to him in his dreams; how often had he hoped and longed to behold her again. How little had he thought he should do so that very night. And now he was actually standing by her side, dancing with her, talking to her. He did not know who she was, he had not caught her name, but in that brilliant gathering there was no one else in his estimation worth looking at. The beauty and attraction of the scene was concentrated in her person. He had eyes and ears for no other.

Fixing her gaze upon him, she suddenly said, with a charming *naïveté*,

"I have seen you before. Not lately, and I am not sure where, but I remember your face distinctly. I did not catch your name when Madame de St. Lys introduced us."

Gerald remembered well enough the time and place of their first meeting. It was not likely he would ever forget it. He did not tell her this, however, but said,

"Nor did I yours. Madame de St. Lys is an old friend of mine, and seeing a young lady who ought to have been dancing and was not, sitting by her side, I did not scruple to beg for an introduction. Otherwise I should scarcely have ventured."

"Oh, my name is Alice Fitzstephen," rejoined his partner. "And what is yours?"

Gerald did not immediately reply, and at that moment a couple of passers-by stopped and spoke to his fair companion, so that she did not observe his silence. He was thinking where he had heard the name of Fitzstephen before. It was familiar to him, and yet he could not remember how. There was a Mrs. Fitz-something who had been at Lethbridge on a visit ages ago, and he had met her there. She had two daughters he remembered, but he was sure "Stephen" was not the end of their name.

Her friends had passed on, and Alice Fitzstephen turned to him again.

"Now I remember where it was I saw you,"
she said, looking up archly into his face. "It
was in London; at a ball in Grosvenor Square.
That was the first time, but I have seen you since
that. I remember asking my cousin, Margaret
Stewart—"

"Your cousin Margaret Stewart?" exclaimed
Gerald in surprise. "Grosvenor Square—I have
a cousin of that name who lives in Grosvenor
Square. At what house was it you saw me?"

"At my uncle Lord Norwood's;" was the
answer.

"Why—then who can you be?" cried Gerald,
laughing, "for Lord Norwood is *my* uncle, and it
is his daughter Lady Margaret Stewart who is my
cousin! This is very funny, certainly," he added,
as she looked at him in astonishment in her turn.

"I think it is for you to tell me who *you* are,"
she answered. "If Lord Norwood is your uncle
as well as mine, I suppose we are cousins—but I
can't make it out."

"My name is Gerald Lennox," said Gerald.
"And my mother is Lord Norwood's only sur-
viving sister. That is how I am his nephew."

"Lennox!" returned his companion. "Of
course, I know who you are now. My father
was Lady Norwood's brother. That is how he is
my uncle!"

"Then you are the Duke of Horningtoft's sister," said Gerald. "I beg your pardon, Lady Alice. How stupid of me not to remember that Fitzstephen was the family name. I met your brother at Dereham's house the other day, and had the pleasure of renewing my acquaintance with him. You came over with him, I suppose? How long do you remain in Brussels?"

"No, I did not come over with my brother," answered Lady Alice. "My cousin Mrs. Temple, who was in London with us in the summer, and always has a house here in the winter, proposed that I should pay her a visit whilst he was here, as it was understood that he was to be fêted and entertained and made a great fuss about. And as I had been to Brussels once before and enjoyed my stay here very much, I was only too glad to come, and some friends brought me over with them the other day."

They had been talking so long that the waltz was now over, and Gerald was obliged to take Lady Alice back to her *chaperone*. As they mixed with the crowd and were making their way slowly towards the window where Madame de St. Lys still sat, they encountered Lady Dereham who was looking for her husband.

"Do give me your other arm, Gerald," she cried, "I cannot make my way at all through all these people, and I want to tell Dereham that I shall not stay much longer, as my head is very bad, and if he likes to remain I shall take the carriage and send it back for him."

"I will just take Lady Alice to her seat," answered Gerald, "and then am at your service."

"Oh, I can get to Madame de St. Lys quite well now," said Lady Alice, slipping her hand out of his arm. "Don't let me keep you any longer."

Gerald wished Lady Dereham somewhere else, but he only bowed and smiled, and departed with her in quest of her lord, with as good a grace as he could muster, resolving inwardly to return to the window where Madame de St. Lys and Lady Alice sat as soon as possible.

"How well Alice is looking to-night," remarked Lady Dereham, as they moved through the rooms. "I suppose you and she are very old friends?"

"Not at all;" answered Gerald, who could not forgive the speaker for carrying him off in the way she had done. "I did not even know who she was till she told me herself. Madame de St. Lys introduced me, and I did not catch the name."

"I do not wonder, if she pronounced it," said Lady Dereham, laughing. "But how very funny that you should not have known each other. Why you must often have met in London, surely?"

"You forget," replied Gerald, "that I have been very little into London society of late years, and not at all since Lady Alice came out. I suppose I should not know one of the young ladies who go to parties now, if I were to go back and begin going to London balls over again."

"Oh! there is Dereham;" cried his cousin. "Thanks. I won't take you any further. You have piloted me beautifully. I suppose you will stay for hours. Good night."

Gerald said good night and hurried off. He pushed through the crowd alone very quickly, and soon gained the spot where Lady Alice and her *chaperone* had been sitting. But much to his disgust, when he reached it they were gone, and although he looked anxiously round—were nowhere to be seen.

He went back to the ball room, passed through all the other rooms again, looked everywhere, but in vain. At last, as he was standing at the head of the staircase, uncertain which way to go next, he heard the announcement below,

"Madame de St. Lys' carriage stops the way."

"*La voiture de Madame la Comtesse de St. Lys.*"

Succeeded immediately by the words,

"Coming out!"

"*Madame la Comtesse descend.*"

He looked over the bannister. Two figures were vanishing through the door-way, hooded and cloaked. He recognized them as those of Lady Alice and her *chaperone*. She was evidently tired of the ball, although it was yet so early, and was going home.   Just before she passed out of sight, Lady Alice looked back for a moment and caught his eye as he leaned over the balustrade watching her. She smiled and gave a little bow.   He had barely time to return it when she was gone.

The ball was over for Gerald too.   He had only danced twice, but that was quite enough.   What was the use of staying now?   Hurrying down stairs, he seized his hat and coat, and passed out through the crowd of servants and others collected round the gateway, into the open street.

He was not tired, or sleepy, and did not think of going home, but lighting a cigar, he walked up and down the Boulevard as leisurely as if it had been a fine night in summer, thinking of the happiness of the past hour.   He did not feel the cold, although instinctively he buttoned up his coat, he was oblivious to all outward things.   At length, when fairly tired out, he sought his lodgings and his bed; his dreams brought back the fair vision of the evening's entertainment, and again he saw that sweet smile, and heard the silvery tones of that gentle voice.

CHAPTER XII.

"Well? How do you feel after your ball?"
asked Mr. Fitzroy, as he entered Gerald's room
the following morning, and found him seated at a
late breakfast, in his dressing gown and slippers.

"Oh, it was delightful; I enjoyed myself
immensely. Will you have some breakfast?" was
Gerald's reply.

"My dear fellow, I breakfasted ages ago.
Thanks all the same. And so it was a good ball
was it? I suppose you stayed very late?"

"No, I did not," answered Gerald, "I never
do stay late at balls, and— But I have not told
you," he added, breaking off the subject, and taking up a letter which lay on the table, "I am
expecting my brother. He writes me word that
he shall probably arrive this afternoon, and stay a
fortnight or three weeks, which is awfully jolly of
him, isn't it?"

"I thought you were looking in high spirits
about something," said Mr. Fitzroy. "Your

brother's visits are generally so short, that I am glad to hear he intends to make a little stay this time."

Gerald coloured up slightly. It was true he felt in particularly good spirits this morning, but the thought of seeing Lady Alice Fitzstephen during the course of the day, which he reckoned upon doing at the Derehams' house, was perhaps the reason, rather than the expectation of meeting his brother, pleased as he always was to see Ferdinand.

"I suppose he will want to be back for Christmas," he said in reply to Mr. Fitzroy's remark, "or else, I should much like him to see St. Gudule at the evening service on Christmas Day. It would do him good, I am sure. Everyone knows that with us there is no obligation upon the people to attend Vespers or Benediction or any service except Mass, unless they like, and when Protestants go into our churches and see them crammed as St. Gudule, large as it is, always is crammed in the evening of Christmas Day, it must strike them, and I know it does strike them very much. The silence, the devotion, the awe which pervades our immense congregations at the moment of Benediction is something they cannot understand, and it impresses them favourably in spite of themselves."

Gerald spoke with enthusiasm, as he always did upon the subject of the Catholic religion, or the services of his beloved Church, and then taking up his brother's letter he began looking through it again.

" But your brother does not consider himself a Protestant, does he?" said Mr. Fitzroy, smiling. "And as to devotion and solemnity, the High Church party are not far behind us in either respect, I fancy. Indeed, from all I have heard, I take it, some of our congregations, especially abroad, might take a lesson from them in such things."

"True, very true," said Gerald, looking up. "But then, you must remember that in England, devotion, nay even the very idea of worship in Church, is a thing which is only beginning to be understood. With Anglicans it is still, and I suspect always will be the exception, to see a church full of people, both men and women, of all ranks and classes, on their knees, really praying to and worshipping God, whereas with us, go where you will, in every country and with all people it is the same as it has always been. Catholics *do* behave in the House of God, as if they knew they were in His Presence, and had come there to worship Him, and it is the exception with us when they appear to forget this, not the rule."

"You converts are always such frightful bigots," said Mr. Fitzroy, patting him fondly on the shoulder as he spoke, "and never can see anything good out of your own communion. Now we—"

"Oh, yes. You old Papists are wonderfully liberal-minded," returned Gerald, laughing, and rising from his seat. "We know that, and you are such a delightful specimen of the popular Catholic, who thinks every other so-called Church is as good, or perhaps better than his own, aren't you? Now, I am not going to hear another word, but if you are going for a walk, as I have nothing particular to do this morning, I will put on my coat and go with you. Just wait one moment."

The Boulevard was full of walkers, as the weather was fine, and at almost every step, Mr. Fitzroy and Gerald met some one they knew personally or by sight. At the corner of the Rue de Trône the Comte de Flandre passed them accompanied by the Duke of Horningtoft and the Prince de L——, both of whom smiled and nodded familiarly to Gerald, as the Count took off his hat and returned his bow. What would the Miss Boltons have done if they had seen that!

After taking two or three turns, Mr. Fitzroy remembered an engagement he had at the other end of the town which he had barely time to keep, and hurried away, promising to look in at Gerald's lodgings the following morning, when he hoped to see Ferdinand as well. As soon as he was alone, Gerald bent his steps towards his cousin's house in the Rue Belliard.

Her ladyship was "at home," the servant said. He knew that to Gerald, if really in the house, she was at home at all hours, and therefore he was at once ushered into the drawing-room where he found her and not alone. A young girl was sitting beside her, playing with the strings of her bonnet, which she had taken off and was holding in her hand. It was Lady Alice Fitzstephen, and she looked up with a pleasant smile of recognition as Gerald approached and asked Lady Dereham how she felt after the fatigues of the night before.

"You are just the man we want," said Lady Dereham, after assuring him that she was none the worse for her dissipation. "Alice and I are going for a drive to the Bois after luncheon, and we are *minus* an escort, as Dereham has of course gone off somewhere, and it is impossible to say when we shall see him again. The Duke promised to come, but Alice says we must not depend on him in the least."

"I saw him a little while ago walking with the Comte de Flandre," said Gerald, "but I don't think they are on the Boulevard now."

"He is most likely at the Palace," said Lady Alice, "and in that case, there is no saying when he will be able to get away. Did you stay late at the ball last night, Mr. Lennox?"

"No," answered Gerald, "I did not. I hear it was kept up till very late, so Roberts told me just now when I met him."

"Madame de St. Lys was tired, and so we came away very early. We had dined there, you know, and she had had enough of it before the dancing began. I was sorry, as I should like to have stayed. If you had not gone away, Selina, I should have asked you to *chaperone* me," said, Lady Alice.

"But Dereham was there. He would have done just as well, and taken you home afterwards. What a pity you did not think of him," said Lady Dereham.

"I took it for granted he had left with you," rejoined Lady Alice. "And it was just as well as it happened, for Julia Temple dislikes the servants being kept up late at night, and she had gone to bed early, so they were waiting up on purpose for me."

Some morning visitors were announced, and Gerald had to speak French for the next half hour to an old lady who did not understand a word of English. Her daughter was talking to Lady Alice a little way off, and he could not help listening to what they said, and thinking how beautifully she spoke French, and with what a perfect accent, indeed, so wandering was his attention that his replies to Madame de ——'s observations were at times decidedly incoherent, and must have caused that good lady to wonder whether he understood what she was talking about.

Lady Dereham had her own carriage and horses

with her, and the elegant equipage with its occupants made no slight sensation as it drove down
the Boulevard, which in the afternoon was again
crowded with people driving and on foot. They
were turning out of the Boulevard de Waterloo
into the road leading to the Cambre, when Lady
Alice exclaimed,

"Who are those girls, I wonder? They are
looking as if they knew us, Selina."

Lady Dereham turned her head in the direction
indicated. Some young ladies, accompanied by
an elderly personage, probably their mamma, were
walking on the *pavé*, and regarding the carriage
as it drove by, with evident interest.

"I don't know them. They must be some
friends of Gerald's, I should think," said Lady
Dereham.

Gerald, who had observed the group, and noticed
the manner in which they stared at the carriage,
shook his head. He did not know who they were,
he said.

Luckily for them they did not hear him say so ;
or how disgusted they would have been! The
party on foot, whom we will now proceed to join,
consisted of the Miss Boltons, who with Mrs.
Richardson and her daughters, were taking a walk
in the direction of the Cambre, and discussing the
various carriages and their occupants as they drove
by.

"That is an English carriage," cried Miss

Edith, as the Dereham equipage appeared in sight. "Those servants and liveries are unmistakable."

"And a Viscount's coronet over the coat of arms. Oh, I see, it is Lady Dereham," observed Miss Kate Richardson.

"Yes, and that is Lady Alice Fitzstephen with her," exclaimed her sister. "I saw her at the ball last night. And Harriet, my dear, I do declare, your friend Mr. Lennox with them !"

"So it is," said Edith Bolton. "And only think," she added in a low tone to her sister, "if we had only known him he must have bowed, and how nice that would have been !"

"They all turned round and looked at us," said Miss Richardson. "I daresay they remembered our faces again, Kate."

"Just as if that was likely, from meeting in a crowd like that," returned her sister, laughing. "They probably wondered who we were, staring at them so."

"I'm sure I saw nothing to stare at," said Harriet Bolton, sneeringly. "I don't admire those pale-faced beauties, and if that is Lady Dereham she must be a good deal older than her husband, that is all I can say !"

Miss Bolton was in a bad humour. Her friend Kate Richardson had come in that morning according to promise, with a full account of the ball of the night before.

" And who do you think Mr. Lennox was dancing with all the evening ?" she had asked, after
giving a list of all the great people who had been
present.

" How do I know ?" Harriet had answered, pet-
tishly.

" Why, with Lady Alice Fitzstephen,—the
Duke's sister," returned Miss Kate. " She was
the belle of the last season in London, and was
the young lady of highest rank in the room."

" Do you mean to say he danced with no one
else ?"

" Why, as to that, I saw him going through a
quadrille with the Honourable Miss Somerville.
You know she holds her head pretty high, but she
didn't seem to think he was beneath her notice."

" What nonsense you talk, Kate," said Edith
Bolton, who knew more about the distinctions of
rank than her friend did. " Miss Somerville is
not an ' Honourable' at all. Her father is, because he is the younger son of a Peer, but that
doesn't make her one. I have heard the Robertses
speak of them. They are dreadfully stuck up,
and she gives herself great airs, though I believe
the title is quite a modern one, and they are nobodies at all really."

" Like Mr. Gerald Lennox," suggested Kate.

Whereupon Miss Edith walked out of the room,
without vouchsafing a reply, and Kate, thinking
she had tormented her dear friends enough on

that point, proceeded to describe the different dresses which people had worn, to Harriet, and assured her that there was not one prettier or which produced more effect than her own.

"What an odd set of English you see in Brussels," remarked Lady Dereham, as they drove on to the Bois. "Such second and third rate people. I suppose it is because it is such a small place in comparison that one notices it, but you are not struck by the same sort of thing in Paris."

"Quite true;" said Lady Alice. "I remember. thinking so when I was here before. You know Brussels well, do you not, Mr. Lennox?" she added, "I think I saw you once last winter, or someone very like you, one evening at St. Gudule."

"I think you did, Lady Alice," answered Gerald, smiling. "I know I saw someone very like you there once."

"It was one evening when Julia Temple went with me to hear the music," said Lady Alice, turning to Lady Dereham. "I had never seen St. Gudule before, and I shall never forget the impression it made upon me. The grandeur and solemnity of the building seen in that dim light, and the silent kneeling figures, (we went round the church when the service was over,) struck me very much. I felt quite a wish to be a Roman Catholic whilst I looked at them, and envied them the right to feel at home in such a place."

"Take care, Alice, take care," said Lady Dereham, shaking her head. "That kind of feeling is a very dangerous one. I advise you not to go to St. Gudule too often. Were you there at the same time, Gerald ?"

"Yes," replied Gerald, "I was ; and I remember seeing Lady Alice and her companion quite well. I could not help noticing the contrast in their behaviour. One appeared to forget the sanctity of the place she was in, and the other," he turned his glance with a meaning smile on Lady Alice as he spoke, " reminded her of it very properly."

"It seems so odd to hear you two 'Lady Alice' ing and 'Mr. Lennox' ing each other," said Lady Dereham, laughing. "Both being my cousins by marriage, I can't help thinking you must be related yourselves."

" No, we are not relations, but we are very near connections," said Lady Alice, " and the best joke was that last night when we were dancing together, we neither of us knew who the other was, till we began speaking of Margaret and Uncle Norwood, and then, it seemed as if, standing exactly in the same relationship to them, as we did, that we must be brother and sister or something of the kind without knowing it !"

"So Gerald told me," said Lady Dereham, " and Dereham was immensely amused when he heard it. But talking of connections who are not relations," she added, turning to Gerald, " Did

I not hear you say that your cousins, the Grahams, were coming to Brussels soon? I remember seeing her the first year I was married, when Aunt Lennox brought her and your sister Blanche to luncheon one day in Grosvenor Square. They were both striking looking girls, but I remember wondering how the dark one, Barbara, would turn out when she grew up. Blanche, I hear, is quite lovely. But that was only to be expected."

"Oh, yes, she is indeed!" exclaimed Lady Alice. "Everyone was talking about her last year in London. She came up for a short time to stay at Uncle Norwood's, and caused quite a sensation. I never saw anyone like her."

Gerald's estimation of the speaker was a tolerably high one, as the reader is probably aware, whether upon sufficient grounds or not, but as she expressed her admiration for his darling sister in such glowing terms, he thought her perfect indeed, and only wondered which was the most beautiful, she or Blanche.

"Barbara is considered very handsome," he said. "But you will have an opportunity of judging for yourself, as I expect that she and Sidney Graham will be here in a few days. They intended to have come much sooner, but he was obliged to go to England on business, and she has been waiting at Spa for his return."

As the carriage drove down the Rue Belliard on its return home, Lady Dereham observed,

"There is Dereham crossing the street. He is walking with Mr. ——. No,—why, Gerald, it is Ferdinand, I declare."

Gerald looked round. He was sitting with his back to the horses, and could not see down the street as his cousin did.

"It is he!" he cried. "He must have arrived by the three o'clock train. Holloa, old fellow!"

The carriage stopped, and the two gentlemen who were waiting for it to draw up, came forward. Lord Dereham had been at the station when Ferdinand's train came in, and telling him that Gerald had gone off somewhere with his wife, he had brought him there to await their return.

"I left my luggage at the station," said Ferdinand, turning to his brother, after exchanging a warm greeting with all the party, for Lady Alice was an old friend of his, he having met her several times at Lord Norwood's house. "I did not know if you would be able to take me in, or whether I should have to take up my old quarters at the Flandre."

Gerald assured him that he could accommodate him easily in his present abode, and after promising to return and dine with the Derehams at seven o'clock, the two brothers set off together in the direction of Gerald's lodgings, a messenger being despatched to bring up Ferdinand's luggage at once.

It was impossible to be with Ferdinand long, without observing what high spirits he seemed to be in, and Gerald remarked upon it very soon. " You do not seem very tired with your journey, and I never saw you looking better in my life," he said, looking at his brother affectionately.

" Oh, we had a capital passage," answered Ferdinand, " and there were some pleasant fellows in the train with whom I struck up an acquaintance, and the time seemed to pass wonderfully quickly. As to looking well, there is not much wonder in that, for I always think happiness is the best possible prescription for health, and I am awfully happy just now !"

And then it all came out. The Colonel and Mr. Lennox had had a consultation on the subject, and it was agreed that as Ferdinand was now in receipt of the income derived from the Newcome property, and it was evident that he and Cissy were mutually and deeply attached to each other, the two " governors" would no longer throw any obstacle in the way of their union, and the wedding was to take place early in the following summer.

" I say it is a great shame to keep us waiting so long as that," said Ferdinand, after acquainting his brother with this arrangement, "but it is something to get them to fix a time at all, and I suppose we must be content with that."

" Well, you are a happy fellow," said Gerald,

giving him a squeeze of the arm as he spoke, "and I don't think she is very much to be pitied either!"

Ferdinand laughed, and said, he hoped not. And then they walked on for a little way in silence.

That night, as the two brothers sat over the fire in Gerald's room before going to bed, Ferdinand touched upon the subject of Gerald's finances, and looking round the apartment, he observed that he certainly had made himself comfortable enough now, and that he hoped he had thought better of his resolution, not to touch that money which had been lying for him in the bank for so long, and which he had told him all along it was a folly not to use.

"No," said Gerald, "I owe all my present 'well-to-doedness' to my success with the Magazine Uncle Norwood introduced me to. That, and the paper I correspond with, keeps me fully employed, and at the same time I am not overworked as I used to be."

"And you have never made use of that money?"

"No. And I never will, as long as I do not know from whom it comes."

Ferdinand looked up at his brother. A meaning smile played upon his lip.

"What if I could tell you who your unknown friend is?" he said.

"Do you know?" cried Gerald. "Do you really know?"

"I do;" answered Ferdinand. "But I am under a promise not to tell."

"Answer me one thing;" said Gerald. "Is it a lady?"

"It is;" replied his brother, looking at him fixedly. "That much I will admit, but I can say no more."

"You need not," said Gerald, throwing himself back in his chair, "for I guess who it is, and I am only more certain than ever that I am right."

"Who do you think it is then?" asked Ferdinand.

"Mrs. Fraser Smith," was the reply.

"Mrs. Fraser Smith!" echoed Ferdinand, in astonishment. "What could have put her into your head? Why, I should not think she had five thousand pounds to bless herself with, much less to give away to other people."

"I am wrong then?"

"Most decidedly. But what could have made you think of her?"

"Well, I cannot tell you exactly," said Gerald, somewhat confusedly. "You know she is a very old friend, and she knew all about my losing that property—and I took it into my head—but, as I was mistaken, it does not signify," he added, hastily, " and as you won't tell me, it is of no use hazarding any more guesses on the subject."

" No, I must not tell you," said Ferdinand, " I wish I might. Apropos to the Fraser Smiths, however, you will be surprised, I daresay, to hear that they talk of coming to Brussels this winter, and very soon too. The girls have never been abroad, and they have at last persuaded old Smith to let them have a taste of foreign life. I believe they had some trouble about it, but it was all settled before I came away, and they will be here next week, I expect."

" You don't say so !" said Gerald. " I shall be very glad to see them. Will they stay any time do you suppose ?"

" As long as they can get their papa to let them, I should say," laughed Ferdinand, rising from his chair. And soon after, as he confessed at last to feeling tired after his journey, the brothers separated for the night.

When Gerald said he should be glad to see the Fraser Smiths at Brussels, he meant what he said. It was clear from what Ferdinand had told him, that Mrs. Fraser Smith at any rate, had nothing to do with that mysterious gift about which he had had so many misgivings, and concerning the donor of which he had formed such a number of conjectures. He had never seen her since that evening in Grosvenor Square, when he had first taken it into his head that it might have come from her, and with that idea still in his mind, it certainly would have afforded him anything but pleasure, to meet either her or her daughters. But now, there was no longer any doubt that he was mistaken on that score, and he only wondered that he had ever thought it possible. It was from something she had said that night in London; but, as Ferdinand had said, it was not likely that she possessed such a sum at her own disposal, and still less so that she should have given it away to anyone else, and been at such pains to conceal from whom it came.

But whom then could it be from ? To him the matter remained as great a mystery as ever. He knew this much now,—that it was from a lady. The donor could not be his own mother or sister, and the very fact that the range of conjecture on his part was now confined to the fair sex, although it rendered it more interesting, at the same time made it impossible for him to guess who it was. Wearied out with his endeavours to think of any female friend or acquaintance who would take so lively an interest in him, he went to bed and dreamed of Lady Alice Fitzstephen, who assured him that she knew who had sent him the money, and would tell him if he promised not to betray her, and then in a fearfully solemn whisper said that it was old Madame de St. Lys, who was desperately in love with him, and had confessed the fact to her ! Lady Alice then changed into Mrs. Fraser Smith, who reproached him with not marrying one of her daughters, and told him she never would have given him all that money unless she had felt sure he was going to do so. Upon which he calmly told her that he knew upon good authority it was not from her it had come, and that it was of no use her trying to persuade him to the contrary. She insisted upon it, however, and in the midst of their argument he awoke. The moon was shining brightly into the room, and it was some time before he closed his eyes again, but when he did so, he fell into a deep, unbroken sleep, from which he did not awake until it was broad daylight.

Two days after Ferdinand's arrival the Grahams came from Spa, and took up their quarters at the Hotel de Belle Vue, intending to move into lodgings when they could find any to suit them. Barbara knew Gerald's address, and sent him a note as soon as they got to the Hotel to apprise him of their advent. He had gone into the country to spend the day with some friends at Tervueren, whom he wished to make known to Ferdinand, and found the note awaiting him on his return. It was then late, but the two brothers at once set off to the hotel, and on enquiring for " Monsieur Graham's" room, were shewn into a spacious apartment in which Sidney was sitting before the fire smoking a cigar, with a glass of hot brandy and water by his side. He sprang up as the door opened, and came forward to receive his cousins, expressing his surprise at seeing Ferdinand as he did so.

"When did you put in an appearance?" he asked, as they seated themselves round the fire. "I did not expect to find you here."

Ferdinand explained that he had come over within the last few days to pay Gerald a visit, and enquired after Barbara. It was so long since he had seen either her or Sidney, and at Wentmore they would expect to hear from him all about them both.

"Barbara is not very well," Sidney answered. She had gone to bed early, and he was sure would be much disappointed at not seeing them, but he hoped they would come round the next morning, and then she would no doubt be able to give an account of herself in person.

As the brothers walked home together, Ferdinand said,

"I can't make Sidney out. He is very much changed, surely. You have seen more of him lately than I have, but he seems to me scarcely like the same person. He is so silent and absent. So different from what he used to be."

"Yes," answered Gerald. "He is changed, I think, in many ways. We used to be great friends, as you know, and now I feel as if I scarcely knew him."

The next morning, as Gerald and Ferdinand

were entering the Belle Vue, they met Sidney
Graham coming out.

"Ah, you were coming to see Barbara?" he
said. "She told me to give you her love, and
say she was not up to seeing anyone to-day. To-
morrow she will be all right, I daresay. Just a
little tired, that's all. So as it's no use your going
in, I will go with you and see something of the
old town again."

They walked about for some time, and then
Gerald proposed that they should go to the Rue
Belliard and join the Derehams at luncheon.

"You remember our cousin Dereham, do you
not?" he asked Sidney.

"Oh, yes," returned he. "That is to say, I
met him once in London ages ago, and was introduced to him. He has a pretty wife, I hear.
I should like to see her, and renew my acquaintance with his lordship."

So they went to the Derehams' house, and
found them as they anticipated, just going to
luncheon. Graham was "more than half a Lennox," Lord Dereham declared, his mother and
wife both having been of that family, and his welcome was a hearty one in consequence.

Sidney had made an appointment which obliged
him to take leave as soon as luncheon was over.
Later in the day, as the brothers were walking on
the Boulevard, they saw him again at a little distance, talking to a man about his own age, who

nodded to Gerald as they passed.   Sidney had his back to them, and did not see them as they went by.

"Who is that with Sidney?" asked Ferdinand. "He looks like an Englishman."

"It is a Captain Lucas," answered Gerald. "He is a friend of Sidney's, and knows the Fraser Smiths, who introduced him to our people at Wentmore, I believe.   He was quartered at Hillsborough, and it seems my father and mother asked him over, as they used to do the other officers occasionally.   I don't know if he has perpetual leave, or whether he has left the army altogether, but he is one of those men who seem always able to go where they please and do as they like.   Sidney and Barbara like him, I imagine, and the feeling must be reciprocal, for he certainly seems to follow them wherever they go.   He was at Spa all the time I was there, and was with them at Aix before that, I heard, and now here he is in Brussels, so I should think they have enough of him.   The little I have seen of him I don't like much, but, of course, he may be a very nice person for all that."

CHAPTER XIII.

THE Curate of Frodsham, (we hope our readers have not forgotten the existence of such a person,) was a bit of an epicure. He was also a conscientious, hard-working man in his parish, and he was gifted with certain powers of discrimination. He therefore did not waste much time in visiting among his wealthier neighbours, or spend his summer afternoons in the cricket field and archery ground, or his winter ones in games of chess and bagatelle, but when he did go out, or call anywhere out of mere civility, he generally selected those houses where he felt pretty sure of being well entertained, and where the *cuisine* was known to be above the average.

Amongst the few places which were down on his visiting list, (although being a person of good family, and having "expectations" of his own, as we have before hinted, he might have extended it as much as he pleased,) was Lethbridge Park, and one morning, early in December, having to visit a poor person in the village, on behalf of one of his own people who was ill, and had expressed a wish to see her brother, a workman on the Colonel's estate, he determined to combine pleasure with duty, (which indeed to perform an act of kindness, always was to him,) and call on his friends at the great house before his return.

As usual, at that time of year, a large party of visitors was staying at Lethbridge, but when Mr. Hayward was shewn into the library, the only person he saw was the daughter of the house, who came forward to receive him, expressing her regret that her father was not at home. He had gone out shooting with the gentlemen guests, she said, and her mother had taken old Lady Oxwick to see her *protégés* in the alms houses. The other ladies were either in their own rooms or out walking, she herself had only just come back from the school, and she was glad he had not come ten minutes sooner, or he would not have found anyone at home. "And after your long walk," she added, "you must want a rest, so I hope you will stay to luncheon."

Mr. Hayward assured her he should be delighted to do so; and then seating himself on a low couch beside the fire, proceeded to make himself very much at home. Cissy begged him to excuse her for a minute, as she wanted to finish a note she was writing to Wentmore, and which a messenger was waiting to take.

As she was sealing her letter, Mr. Hayward looked up at her, and said in a sudden sort of way, peculiar to himself,

" I declare, Miss Lethbridge, everyone is turning Catholic now-a-days ! First, Mr. Gerald Lennox goes over,—then his sister—and now I am told that young Woods, who was curate at Wentmore, if you remember, a year or two ago, was received into the Church somewhere abroad before he died. I suppose we shall all end that way at last, but it is startling to hear of so many conversions in so short a time, isn't it ?"

Cissy rang the bell, gave her note to the servant who answered it, and then turning to Mr. Hayward, who was staring vacantly at the fire, she said,

" I cannot think how you, a Catholic Priest, can speak in that way about such things. You know what a grief dear Blanche Lennox's change of communion has been to us. *If*, as you put it, she has *become a Catholic*, instead of lamenting such a step on her part, we should do well to follow her example."

" Oh, of course, I beg your pardon. I know I ought to have said ' Roman' Catholic, and that I am myself a ' Catholic Priest' and all that. But —you see, Miss Lethbridge, they are so much more like the ' real thing' when they have gone over, that one cannot help envying them a little. Can one ?"

"Really, Mr. Hayward, I have no patience with you. Envy them! Why should we envy them? And as to calling them 'Roman' Catholics, I do not admit that they are Catholics at all in this country. It seems to me as clear as possible that if *we* are Catholics, and our Bishops are *the* Catholic Bishops, and our Church *the* Catholic Church, then those who do not acknowledge our Bishops and are not in communion with us, are not Catholics in any sense whatever. To talk of 'Roman' Catholic, and 'Anglo' Catholic, in the same breath, as people do, is the same thing as saying that there can be *two* Catholic Churches at the same time, and in the same place, differing from and anathematizing each other, which is absurd. Either we are Catholics, and the *only* Catholics in England, and the Romanists in positive error and schism, or they are the only Catholics, and we are—nothing at all!"

"I like to hear you talk, Miss Lethbridge, I do indeed," said Mr. Hayward, rubbing his hands. "I only wish some people could hear you. It would make their hair stand on end I verily believe. But it would scarcely do for all of us to be so bold and decided in our views. Or, at least, if we think as you do, we must keep our thoughts to ourselves!"

"Now, that is what I can't understand," returned Cissy. "If a thing is true, why should anyone, least of all the clergy, be afraid to say it?

Much as we have in common with Romanists, much as we may love and admire individuals amongst them, surely we ought not to forget, or slur over the fact, that schism is a deadly sin, and that to be out of communion with the True Church is a frightfully dangerous thing. If we are Catholics, and if our Church is, as we believe, the only True One, in this country, then why on earth don't we try and convert both Romanists and Protestants as we ought? What I admire and like in the Romanists above everything, is their eagerness to make converts. They get more blamed on all sides for that than anything else, and it is what I would praise them for most of all. If one believes one alone has the Truth, it is one's *duty* to try and make others see it. They say they have it, and they are consistent in doing all they can to win others over to their views. They are bound to do so by the position they take up. If we were true to ourselves, we should do the same. But we are not. You and I know that we are all right ourselves, and with that knowledge we are content. Our next door neighbours may become Romanists or Presbyterians, or anything they please. It is nothing to us. If they are born out of the Church of England, they may remain so. If they leave it, no effort is made to win them back again. Now, that is not the spirit of the Gospel, I am certain, and it is as wrong a state of things as can possibly be."

"You are right, quite right. I agree with every word you say!" exclaimed Mr. Hayward. "But do you not think that one reason why, as a rule, Anglicans take so little pains to make converts, is, that they don't feel that perfect assurance which Cath— which Romanists boast of, that they, and they only, possess the Truth? We feel quite certain that up to a certain point,— what shall we say—as far as contending for everything which is contained in the Three Creeds, for instance, goes? that we are right. But, there you see Rome and the East are one with us, and it is when we get beyond that, that we differ, and in differing, lose all certainty of our being *alone* in the right. That is our weak point, that is what makes us shy of making converts amongst Romanists, don't you think so?"

"If, where we differ, we are right, and they are wrong, why should we hesitate to say so?" answered Cissy. "If there is any doubt as to our position,—any question as to which is in error, on any single point of difference, the doubt should be removed—the question set at rest. I don't often speak to Blanche Lennox on the subject, but I remember her saying one day, that the only fault she found with me, was that I would not enquire sufficiently, and took things too much for granted. I said—what was the use? I believed that our Church was the right one, and that was enough. If I began to doubt about that, I should be miserable. What I insist upon is, that there should be no room for doubt. She says she *knows* she is right in all she believes, and I say the same, and there the matter is ended. Of course we can neither of us convince the other, and we never now touch upon the question."

Mr. Hayward was silent for a few moments. Then looking up at Cissy, who in her excitement was walking up and down the room, he said, thoughtfully,

" There is one thing which always strikes me as awkward for us, Miss Lethbridge. I do not know if you have ever thought about it, but I daresay you are familiar with the axiom that 'to be in communion with schismatics, is tantamount to being yourself in schism.' Now, when you come to think of it, these Romish Schismatics, (as we call them,) in England, and Scotland, and Ireland, everywhere in short, where the Anglican Reformed Church exists, are in full and undoubted communion with Bishops and Churches we recognize as Catholic. For instance, no one questions the fact of the Archbishop of Paris, or the Pope of Rome, being Catholic Bishops, and if they were asked whom they considered as their Brother Bishops and fellow Catholics in this country, the Archbishop of Canterbury, and the Anglican Hierarchy, or the Archbishop of Westminster, and his Romish brethren, I am afraid they would say the latter and not the former,—in other words, they, as

Catholic prelates, would offer the right hand of fellowship to those whom we consider schismatics, and ignore our Anglo-Catholic Bishops altogether."

"But if we *are* Anglo-Catholics, and our Bishops the right ones, all the foreign Bishops and Patriarchs in the world can't make us or them anything else. What I maintain is this. Either the Archbishop of Canterbury is as much a Catholic Bishop as the Pope of Rome, and Mr. Lawrence the vicar of this parish, (or yourself, if you like it better,) as true a Catholic Priest as any Italian, French, or foreign Priest you choose to name, and I myself, papa and mamma and all of us, as certainly members of the Catholic Church as M. de Montalembert, the Empress Eugénie, or any Spanish, German or other sort of Catholic in the world, or we have no standing ground whatever. If we are Catholics we ought never to give way to the Romanists in this country and their pretensions, in the least, and if we are not, why, then they are right and we are the veriest humbugs and impostors possible. Now, Mr. Hayward, do you allow that ?"

Cissy paused, and turned towards the curate, who was leaning his head on one hand, in an attitude of thought, and awaited his reply.

" Yes," he said, slowly, and more as if speaking to himself than to her, " if they are right, we who think ourselves and call ourselves 'Catholics' must be deceiving ourselves most awfully. But, God knows, I would not remain where I am one hour, if I felt convinced that the Church of England was not a true branch of the Catholic Church. Would you, Miss Lethbridge ?"

" How do you do, Mr. Hayward ?" said a voice, before Cissy could answer, and turning at the sound they perceived Mrs. Lethbridge standing in the doorway. "You are going to stay to luncheon, of course ?" she added, advancing towards him, "it will be ready directly. My husband and all the gentlemen are out, but we ladies shall be very glad to get you to carve for us."

"Yes, dear mamma, Mr. Hayward will stay to lunch," said Cissy, as the curate shook hands with Mrs. Lethbridge, and thanked her. " And there is the gong."

" Then I shall not go upstairs," said Mrs. Lethbridge, taking off her bonnet. "Lady Oxwick and I have been visiting the old people at the alms houses. She is quite in love with the porches I had put up to them last year, and declares she shall have some made like them in Norfolk as soon as she goes back."

Amongst the other lady visitors at Lethbridge at this time, was our friend Mrs. Vernon, and after luncheon Cissy proposed, as the day was bright, to drive her and Mr. Hayward to Frodsham in her pony carriage. Mrs. Vernon had not seen the church since its restoration, so it would be something for her to do, and Mr. Hayward would be saved the walk back. Lady Oxwick was going to remain at home, and Mrs. Lethbridge would take the other ladies with her in the *barouche*. Should it be considered as arranged?

Mr. Hayward protested that the walk was nothing to him, he was a great walker, and four miles out and back again was no consideration whatever; but if Mrs. Vernon wished to see the church, and Miss Lethbridge would take him, he should be delighted.

Mrs. Vernon declared that she should infinitely prefer a drive in the pony carriage, to going with the others to call on the swells of the neighbourhood, all of whom she knew, and none of whom she liked, and as to Frodsham Church, it would be as good an object for a drive as anything else. So it was settled, and in half an hour's time they set off. Cissy and Mrs. Vernon in the front seat, and Mr. Hayward compressing his long legs as well as he could, behind.

They had gone about a mile from the lodge gates at Lethbridge, and were just branching off to the left from the main road which led on towards Wentmore, when Mrs. Vernon exclaimed,—

"Are not those the Lennox ponies coming? I am sure that is Mr. Lennox driving Lady Frances, and a servant or someone behind."

"You are right," said Cissy. "But it is Blanche, not a servant, who is on the back seat.

She is bending down her head, don't you see?—she is knitting or something. She always takes her crochet or work whenever she goes in the carriage and does not drive. I never knew such a girl. She is never idle for one moment!"

"So she is! Crocheting, I declare," said Mrs. Vernon in astonishment. "She is industrious, certainly."

"She is a darling," said Cissy. And at that moment the two carriages drew up alongside of each other, Mr. Lennox having seen and recognized Cissy's pony in his turn.

"Were you going to Wentmore, young lady?" he asked. And it was easy to see from the affectionate smile with which he regarded her, that his daughter-in-law elect, was a favourite with the Rector.

"No, I am taking Mrs. Vernon to see Frodsham Church," answered Cissy, "and giving Mr. Hayward a lift home at the same time. May I ask if you were bound for Lethbridge?"

"Ah, Hayward, how are you?" cried Mr. Lennox, and the curate, getting down from his seat, came round and shook hands with the Rector and Lady Frances.

"We intended to take Lethbridge on our way home," said Blanche to Cissy. "Mamma wanted to do some shopping in Westling, and so we were going there first. Shall you be back, do you think, before we leave?"

"I daresay we shall," answered Cissy. "Polly goes along at a good pace, and especially when her head is turned homewards. Do stay as long as you can, if we are not at home when you get there, as I want very much to see you."

Blanche stretched out her arm, and put a letter into Cissy's hand.

"I was bringing you that," she said.

Cissy coloured and laughed as she recognized Ferdinand's writing. Then slipping the letter into her pocket, she kissed her hand, gave Polly a touch with her whip, and Mr. Hayward having jumped up again, they drove off.

"How well Blanche is looking," said Mrs. Vernon. "That hat is very becoming to her. I wonder where she got it from."

"Everything she wears is becoming to her," said Cissy. "She is looking very well. That visit to Kingstanton did her so much good in the summer. I was quite frightened about her before she went there, but she has not been like the same creature since."

"I suppose she is in greater hopes of your brother's conversion," laughed Mrs. Vernon. "By the way, when do you expect him down? He will get leave again before long, I suppose?"

"He had so much in the summer, I am afraid they will give him very little now," answered Cissy. Then in a thoughtful tone, she added, "I hope Blanche is not deceiving herself about him.

I am certain, from something he said in a letter to me the other day, that he is further from having any leaning towards the Roman Church than ever. She never says a word to me about it, but I have sometimes suspected of late, that her improved spirits were owing to her being more sanguine about him in that way, and if so, I know she will be disappointed. I am sure of it."

" I can't think why she should care about it in the way she does," said Mrs. Vernon, " Catholics marry Protestants every day, and it is thought nothing of."

" I wish, Madeline, I could teach you not to talk in that way," said Cissy, impatiently. "Protestantism in every shape and form is Heresy. We, as members of the Church of England, are Catholics, and have nothing in common with Protestants whatever. It always enrages me to hear people class us with non-Catholics, as if we were the same as Lutherans, and Presbyterians, and those sort of creatures. They are Protestants if you like. We are not, and I wonder you don't see that, when every Sunday of your life you get up in Church and profess your solemn belief in the ' Holy Catholic Church.' "

" Cissy is giving me a theological lecture," exclaimed Mrs. Vernon, looking back and addressing Mr. Hayward. " Pray come to the rescue, and tell me what to say. She is trying to convince me that I am a Roman Catholic ——"

"I am trying to do nothing of the kind," interrupted Cissy, giving Polly a gratuitous cut with her whip, which that spirited animal resented by whisking her tail and giving her head an indignant toss. "But I will not let her call herself a Protestant, and I am sure you will say I am quite right, Mr. Hayward?"

"Miss Lethbridge and I agree in everything," said the curate, smiling. "I advise you, Mrs. Vernon, not to attempt any argument with her. She would be a match for a real Catholic any day."

"I declare, Mr. Hayward, you are worse than she is," cried Cissy, looking as if she would like to give him a taste of the whip, as well as Polly. "I suppose you don't consider yourself a *real* Catholic then? If you are not one, what are you?"

"Oh, Miss Lethbridge, I meant a *Roman* Catholic, when I said a *real* one," said Mr. Hayward, confusedly, "but—"

"And you were quite right," interrupted Mrs. Vernon, who rather liked teazing Cissy on these points sometimes. "But, for goodness sake, don't you two begin disputing, Cissy, that pony is running away, I am certain. I do wish you would attend to it, instead of taking up the cudgels in a war of words. I will be any sort of a Catholic you like, if you will only not upset me, but when you drive so furiously it frightens me out of my wits."

Cissy laughed, and said, she thought they both deserved turning over. Then devoting her attention to Miss Polly in compliance with Mrs. Vernon's request, she soon reduced that young female to order, and in a few minutes more they drew up in front of the churchyard gate at Frodsham.

"The door is open," said Mr. Hayward, as he assisted the ladies to descend. Then calling a boy who was standing near to take charge of the pony, he led the way into the church.

Frodsham Church, since its restoration, had become one of the lions of the neighbourhood. Wentmore had always been considered the *beau ideal* of a Parish Church in those parts till now, and many persons still preferred it in some respects to Frodsham; but a large sum had been expended on the latter edifice, and the interior arrangements, especially with regard to what one set of people called the "altar," and another set, the "table," were much more elaborate in their detail. The stained glass at Wentmore was very fine, but connoisseurs had pronounced the east window at Frodsham, infinitely superior to anything of the kind at Wentmore. Cissy Lethbridge was rather offended when she heard any comparisons being drawn between the two churches, to the disadvantage of Wentmore, but she could not but allow that on the whole, Frodsham was more

as she would like to see every church in the king-
dom, than Wentmore. Mr. Lennox had two large
candlesticks on his altar, but they were never
lighted except in the evening. At Frodsham,
they had six large, and two smaller ones, and
these latter were always lighted during the Communion Service ; this Cissy highly approved of,
and she was often heard to express a wish that
Frodsham was a little nearer Lethbridge, in order
that she might gladden her eyes more frequently
by the sight of them.

When they entered the church, Mrs. Vernon,
uttering an exclamation of delight, rushed off to
admire the painted windows in the chancel, but
Cissy quietly slipped into a seat, and kneeling
down, said a short prayer before she did anything
else. Mr. Hayward observed her, and wished that
he had courage to do the same, but he was afraid
some one would notice him, and think it strange,
so he remained fidgetting first on one foot and
then on the other, in the passage of the nave.
Presently, Cissy rose, and looking round, asked
in a low tone, if she might be allowed to go into
the sanctuary and examine the reredos which she
had never been able to do quite closely.

"I know, women are not admitted within the
rails, as a rule," she said, "but with your permission, I should very much like to go close to it,
just for one minute."

"Oh, certainly," said the curate. "There can

be no possible objection. It is not everyone who is so particular as you are. Look at Mrs. Vernon, she has gone inside the rails without asking leave of anybody."

Cissy did look, and was shocked to see Mrs. Vernon, standing unceremoniously close to the altar, examining the vases and other ornaments which stood upon it, and doing so with anything but a reverential air.

" That window is beautiful," she exclaimed, as Cissy and Mr. Lethbridge approached, " but I am disappointed in the stone carving; I had heard it was so very good."

Then without waiting for any answer, and not seeing the reproving glance which Cissy bestowed upon her, she hurried off to look at the font at the other end of the building.

If Cissy's behaviour in the body of the church was " particular," inside the altar rails, she seemed quite awestruck. Never, in church, as a rule, did she speak much above her breath, but now in answer to Mr. Hayward's observations on the reredos and east window, she scarcely dared to whisper. In the midst of an explanation the curate was giving, of what it was intended to do in the way of further decoration when the funds permitted it, Mrs. Vernon suddenly came back, and interrupted them with the request that Cissy would try the organ, which stood in the north

aisle, and which she had heard was quite a splen-
did one.

"Do, Cissy dear," she said, laying her hand on
Cissy's shoulder. "Come at once, like a dear
girl, just play something and then we will go."

"Hush!" said Cissy, looking very grave.
"Don't talk so loud, Madeline. What can you
be thinking of?"

"What do you mean?" asked Mrs. Vernon,
staring at her. "Why shouldn't I? There is no
service going on!"

"You forget where you are," whispered Cissy.
"You forget who are listening!"

"Listening?" cried Mrs. Vernon, looking at
Mr. Hayward, and then round the chancel, in
which there was no one but themselves. "I don't
see anyone, and what would it matter if there
were?"

"This is God's House," said Cissy, "and the
Angels are listening."

Mrs. Vernon understood her now. She felt
herself reproved, and turned away her head impatiently.

"Bother the angels," she muttered, half crossly.
Then recovering her good humour, and taking
Cissy's hand in hers, she whispered, "You are a
dear little goose, and I am sorry if my speaking so
loud has distressed you, but I am wanting in the
bump of reverence, I believe, so you must forgive
me, and I will try not to offend in the same way

again. Now come and play for me like a dear child, and I will be as quiet and orderly as a mouse."

Cissy at once proceeded to the organ, and as Mr. Hayward knew where to find the key, they opened it, and she commenced playing the Kyrie from Mozart's Twelfth Mass.

Mrs. Vernon went to a little distance, where she stood listening with delight. She was passionately fond of music, and Cissy performed with no ordinary skill.

"Please play something else," was the joint request of both her auditors, as she took her hands off the keys.

And then, calling forth the whole strength of the magnificent instrument, Cissy began the Hallelujah Chorus, the jubilant strains flooding the church with their sound, and seeming to linger in the vaulted roof long after they had died away in the space below, and Cissy had ceased playing.

"Now we must go," she said, rising, and closing the organ. "Do you remember the day we drove over to Wentmore, and found Miss Barbara Lennox playing in the church there?" she added, turning to Mrs. Vernon. "It was just after they had heard of Gerald's having become a Romanist."

"Yes," said Mrs. Vernon, "I remember."

"But she did not play like you. It was my first visit to Wentmore. Sir Edward Bateson was with us."

She said these last words as if talking to herself, and seemed lost in thought as she followed Cissy down to the gate where the pony carriage was standing.

Having taken leave of Mr. Hayward, the ladies then drove off, and Polly, who no doubt knew she was returning to her stable, took them over the ground rapidly in the direction of Lethbridge.

When they arrived, they were met in the hall by Mrs. Lethbridge, who informed Cissy that she had seen the Wentmore party in Westling, and, in consequence, they had altered their plans and were not coming there on their way back, as Lady Frances wanted to get home early, so Blanche had sent her love, and hoped Cissy would be able to go over to Wentmore the next day, instead.

Cissy was disappointed, as she had hurried back in hopes of seeing Blanche, whom she had not seen to "speak to" for several days, and to wait till "tomorrow" seemed rather hard. However, she consoled herself with the perusal of the letter Blanche had given her, and retired at once to her own room to devour it in private. She herself had received an epistle from Ferdinand by that morning's post, indeed if the truth must be told, it was seldom a morning passed without bringing her a letter from him, but it had been an agreement with Blanche whenever he was away, that his letters to her should be common property, and it was from them that Cissy chiefly learned any news of his movements or what was going on around him at all, as when he wrote to her, although his letters were far from short ones, they were somehow or other taken up with what was undoubtedly very interesting matter to the recipient, but did not convey much in the way of news, or information of a general character.

Availing ourselves of our author's privilege, we will look over the young lady's shoulder as she reads, and make our readers acquainted with the contents of the closely written epistle.

It ran thus:

"I know, my darling Blanche, that you have been expecting to hear from me, but I assure you I have not had much time for letter writing," ("Excepting to me," thought Cissy,) "and I know Gerald keeps you *au fait* with our proceedings from time to time. I am enjoying my stay at Brussels immensely, and you may imagine how jolly it is for us two to be together again for a time. It is so nice for us, having the Derehams here, and their cousin Lady Alice Fitzstephen is staying on the Boulevard with Mrs. Temple, who is also a relation of theirs, you know. Lady Alice is prettier than ever" (Cissy frowned and pouted as she read this,) "and I rather think Master Gerald is smitten in that quarter," (Cissy smiled again and looked relieved,) "but don't you take any notice of this, as I don't think he would like it.

I know you will be wanting to hear all about Bibi
and Sidney, and I would have sent you a full
account of how I thought her looking, etc., before
this, but the truth is, till yesterday (which was a
whole week after they got here,) I never actually
saw her. Gerald and I called several times at
the hotel where they are staying, but she was
always ill, or out, and when we did meet at last,
it was quite by accident. I never saw anyone so
altered as she is. I told you how different I
thought Sidney to what he used to be, but she is
much the more changed of the two. Gerald and
I were passing a shop, when suddenly she came
out of it. Gerald called out, ' There is Barbara,'
or I should not have seen her, for I was looking
another way. She did not seem to recognize us,
and was getting quickly into a cab, but Gerald
touched her arm, and then she turned round and
saw us. Her veil was down, but I could see
through it how pale she looked. She was in a
hurry, and we only kept her one minute, but
arranged to go and have tea with them in the
evening, which we did. She has been very ill, I
am afraid, and looks far from well now. When I
shook hands with her, she trembled, and seemed
as if she was going to faint, but laughed when I
asked her if anything was the matter, and drove
away before there was time to say another word.
In the evening, she appeared more like her former
self, but all her cheerful old manner is gone, and

I told her several times, that if it had not been for her voice I should scarcely have known her again. I am afraid that she is not happy. I do not know why. Sidney seems kind to her, but he is very little with her, I know. She seems low and out of spirits, but that may be from not feeling well. I will write again when I have seen more of her, and tell you what I think then. She spoke of you and my mother with much affection, and was much interested about C. I told her I thought there ought to be a double marriage on the same day, but Sidney called out that they were horrid inventions, and she did not give an opinion. The Smiths are here, and talk of remaining the winter. I know Miss Minnie is a correspondent of yours, so I have no doubt you hear all about their impressions of Brussels, etc., from her. If you see any of the Lethbridge party you may give them my love. With heaps of the same from us both to the dearest of mothers, the Pater and yourself. Ever, my darling, I am your most loving brother,

" FERDINAND."

CHAPTER XIV.

LADY FRANCES LENNOX was one of those women (of whom, happily, there are many to be found in our English homes,) who habitually think of others rather than themselves. Unselfishness was an attribute of the Lennox family, and in no member of it was it more conspicuous on all occasions than in the high-born gentle mother, the tender devoted wife, and the loved and honoured mistress, to whom children, husband and servants turned at all times of doubt or difficulty for counsel and sympathy, sure of finding both in her.

Lady Frances, never a very strong or robust person, had of late years been subject to severe attacks of headache and indisposition which often confined her for days to her room. She did not keep her bed, but she would lie upon the sofa, her eyes closed, and the room darkened, hour after hour, trying in vain to obtain relief by sleep. But although soporifics were administered, and every means employed to induce that repose which she so greatly needed, they seldom had any effect, and when others hoped and thought she was sleeping, she was alive to every sound and movement around her. Her brain, always active and busy, would at such times work itself into a state of almost feverish excitement, and she would live over again scenes and sorrows in her past life which brought back as freshly as ever, feelings of the most harrowing nature and most injurious to her in her then weak and exhausted state. It was on one of these occasions, when she was labouring under a more severe attack than usual of headache and neuralgia combined, that a note was brought to her by her maid, which she was told a lady had written in the hall, and was awaiting an answer.

The woman had not long been in her place, and if Blanche or Mrs. Statham had been at hand, they would not have suffered Lady Frances to be disturbed by any message or note whatever, but the former had driven out with her father, in compliance with her mother's earnest entreaty, as she had been sitting with her in her room all day; and the housekeeper had gone into the village with a message to a poor woman from her mistress, which she had been especially directed to deliver herself.

" Who is it ? Do you not know ?" asked Lady Frances, raising her head which throbbed painfully.

"No, my lady," answered the maid. "I told her your ladyship was confined to your room, and she took out her pencil and wrote that note, and asked me to take it to you."

"Open the shutter a little way," said Lady Frances, and then putting on her glasses, she read the following lines :

"May I come up and sit with you a few minutes? I want to ask your advice. I am ashamed to disturb you, but am obliged to write by this post or would not think of doing so. A. J."

Lady Frances recognized the writing and the initials as those of Miss Jones. She sighed as she put the tiny missive on the table, for she felt that her chance of rest for that time was over, and she was weary with pain. But she did not hesitate. There was certainly need of her counsel, or Miss Jones, knowing that she was unwell, would not so urgently have sought it. (Thus Lady Frances argued ; imputing to another the thoughtfulness she would have had herself.) And turning to the servant, she said,

"Tell Miss Jones I shall be very glad to see her."

"My dear Lady Frances, I am quite ashamed of myself," began Miss Jones, as soon as she entered the room. "I am afraid you will never forgive me for disturbing you, dear, dear! But I am obliged to send my answer this afternoon, and I could not decide without having your opinion. It is altogether such a surprise, and I have no time to think it over. I don't in the least know what to do, dear dear!"

"Sit down, dear Miss Jones," said Lady Frances, in her gentle kind way, "and tell me what it is I can do for you. I feel very stupid to-day, for my head and face are both aching, but I will do my best to help you if you will let me know what your difficulty is."

Miss Jones sat down, and took a letter from her pocket.

"I have heard from Minnie Smith this morning," she replied, "and she says that her mamma and papa will be very pleased if I will go over and be with them during the remainder of their stay in Brussels. It seems that one of the servants they left behind at the Oaks, is going to them with some things they want, and so they propose that I should travel with her. The journey by way of Ostend is not a long one, and I feel very tempted to go, but I am so unprepared,—and the proposition is so sudden,—and I have so little time to make up my mind, as the servant is going directly, that I really don't know what to do, dear dear !"

"Will you let me see Minnie's letter?" said Lady Frances. "It seems to me a pity that you should not go, as they have asked you. Gerald and Ferdinand (who is still with him, you know,) will be so pleased to see you, and I am sure you will like Brussels."

Miss Jones put the letter into Lady Frances' hand, and when she had glanced through it, she returned it with a smile, saying,

" I should certainly make up my mind to go, if I were you."

Miss Minnie had written a most pressing invitation, urging her " dearest Miss Jones" to come and pay them a visit in Brussels, which was the *most* charming place in the world ; she said. They had a large house, with plenty of room. There would be lots of people she would know, the two Mr. Lennoxes, their cousins Mr. and Mrs. Graham, etc., and she, Minnie, would be so delighted to take her about, and shew her all there was to be seen. In short, all she wanted to complete her happiness was to have Miss Jones with her ; and she really must come. Turner would take great care of her on the journey, and there would not be the slightest difficulty, as her papa would meet them at the station, etc., etc.

" It sounds tempting, doesn't it ?" said Miss Jones, still hesitating. " I have never been abroad but once in my life, and that was to Boulogne, for a week, with my dear father and mother years ago ! I should like to go—if you thought—if it wasn't— I'm afraid it is like trespassing on Mr. and Mrs. Smith's kindness. But if you see no objection—— ?" and she looked anxiously at Lady Frances as she paused for a reply.

"I see no objection whatever," said Lady Frances, smiling, "since you ask my opinion. But of course it is a matter you must decide for yourself. I think the change would do you good, and as there is this servant of the Smiths going, it is not as if you would have to travel alone. When does she start ?"

" On Monday, I believe, and this is Thursday."

" Then I should write at once and say I was coming, and lose no time in making my preparations. You will not require to take much luggage with you, for I think Miss Minnie says they do not stay more than a fortnight or three weeks longer, doesn't she ? I am sure you need not hesitate about it, and if you take my advice you will go."

" Then I will. Thank you very much," said Miss Jones, starting up, and kissing Lady Frances on the forehead. " I will go and write at once. I am so much obliged to you. I hope I have not made you ill. I should never have been able to decide without seeing you, but it was very wrong of me to burst in upon you in this way. I don't know what Blanche would say to me. Pray forgive me. And you really think I may say—yes ?" she added, stopping in her way to the door, as if still in doubt as to whether Lady Frances fully approved the idea.

"Most decidedly," laughed Lady Frances, who in spite of her suffering, could not help being amused at her old friend's uncertain state of mind. "We shall see you before you start, and I daresay Blanche will have some little commissions for you to execute, if you will be so kind. Only remember, that if you do not wish to get into disgrace, you must not omit the 'Fraser' before Smith when you speak of your host and hostess!"

"No, no!" answered Miss Jones, running back, and pressing another kiss on Lady Frances's forehead, "I won't forget indeed, dear dear! It is so kind of you to remind me. Goodbye, dear Lady Frances. A thousand thousand thanks," and kissing her hand as she stood in the doorway, she disappeared.

"Poor thing!" said Lady Frances to herself, when she was left alone. "She thinks she owes all her happiness to me, for merely telling her to do as she wished! Good, simple soul. It is really kind of the Smiths to ask her, and I am sure the trip will do her good."

Ten days after Miss Jones had taken her departure from Rose Cottage *en route* for Brussels, Blanche Lennox went up to town, accompanied by her father. There was to be a family gathering in Grosvenor Square. News of a startling nature had arrived one morning by post at Wentmore.

An express had been sent to Brussels summoning Gerald and Ferdinand to London, and Mr. Lennox and Blanche were there to meet them on their arrival. Ferdinand's stay in the Belgian capital had been prolonged from day to day and week to week, and he was with his brother when the telegram was put into Gerald's hands. It was brief, but peremptory. They were to start at once on receiving it, and proceed direct to Lord Norwood's house, where their father was expecting them. Lord and Lady Dereham, who were meditating a return about the same time, talked of accompanying them, but they were not quite ready to start, and Gerald felt that it was impossible for them to delay, so a few hours after receiving the despatch, he and Ferdinand were on their road.

Lord Norwood and his daughter had both come up from the country, and as Gerald had telegraphed to say what train they should arrive by, his father and uncle were on the platform to meet them. The telegraphic message sent to Brussels, had contained the reassuring words, " All well," at the end of it, and so the brothers did not feel uneasy as to the cause of their summons, but their curiosity on the subject was great. In a few minutes they were seated in Lord Norwood's carriage, on their way to Grosvenor Square, and then Mr. Lennox turning to Gerald, took both his hands in his, and drawing him towards him, said, with scarcely repressed emotion,

"My boy. An unexpected thing has happened. Most unexpected by me, by all of us, and I am certain by you. Old Ernald Lennox of Stanfield is dead, and has left all his fortune,—no inconsiderable one as you know,—to you. He was an eccentric old bachelor, but one of the most generous-hearted men that ever lived. He had no great love for Roman Catholics," (here the speaker smiled, though the tears glistened in his eyes,) "and knew but little of you personally, but he heard of your—your conversion, and of your having given up what you did for your religion, and he made, it seems, a fresh will immediately, leaving every penny he had in the world to you. I believe there are some injunctions and bequests in the will, with regard to a few of his old servants and others which it will be a pleasure to you to carry out, but that is all, and at this moment you are one of the wealthiest commoners in the land."

Gerald listened with a bewildered air to what his father was saying, and when the latter paused, seemed as if he scarcely understood what he had heard. His hand lay in his father's, and his eyes were fixed upon him with a look of strange wonderment, but he did not speak or move. The first thing which roused him from the state of stupor into which he seemed to have fallen, was feeling an arm round his neck, and Ferdinand's voice whispering in his ear,

"God bless you, my dearest fellow. How awfully glad I am!"

Then he put one hand before his eyes, and pressed Ferdinand's with the other. He tried to speak, but could not steady his voice sufficiently to do so. The surprise had been so great, and a thousand different emotions seemed to rise up and choke him as he made the effort.

Lord Norwood put his hand caressingly on his nephew's shoulder. "I wish you joy, my boy. Your cousin Ernald, is not the only member of your family who has admired your conduct, however much they might differ from you in opinion, and to every one of us the way in which he has marked his sense of it will be a cause for rejoicing."

Ernald Lennox of Stanfield Hall, (a fine old mansion, situated in one of the midland counties,) was a younger brother of Mr. Lennox of Bentley. He had succeeded to a large fortune on the death of his mother who had been an heiress, and whose property was entailed upon her younger son, in addition to which, a wealthy relative on his father's side had also left him a considerable sum, in accordance with the rule which seems to guide persons in such matters. Both Ernald Lennox and his elder brother (as head of the family and owner of the Bentley estate) were well off, but the younger was, if anything, the richer of the two, and therefore, although their cousins, Reginald

and Geoffrey, who were related exactly in the same
degree to old Colonel Lennox, were much more in
need of such assistance than either of them, this
additional amount of wealth, fell as a matter of
course to Ernald. Perhaps some feeling of com-
punction for having absorbed so large a portion of
what might have been more equally divided amongst
them, may have actuated the old bachelor when
he altered his will in favour of his cousin Reginald's son, but he had also been much struck by
the story of Gerald's self-abnegation in the matter
of his religious change, and upon hearing it, exclaimed, "By Jove. That fellow is in earnest.
Right or wrong, there is no humbug about him,
and if he has turned Papist, it is only going back
to the faith of his ancestors after all. I'll ask
him down here to stay with me as sure as fate!"
And Gerald had received an invitation as he now
remembered, but he was just on the point of leaving England when it arrived, and never having
seen his cousin but once, years before, and taking
it as merely an accidental mark of friendship and
good feeling on the old fellow's part, he had
thanked him and declined it at the time, and
never given him or his kindness a moment's
thought since. Now, however, it flashed back
upon him, and he regretted having lost the opportunity which had been afforded him of becoming
better acquainted with one to whom he found that
he owed so much.

The carriage stopped at the door of Lord Norwood's house. In another moment they were in the entrance hall, and Gerald felt a pair of arms flung round his neck, and someone whose tears mingled with her kisses, whispered in his ear,

" My darling. How happy I am. Mamma so longs to see you, and I was to give you my first kiss for her."

He returned that sisterly embrace with warmth. It was the first time Blanche and he had met, since she had become a Catholic, and the thought was in both their minds. The clinging pressure with which their lips met, denoted the fulness of each heart, but still Gerald did not speak, and when he met Lady Margaret, who stood at the top of the stairs, waiting to receive him, he squeezed her hand in answer to her few words of earnest congratulation, and then proceeding at once to the room which he always occupied when at Norwood House, and which was reached by two steps from the drawing-room floor, he closed the door, and it was understood by all that he wished to be left alone.

" He is quite overcome, I can see that," said Mr. Lennox to Blanche, as she stood with her arms round him, asking what Gerald had said, when they told him the news, " and it is best to let him be quiet for a while. He will have enough to think of bye and bye, and needs a little time to recover himself."

The first to appear when the party assembled for dinner was Gerald. As Lady Margaret entered the drawing-room, he came forward with his usual calm, pleasant manner, and apologized for his abrupt behaviour on first arriving.

"You must have thought me a regular bear," he said, "dear Margaret. But I was so utterly unprepared for the news that awaited me when we arrived at our journey's end this afternoon, that I really did not feel able to collect myself for a time. I don't think I even spoke to Blanche when I came in."

"No, that you did not, sir," said Blanche, who at that moment came into the room. "And so I shall expect you to make up for it, during the rest of the evening."

Gerald turned round, and caught her in his arms.

"My Beauty B!" he said, "how are you? Sit down, and tell me all about Wentmore, how you left my Lady Mother, and how everything and everybody is going on there."

"A likely thing indeed, until I have heard all your news—how Barbara is—what Miss Jones thinks of Brussels—when the Derehams are coming back—and all the things you have got to tell me," returned Blanche, laughing.

When dinner was over, and the ladies had gone upstairs, Gerald whispered to Ferdinand that he was going round to Hill Street for half an hour.

"I must see Father Clifford," he said. "But do not take any notice of my absence, and if any-one asks where I am, say I shall be back directly."

Ferdinand nodded, and Gerald quietly left the room, put on his hat and coat, and quitting the house, hastened in the direction of Hill Street.

"Is Father Clifford at home?" he asked, as the servant appeared in answer to his ring at the bell of No. —

"No sir. He has just stepped out to a sick call," was the answer, "but I expect him in shortly."

Gerald hesitated a moment. "Can I get into the church?"

"Yes sir. One of the Fathers is in the church, and you will find the side door open. You can go through this way, if you please, sir."

Gerald entered, and the man shut the door. Then leading the way, he ushered Gerald through a kitchen at the back of the house, across a small court, from which they entered a building which was used by the Fathers as a school for the poor Catholic children of the neighbourhood. A passage through this led to a door opening into Farm Street, almost opposite the church.

"Thank you," said Gerald. "I will just go into the church for a few minutes, and I daresay Father Clifford will have returned when I come back."

"If you ring at this bell, sir," said the man,

"I will let you in, and it will save you going all the way round."

The side door of the Church was open, and Gerald entered. The greater part of the holy building was in darkness, but the sanctuary, as usual, was lighted by a small lamp, which hung in front of the altar, and a light streamed from the open door of the sacristy. As Gerald approached the altar rail and knelt down, he heard some one come out of the sacristy and return again. It was doubtless the priest whom the servant had mentioned as being in the church, and who, hearing footsteps, had been to reconnoitre. He was conscious of a slight movement from time to time in the sacristy, as he knelt, gazing at the tabernacle, but otherwise not a sound broke the stillness of the place. He was alone with God and the Angels.

And that was what he wished to be. How long he knelt there he did not know. Thoughts seemed to crowd themselves upon his brain, and oppress him with their weight. He tried to pray, but he could neither fix his attention nor find words to suit his need. Still, there, in THAT PRESENCE he felt at peace. The Eye which was upon him, could read the inmost desires of his soul. The Sacred Heart which beat beneath the Sacramental Species, knew better than he did what it was he longed to express, and feeling that it was so, he continued prostrate and immoveable before the

altar, as minute after minute went by. He thought
of the day when he had risen from his knees in
that church and knew himself to be a Catholic. He
remembered Father Clifford's words to him as he
took leave of him when the ceremony of his Reception was over. "Now you are a Papist—and I
do not pity you in the least!" How much of true
sympathy and of strengthening power had lain
concealed under those seemingly rough words.
The good priest knew that he was going to do
battle with the world, that he was giving up much,
and would have to suffer much, but he wished him
to see that there was nothing to be pitied for in
that. Rather was the servant of Christ to be
envied, who had anything to bear of pain or reproach for his Master's sake. And then he thought
of the grief his parents, his brother and sister had
felt in consequence of his conversion, of his own
loss of wealth and position, and all he had gone
through since. He had been tried sorely, far
more severely than he had ever supposed would
be the case when he first joined the Catholic
Church, and yet how little it all seemed when
compared with what others had been called upon
to endure. Indeed, as he looked back upon the
past, it seemed as if the happinesses he had experienced, far outnumbered the trials he had under-
gone. Blanche's conversion, and that of poor
Arthur Woods—two souls gained already, and
one of them so unutterably dear to him. And

now, this sudden restoration to wealth, such wealth as he had never before possessed. It seemed all Mercy and Goodness, which had been dealt out to him. His heart swelled up with a sense of intense overpowering thankfulness, and with a deep sob, he buried his face in his hands, and from his innermost soul begged of God the grace to serve Him in the future more faithfully, more worthily, than he had done heretofore.

As he thus knelt and prayed, forgetful of the lapse of time, and indeed of all outward things, he was startled by feeling a hand laid on his shoulder, and looking round, he saw in the dim light the figure of a young priest in the garb of a Jesuit, standing by his side. For a moment, Gerald looked at him with a half-puzzled air, as if striving to recal his thoughts and remember where he was. Then seeing the gentle smile with which the Father regarded him, he rose hurriedly, murmuring an apology for having kept him in the church, as he feared he must have done, and explained that, having called to see Father Clifford, and finding he was out, he had asked permission to visit the Blessed Sacrament, and been told he might do so, as one of the Fathers was in the church, and he would find it open.

"I am sorry to be obliged to disturb you now," said the young priest, "but I am about to leave the church, and must close it after me. Still, if you wish to remain a few minutes longer, pray do so."

Gerald smiled his thanks, but having said a short concluding prayer, he at once rose from his knees, and followed the Father from the church.

"I am afraid I have been keeping you," he said, as they quitted the building. "And indeed I ought not to have remained so long myself, for I only came out for a short time."

"I was engaged in the sacristy, and had only just come out when you saw me. I heard you enter the church, and thought it might be some Protestant who had looked in out of curiosity, but I soon perceived you were a Catholic, and only regret having had to disturb your devotions as I did."

On entering the Clergy House, they were informed that Father Clifford had returned, and would see Mr. Lennox in his room at once. Hearing Gerald's name, the young priest bowed, and said with a smile, that he had often heard of him, although he had not had the pleasure of meeting him before.

"May I ask your name, father?" said Gerald, holding out his hand, as the servant stood waiting to open the door of Father Clifford's room.

"Father Merton;" was the answer. "I have not been attached to this mission long, as my health is not very good, and the country was thought better for me, but I hope I shall be able to remain in town now, and have further opportunities for renewing our acquaintance."

Then wishing Gerald good-night, he turned away, and Gerald noticed how delicate and pale he looked. With his usual inclination to take a strong liking for anyone or the reverse, at first sight, he felt strangely prepossessed in favour of this young priest, whose voice, manner and appearance interested him greatly, and involuntarily he heaved a sigh as he remarked how far from strong he seemed.

To his surprise he found Ferdinand speaking to Father Clifford when he entered the latter's room. The Father advanced towards Gerald, and grasped his hand warmly.

"I have heard from your brother all about your good fortune," he said, "and I need not say how sincerely I rejoice at the news."

"I thought I would call for you," said Ferdinand, "knowing you were here, and was told you were in the church, but that Father Clifford was expecting you every moment, and hearing I was there, he kindly asked me into his room."

"And we have had a most interesting talk," said the Father. "I have great hopes of you," he added, taking Ferdinand by the hand. "Only enquire fearlessly, and pray hard, and you will be safely landed in Peter's net at last."

Ferdinand smiled, and shook his head. Then turning to Gerald, Father Clifford informed him that he was obliged to go out again immediately, so that he could not speak to him then, but would be at home any time the following morning, if he liked to call.

"I will come round directly after breakfast," said Gerald.

Father Clifford detained him a moment, as he held open the street door for them to pass out.

"When you get home, my son," he said, "read over the tenth chapter of St. Mark's Gospel, and note how the twenty-ninth and thirtieth verses apply to your own case. You, who gave up somewhat for your Master's sake, have already received 'a hundred times as much, now in this time'— but even with the earthly blessings which are promised to the faithful, are coupled 'persecutions,' and these can reach us in many ways."

There was an anxious ring in the tone of his voice, as if he would warn Gerald and prepare him, now, in the moment of his prosperity, for unforeseen trials in the future, of a different kind, perhaps, to those which he had hitherto encountered, but equally severe in their way. Gerald pressed his hand warmly in reply, and then followed his brother into the street.

Some ten days after, Gerald was sitting in Lady Margaret's morning-room, reading, whilst she was occupied with a drawing to which she was putting the finishing touches. He was expecting a visit from his lawyer, and had asked leave to visit his

cousin in her sanctum, as Lord Norwood and
Ferdinaud had gone off somewhere after breakfast,
and Mr. Lennox and Blanche had returned to
Wentmore, whither the brothers were to follow
them as soon as Gerald could get away, and he
found it dull work by himself in the dining-room
below. Throwing down his book, he exclaimed,

" I wish Mr. Gooch would come. I have to be
in the city to see the steward from Stanfield at
one o'clock, and arrange about my going down
there to take formal possession bye and bye, and
he always stays such a time when he is here. I
have no chance of getting away under an hour at
the earliest !"

" That comes of being such an important person, you see, Gerald," said Lady Margaret, de-
murely, as she took up her drawing and held it at
a little distance for inspection. " The cares and
troubles which a large fortune entails, are beginning to make themselves felt already !"

"*Apropos* of large fortunes, Margaret," said
Gerald, getting up and walking about the room.
" Did I tell you that Ferdinand knows who it was
sent me, what certainly seemed like one at the
time it came ? That money which I have never
made use of, and which is lying at my bankers
still in my name. I always meant to ask you if
you had the least idea who the mysterious *lady
friend* could be to whom I am indebted for the
same. Now, that I do not absolutely want it, I

am more inclined to keep it, and make use of it
than ever I was before, and if I could only guess
from whom it came, that would decide me one way
or another."

Lady Margaret's drawing suddenly fell into disgrace. Something was wrong about it, she could
not make out what, and was obliged to move to
the window to examine it more closely.

"I think you were very foolish not to take
advantage of it when it was sent you, and when it
would have been of use," she said, presently, in
reply to Gerald's remark. "As to its coming
from any lady, that must be Ferdinand's nonsense.
Just as if such a thing was likely! Talking of
ladies," she added, hurriedly, "how did you think
Alice was looking last night? Everyone's glass
seemed turned on our box, and although I tried
hard to persuade myself I was the object of part of
the admiration we excited, I am afraid I came in
for a very small portion of it myself!"

"She looked very well," said Gerald, with an
assumption of indifference. "By the way, I must
go and call there this afternoon. It will be a
wonder if she has not taken cold after our adven-
ture in the Park."

"Which reminds me that you have never asked
after my health this morning," said Lady Margaret, whose drawing seemed once more restored
to favour. "I don't see why I should not be as
likely to suffer from the effects of our terrific ex-

posure as Alice, especially as no one offered me a covering for my head, and so I really was much the worse off of the two!"

"I am so disgusted at myself for not having told that girl where we lived," exclaimed Gerald, seizing the poker, and giving the fire a vigorous poke. "But I was in such a hurry to get you both into the cab, and drive off, that I did not think of anything else. I declare I never saw anything so nice as the way in which she took off her warm neck-kerchief, and begged Lady Alice to put it over her head, although she had no chance of ever seeing it again. Her face put me in mind of someone too, I think I must have seen her before, but that may be only fancy. Still, I would give something to find out who she is, and thank her properly for her kindness."

"Yes," said Lady Margaret. "It was the most unselfish thing I ever saw. Giving away what she must have wanted herself such a cold night, to an utter stranger. And when I told her we should have no means of returning it, she said, 'It did not signify, and we were not to mind in the least!'"

To explain what Gerald and his cousin were referring to, we must inform our readers, that on the previous evening, he had escorted Lady Margaret, and her cousin Lady Alice Fitzstephen (who had arrived in London a day or two previously with Lord and Lady Dereham from Brussels) to one of the theatres. The roads were very slippery, and in the Park, just opposite Buckingham Palace, the horse they were driving came to a stand still, and the coachman told them he was afraid they could not go on. The two ladies were, of course, in evening dress, and utterly unfit for exposure to the open air, but Lady Alice immediately sprang out of the brougham, and Gerald found himself standing with his fair companions in the centre of an admiring group of bystanders, whilst the coachman in vain attempted to make his horse proceed. Luckily a cab drove up with a horse which had been roughed, and into this they got, and proceeded on their way. Not however, before Lady Alice had slipped in attempting to walk a few steps, and must have fallen to the ground, had not Gerald, who was speaking to his uncle's servant, sprung forward and saved her. She laughingly declared that she was not hurt, only frightened, and would not hear of their doing otherwise than going on to the theatre. Whilst they were standing in the cold, a respectable looking young woman had stepped out of the crowd, and taking off the wrapper she wore round her neck, had begged Lady Alice to accept it and put it over her head. "Pray take it, Miss," she had said, "you will catch cold, I am sure, and I can quite well do without it." It was no time to hesitate, Lady Alice had accepted the offer with thanks, and immediately after, the cab drove up, and they went

off. Gerald had noticed the girl as she spoke to
Lady Alice, and looked round for her before they
started, but she was gone.

It had been a very pleasant evening. Lady
Alice had heard of his good fortune, and was warm
in her congratulations. Gerald had even fancied
there was something more than usually kind in
her manner, and his heart beat the faster in consequence. In the silent hours of the night he
asked himself what it was that gave him the deep-
est satisfaction in this sudden and unlooked for
acquisition of wealth, and the answer which he
felt to be the true one, was the consciousness that
now he could without presumption raise his eyes
to the Duke's daughter, and ask her to be his
wife.

Well-born and highly connected as he was, if it
had not been for the unforeseen and amazing piece
of good fortune which had befallen him, he could
never have supported her as became her rank, or
ventured to speak of his love. But now, how
differently was he situated, and how joyfully did
he recognize the difference, and look forward to the
future which awaited him!

CHAPTER XV.

THE weather at Brussels, that winter, had been unusually sharp. During the month of January, its severity had in some measure abated, but early in February the cold again set in, and amongst the poorer classes much suffering ensued. Ill-fed and scantily clothed, they felt the keen blast and nipping frost more acutely than those who were able to draw near their fires, and were surrounded by other comforts as well, but even these complained bitterly of the sharpness of the season, and some of the English residents declared that the cold exceeded anything they had ever known in their own country.

Barbara Graham sat shivering over the fire in her drawing-room. They had taken a house in the Rue du Commerce for three months, and with the taste for " having things nice about her," as she expressed it, which was inherent in the Lennox family, she had made her temporary home as much like an English one in its arrangements as possible. A good coal fire blazed in the grate, and Barbara had pulled her Eugénie chair close to the fender upon which she had placed her feet. A warm shawl was drawn over her shoulders, and she certainly looked comfortable enough, but with every blast which shook the windows, she drew it closer round her and shivered afresh. She was pale and thin, and an air of depression sat upon her features. She had been reading, but her book was lying on the ground beside her. She had evidently tired of it, and was absorbed in reverie as she sat gazing at the fire.

She was, as her cousin Ferdinand had said, indeed changed, since the days of old at Wentmore. It was not quite two years since she had left her uncle's roof, and the happy home of so many years. She had been quite a girl then, and looking at her now, you would imagine, had you not known to the contrary, that she was a married woman who had experienced much both of care and sorrow, and had long bid adieu to the carelessness and elasticity of youth. But Barbara Graham, although much altered, and not so young looking as many of her contemporaries in age, was a distinguished, not to say handsome looking woman still. Lady Dereham had exclaimed to Gerald, after first seeing her, "Mrs. Graham is not in the least like what I expected. She must be a great deal older than Blanche ?"

"Yes, she is some years older," Gerald had

answered, "but if you had seen her before she married, you would not have thought there was much difference between them. She has been a good deal out of health lately, and that has changed her in appearance greatly."

Lady Dereham thought there must be some other cause besides ill health, to produce the care-worn look which often sat on Barbara's features. She did not say so to Gerald, but she suspected that Sidney Graham's wife was not a very happy woman, and that an aching heart had as much to do with her pale looks as bodily weakness. And she was right.

Barbara was aware, when she married her cousin Sidney, that she was embarking on a venture which from the outset promised badly. We know that she had felt undecided up to the last moment, and that even then she had had more than half a mind to draw back ere it was too late. But the fatal step once taken, she had resolved to make the best of things, and for a time had flattered herself that she might have done worse than give her hand, where the heart was not. All this we know, but before long (as is ever the case with those who delude themselves in like manner,) she had discovered how fallacious was this hope, and from that time her life had indeed been a sad one. To the outward world she appeared a hard, cold sort of woman, with whom it was difficult to get on, and for whom it was impossible to feel much

either of interest or sympathy. Only very few
penetrated beyond the exterior show of coldness
and reserve which surrounded her, and got sight
of the woman's heart beneath, and if by chance,
any succeeded in doing so, they would leave her
with feelings of sorrowful amazement and wonder
as to the cause which had so darkened and blighted
that young life.

The first bright gleam which had crossed her
path, had been that meeting with her cousin Gerald
at Spa, and she had looked forward eagerly to the
winter in Brussels, where she hoped to see him
often again. In the old 'Brother and Sister'
days at Wentmore, although never great allies,
they had been up to the time of Gerald's "perversion" very good friends. Barbara had turned
against him then, more out of indignation at the
grief he had brought upon Ferdinand and Blanche,
who had always been her two favourites in the
family, than from any other cause. But now,
when after both had gone through much trouble of
a different kind, they met again, that temporary
soreness of feeling had passed away on Barbara's
part, and she saw in her cousin Gerald only the
friend and companion of her happier days. She
thought too little of religion in the abstract to
make any difference on that point a cause for dis-
sension, and since she had been living in Catholic
countries, she had imbibed somewhat of a liking
herself for the churches which she had visited

from time to time, partly out of curiosity and partly because their still solemnity, or the beauty of the music and services, had a soothing and tranquillizing effect upon her which was peculiarly their own.

No sooner did she hear that Ferdinand had arrived unexpectedly upon a visit to his brother, however, than her feeling of satisfaction at finding herself at Brussels, departed, and she endeavoured anxiously to persuade her husband to go elsewhere. She pleaded ill health, and a variety of reasons, for cutting short their stay in the Belgian capital. It was a dreadfully cold place, and she was sure it would never agree with her. The difficulty of finding suitable lodgings was immense, and living at a hotel for any length of time, ruinous. She did not care where they went to, any other place would be preferable, only let them get away from Brussels! But Sidney was inexorable. He was very well satisfied with the place himself, and as to his wife's health and nonsensical fancies, he did not believe but that Brussels would suit her as well as anywhere else. With regard to not getting apartments at once, exactly to their liking, it was preposterous to suppose they would do so, she must just take a little more pains in looking about. In the meanwhile he was very well contented where he was. They gave him good dinners at the hotel, the wine was better than he had tasted for a long time, and he was not going to move to please anybody.

Compelled to remain where she was, Barbara resolved to delay the meeting she dreaded as long as possible. She had hoped never to see Ferdinand again, or at least not for many years, and now he was thrown by accident across her path in such a way that to avoid him was almost impossible. If the brothers called she was "not at home" or "unwell," and for a while she succeeded in eluding them. What she wanted was time. Time to school herself into composure. Time to determine what she should say, and how she would act when the rencontre which she felt was inevitable, took place. And then she would ask herself, why she needed anything of the sort? What if she had loved her cousin Ferdinand? What if (miserable woman that she was) she loved him still? He did not know it. He would meet her simply as the friend and cousin, the "sisterly cousin" of former days, and why should she shrink from so natural an encounter? Twenty times a day she told herself it was absurd. She would see them the next time they called. She would ask Sidney to take her and call upon them. And yet, whenever it came to the point, if she was informed that "*Les deux Messieurs Lennocks*" were asking for her below, or her husband volunteered to take her anywhere, which however, he did but seldom, she trembled and turned pale, and her resolution to seek the encounter herself would forsake her entirely. Once she caught sight of the receding forms of the two brothers from her window as they were leaving the hotel, and the colour rushed to her cheek and her heart beat fast as she did so. She all but rushed to the bell, to summon the waiter, and have them called back. But no. She was not ready yet—she would put it off a day or two longer, and then she really would admit them if they came again. And after all, she met them suddenly and without preparation. She had been shopping on the Montagne de la Cour, and was stepping into the *vigilante* which was waiting to convey her elsewhere, when she felt a hand laid upon her arm, and turning round, she beheld her cousins standing beside her. What she said in the confusion of the moment, or what she did, she could not afterwards remember, but they had met, they had spoken, and they were coming to spend the evening with her at her own invitation. She greeted them when they came as calmly and collectedly as though they had seen each other daily for the last twelvemonth. Her reception of Ferdinand was as unconstrained as possible, and no one who saw her or heard her speak that evening could have told by change of colour or intonation of voice, of the heart-burning, the struggle, and the pain which was passing within.

Since that she had seen them often. They had

moved from the hotel to their present quarters soon after she first met her cousins, and they were both constantly at the house during the next few weeks. On getting their summons to London, they had hastened to take leave of her. She had heard from Gerald since, of his unexpected good fortune. He had mentioned Ferdinand's name, sent his love, and made some remark about his being a bad correspondent save in one direction just then, that was all. She was not likely to hear from him, or of him in any other way. They were gone, and she was alone once more—more alone than ever. She did not know how much she had enjoyed seeing them, enjoyed being with them (she always put it to herself in the plural number) until now, and her life seemed more desolate, more sad, more unbearable than before.

Amongst other people, with whom the Grahams had become acquainted since their arrival in Brussels, was Mrs. Bolton, and that lady was suddenly announced to Barbara whilst sorrowfully meditating over the fire, as we described her at the opening of this chapter. On such a cold, miserable day, she had not anticipated morning visitors, but suppressing an exclamation of annoyance which almost escaped her, and inwardly resolving to scold the servant for having admitted anyone without warning, she advanced with her usual courtesy to meet the widow.

Mrs. Bolton's visit was not a very long one.

She had come for a certain purpose, and when
that had been accomplished she took her departure. But she did not look so pleased or so smiling when she left No. — Rue du Commerce, as
she had been when she rang at the bell some
twenty minutes before. She had hoped and intended to establish herself on a footing of intimacy
with young Mrs. Graham, and in her own mind
had determined that Barbara in return for the
information she considered it her painful duty to
impart, would throw herself into her motherly
arms, and be her devoted friend for ever after.
And she was not altogether satisfied with the
manner in which her communication had been
received. At any rate it had failed to produce the
impression, or the results she had anticipated.

Barbara had listened with apparent unconcern
to her visitor's whispered communication, after
being told that nothing but a stern sense of duty
and a feeling of womanly compassion had induced
Mrs. Bolton to say a word upon the subject. She
had replied shortly and coldly to that lady's assur-
ances of sympathy and kindly feeling, and as soon
as she could do so with civility, had got rid of her.
But no sooner was the door closed and she was left
to herself, than every vestige of colour forsook her
cheeks, and she sank back upon her chair, trembling in every limb.

This exhibition of weakness, however, was only
momentary. Starting from her seat, she clenched

her fist and stamped her foot on the ground, exclaiming, "If what she says is true, *and I am
sure it is true*, I will remain with him no longer.
I have borne too much already, and there is a
point beyond which endurance cannot go. I will
leave him!" she continued, excitedly, "I will go,
—I care not whither. But stay with him, beneath his roof, as his wife, any longer,—I will
not!" And then throwing herself on a sofa, and
burying her head in a cushion, she burst into a
passionate fit of tears.

Meanwhile, Mrs. Bolton had taken herself home
where her daughters, who knew the purport of her
visit to Barbara, were awaiting her return with
curious expectancy.

"Well, mamma," they both exclaimed, as she
entered the room, "What did she say?"

"Little or nothing," answered Mrs. Bolton,
tearing off her gloves and sitting down before the
fire to warm herself. "It is precious little thanks
one gets in this world for doing a goodnatured
thing. And I am sorry now that I took the
trouble of going near her."

"But wasn't she shocked? And didn't she
think it very kind of you to open her eyes to what
was going on?" asked Harriet.

"She was as high and mighty as possible.
Thanked me for my good intentions, but assured
me that she did not believe half the reports that
were spread about people, whether well founded or

not. She had often heard of Madame ———,
and had heard her husband express an admiration
for her, as she supposed most men would do, but
she was sure (mind you, I didn't believe her
one bit myself,) that he did not frequent her
house, and she had no patience with the way in
which some people were ready to make a scandal
out of nothing. I told her that nothing but a
sincere feeling of interest in her and of fear lest
she should hear the report in another and more
painful manner, would have induced me to mention the subject, and then she gave me to understand that she was busy, and so evidently wanted
to get rid of me, that I got up and came away."

"Oh, mamma! how rude!" cried Edith. "She
might have been civil at any rate !"

"I do not mean that she was absolutely rude,"
said Mrs. Bolton, "but I suppose she thought I
was interfering, and she is just one of those people
who keep one at arms' length in a quiet way, and
with whom one can never get an atom more intimate than they choose. It will be some time
before I go to call upon her again, I know that."

"I am sure I don't know why she should give
herself airs," said Harriet. "I suppose it is because she thinks herself in a better set than we
are, being intimate with Lady Dereham, and all
that sort of thing. I have no patience with that
kind of person !"

"And as to that," observed her mother, "she

is not the only person who is on visiting terms
with people of rank, and Lady Dereham, though
she may be a Viscountess, is not everybody. I
should like her to see my card dish in London!
Perhaps she would be astonished to find that I
exchanged calls with such persons as the Countess
of Pattesley, and Lady Godwick, and—"

"Mamma!" cried Miss Harriet, "how can you
be so vulgar! No one speaks of 'Countesses' and
'Viscountesses' in good society. You are as bad
as Kate Richardson with her 'Honourables.'
The wife of a Marquis and the widow of a knight
are called 'Lady So and So' alike, and none of
her friends (amongst whom, I suspect, she would
not number us,) would call the solitary Countess
we can boast of in our visiting list, anything but
'Lady Pattesley.'"

Mrs. Bolton was quite aware that her daughters,
who kept their ears and eyes open upon all occasions, were much more "up" in the ways of the
world than she was herself, and had little doubt
therefore that Harriet was right, but she did not
like being called to order so unceremoniously by
her own child, so getting up from her seat she
desired the girls to get their things on at once,
if they wished to go out with her, and left the
room.

A little later on that same day, a *vigilante* drew
up at the entrance of the Station du Nord, and
three ladies alighted from it. Another conveyance,

loaded with luggage, (of which there was a plentiful supply on the roof of the first one also,) followed close behind it, and out of this got a female servant who evidently belonged to the other party. One of the ladies remained outside to assist the servant in looking after the boxes, and to give directions to the porters. The other two went forward in the direction of the " Salle d'Attente," and taking possession of one of the compartments, they piled their cloaks and wraps and all the other articles without which ladies in these days cannot move about the world, on one of the seats, and then one of them, addressing the other, who was her junior by some thirty years or so, observed,

" We are in plenty of time, my dear. More than half an hour I see before the train starts, but I would much rather wait here and take things comfortably, than have to rush about and get one's ticket, and look after one's luggage and everything just as the train is starting, dear dear !"

" Yes. It is much better to be ready," remarked the younger, " but I don't see why we should sit here all the time. Here is Clara. She will mount guard over these things, and we should just have time to go and see the new church the Jesuits have built in the Rue Royale, if you will come at once ?"

And jumping up, she made a step or two towards the entrace of the *salle*, through which the lady who had remained to help the servant with the luggage was now advancing, whilst her companion seemed to hesitate as to whether she should follow her or not.

Minnie Smith and Miss Jones. The reader will already have recognized them? The latter was leaving Brussels on her return to England, accompanied by Clara Smith and the servant who had travelled out with her, Mr. and Mrs. Smith, Laura and Bella having started the day before. Minnie was not going with them, as she had been asked to stay with the Robertses a little while, and Mrs. Fraser Smith, who was only too happy to be able to tell all her friends in Southshire, that "Dear Lady Sophia had begged so earnestly to keep Minnie for a time; she was such a nice companion for the two Miss Robertses, who were just about her own age!" had easily persuaded her husband to consent to the proposal.

Clara Smith, who had seen the church in question, was quite content to remain in the waiting-room till their return, only begging them not to be late, and the other two set off. The "Eglise de Jesus" was not far distant, and having duly inspected and admired it, Miss Jones and Minnie were soon on their way back to the station.

"My dear Minnie," said the former, as they walked along, "mind you write to me, and do not let those Miss Robertses knock you up by taking you about too much. You are not strong, and

must take care of yourself. And Minnie, dear—
you will not be angry if I say something ?"

"What ?" asked Minnie.

"Don't go too often to those churches, dear.
You are being left among Papists in a Popish
land. You know I am not bigoted, and that I
think there is a great deal of good in them—but
you are young and enthusiastic, and such natures
as yours are easily led away. It is not all gold
that glitters, dear, and do be careful how you let
yourself be influenced by their services, and the
beauty of their churches, and all that sort of
thing."

Miss Jones took Minnie's hand, and looked
anxiously in her face as she spoke.

"You need not be uneasy, dear," answered
Minnie. "You know I feel quite at home in
Catholic churches and with Catholics, because I
am a Catholic myself. Not a *Roman* Catholic,
you know—but still a Catholic."

"Oh, yes, dear ; I know what you mean. But
you always frighten me when you talk like that,"
said Miss Jones. "Our religions are so very
different."

"I beg your pardon. My religion is the same.
Don't look so horrified. But I mean what I say.
There is only one True Religion, only one True
Faith, which I have been taught, and professed
since my infancy, the Catholic Religion, the
Catholic Faith."

"But, Minnie, dear. *They* have corrupted it so. What with their Mass, and their Confession, and—"

"Stop, dear," interrupted Minnie, gravely. "You know Confession is as much taught in our Church as in theirs. And the Mass is the same as our Holy Communion. I daresay you will be shocked, but I say my prayers just as happily at St. Gudule, as I do at St. Barnabas in London, and I would go to Confession and Communion here too, if they would let me. Only they won't."

"Well, my dear, you may understand those things better than I do," said Miss Jones, "but one thing you must allow. Those horrid images of the Virgin Mary which you see everywhere— surely you cannot like them, or think them right?" And the speaker looked as if she had advanced, in her own opinion, an unanswerable argument.

"As to their being 'horrid' images," answered Minnie, "that is merely a question of taste. I agree with you that most of them are unartistic and ugly to a degree. But I must say I like to see them in the churches, or carried in procession. I have a great devotion to the Blessed Virgin."

Miss Jones was struck dumb. After such an avowal, she could only conclude that "those Jesuits" had made a convert of poor Minnie already, and any attempt on her part to rescue her from her delusion was utterly hopeless. The remainder of their walk to the station they pursued in silence, but Miss Jones was in very low spirits when the moment came to say good-bye.

"Give my love to Mrs. Graham when you see her," she said to Minnie, as the latter stood at the door of the railway carriage before the train moved off. "And do tell her, if you have an opportunity," she added, in a lower tone, "not to let that Captain Lucas come so often to the house. He is dangling after her from morning to night. She is seen much oftener with him than with her husband, and I assure you, people make their remarks."

Minnie laughed, and said, she should not dare to be so impertinent. "I should just as soon think of flying over the moon, as venture to tell her such a thing. I was always rather afraid of Miss Barbara Lennox in old days, and coming from me, such a warning would be in the worst possible taste—as Captain Lucas was at one time supposed to be an admirer of mine!"

"No! my dear—was he?" exclaimed Miss Jones, quite seriously. "There is something about him I cannot endure. I don't know if it is his voice, or his manner, or what it is, but I don't like him. I did not know he was a friend

of yours, dear, dear. I don't think I ever saw
him at your house ?"

"Oh, it was ages ago, when he was quartered
at Hillsborough. He used to come over to the
Oaks, if he had nothing better to do, and do
me the honour of noticing me a little. That
was all. Goodbye, dear, goodbye, and mind you
write !"

Miss Jones drew back hastily as the guard
slammed-to the door, blew his whistle, and the
train started. She and Clara looked out of the
window, as long as Minnie was in sight, waving
their handkerchiefs and kissing their hands.
Then sinking back into her corner, Miss Jones
closed her eyes and had a "good think." She
was not happy about her friend Minnie. She
thought the poor child was in a bad way, and
leaving her in the hands of Papists in that manner, with her mind already deeply imbued with
their principles, was a thing which troubled her
very much. She would certainly tell her mother
what danger she thought she was in, when they
met, and urge her being sent for home, as soon as
possible. She then thought of her other young
friend, in whom she took, for many reasons, a
strong and deep interest, although she had never
been so intimate or friendly with Barbara, as with
the other members of her family. She had been
anxious to see her in her new aspect, as a married
woman, and in so different a scene to any in which

she had formerly known her. From what she had heard before they met, she had feared that Barbara's marriage had not turned out as happily as might have been wished, but she was not prepared for the utter estrangement which even a casual observer could not but see, existed between her husband and herself, and above all she was startled and distressed at the way in which the young wife had become the subject of comment in a place like Brussels, where comments were generally of an ill-natured kind, in regard to her intimacy with a young man like Captain Lucas, of whom no one seemed to entertain the highest possible opinion.

And Miss Jones was not the only person who, taking a kindly interest in Sidney Graham's wife, felt uneasy at the things which were said both about her and her husband. Ever since his first meeting with her at Spa, Mr. Fitzroy had entertained a great liking for the daughter of his old friend, and had resumed his acquaintance with her as soon as an opportunity offered, when she arrived in Brussels. He had feared, when at Spa, that she was not happy, and now that he saw more of her, he was convinced of the fact. Sidney Graham he seldom saw, for he was never at home when Mr. Fitzroy called at the house, and they did not often meet elsewhere. Sidney had become one of an English set, who rather prided themselves on their fast reputation in the town. It was chiefly composed of young officers on leave, and a certain number of choice spirits who had no particular calling of any kind, and whose chief aim and object seemed to be to "kill time," but they reckoned few married men amongst them, and Sidney's adhesion to their ranks therefore, was noticed the more. Sundry stories, which did not exactly redound to his credit, in a moral point of view, had reached Mr. Fitzroy's ears, and he felt that if even a portion of these was true, the young wife was to be pitied indeed.

Late in the afternoon of the same day on which Miss Jones and Clara Smith took their departure from Brussels, Mr. Fitzroy called at No. — Rue du Commerce, and enquired for Mrs. Graham. He was told she was not at home. Leaving his card, with a message about some tickets for a morning concert which Barbara had asked him to procure for her, he walked away, and as it was still too early to return home to dinner, he crossed the street a little lower down to call on a bachelor friend who lived on the opposite side, and upon whom he often looked in for a chat at that hour. This friend too, was out, as it happened, and Mr. Fitzroy was in the act of turning away with the intention of taking another short turn on the Boulevard before going home, when his eye fell on the door of the Grahams' house on the other side of the way, and he saw a man come out of it. At first he thought it was Sidney Graham, but a second glance shewed him that he was mistaken. It was not Barbara's husband, but her friend Captain Lucas, who was leaving the house, and who, seeing Mr. Fitzroy, nodded to him across the street. That gentleman remembered the "Not at home" which had been said to him a few minutes before, and seeing a visitor leaving the house so soon after, felt that the words must have had a personal meaning. He returned Lucas's nod coldly, and walked thoughtfully away. He did not like what he knew of this man, and it vexed him to think that he was a privileged visitor at Mrs. Graham's, to whom she was "at home" when she was not to others. But after all, he might have been visiting her husband. Mr. Fitzroy had not asked for him, and Captain Lucas might have been calling upon him and not upon his wife. Assuring himself that this was the case, he walked on with a lighter air, resolved to think no more about it, but nevertheless he did think about it several times in the course of the evening, and the more he did so, the less satisfied he felt as to whom the Captain's visit had been made.

Two days later, it was getting dark, and Barbara again sat alone in her room over the fire. Sidney was dining out. He seldom dined at home now, and that morning he had left word that she was not to expect him again that day, as he was going by train to Antwerp after dining with some friends, and should not return till the following afternoon. The note which he had written to this effect was brought to her, whilst she was seated at her late breakfast. Her lip curled disdainfully as she read it, and throwing it into the fire, she had desired the servant to deny her to all visitors that day "excepting Captain Lucas."

Captain Lucas called that afternoon, and remained for some time in Barbara's pretty drawing-room, talking to her long and earnestly. When he left, the servant who shewed him out, exchanged looks of intelligence with "Madame's" maid, who was standing on the stairs. Both glanced at the door of the room where their mistress was sitting, shrugged their shoulders and laughed. The action was expressive, and said more than words could have done, of what was passing in the mind of each.

The evening closed in. The footman came in to shut the shutters, and to ask when "Madame" would choose to have the dinner served. She dismissed him abruptly, saying she should not dine at all, and would ring when she wanted a cup of tea which the maid was to bring her. Should he light the candles? No. Madame preferred the fire light, and did not wish for candles. So he retired from the room, and Barbara was again left alone.

For two hours she sat motionless on the same low couch before the fire, thinking. During the

greater part of the time, she kept her elbows on
her knees, and her hands pressed tightly against
her forehead, concealing her face almost entirely
from view. Once or twice she looked up, and her
lips moved as if she was speaking to herself, though
not a sound escaped them. Perhaps she was
praying? Alas! No. Prayer with Barbara, had
for long been a thing of the past. She was
dwelling upon days gone by, and breathing
words which she did not dare to utter aloud, even
to herself. It was not her early life she thought
of, the happy innocent days when care and sorrow
were known to her by name only. She did not
venture to look back upon these, but she was
thinking of her married life and all the misery she
had experienced since the day on which she became Sidney Graham's wife. She was thinking of
what Mrs. Bolton had said to her,—of the manner
in which her husband's name and that of the
notorious Madame —— were coupled together in
the idle gossip of the town,—of the open way in
which he shewed himself in her society, on every
occasion, and of the hours he spent at her house,
whilst she sat lonely and miserable at home. She
had affected indifference and incredulity when she
was told these things, but she believed them all
the same. The remembrance of them sank into
her heart and rankled there. She had never loved
her husband, nor had he ever professed any deep
attachment for her. It was not jealousy, so much

as anger and indignation that possessed her as she sat and thought, for even in marrying *him*, she had not expected such treatment as this. And she thought too of what had passed that afternoon when Henry Lucas sat beside her, and spoke such soft and honied words into her ear, of the proposition he had made, and of the consent she had yielded,—and she shuddered as she remembered it all.

But she was resolved, and thinking was of no use. That very night had been agreed upon for their flight, and she had several preparations yet to make. She must rouse herself, and stifle the still small voice of conscience which endeavoured to make itself heard, by occupying herself in such a way as to leave no time for reflection.

Ringing the bell, she desired her maid to carry the tea into her bed-room. She would take off her dress at once, she said, and then Marguerite might go to bed, she should require nothing more that night.

As soon as the woman had withdrawn, and she was left to herself, Barbara locked the door, and opening a travelling bag which was already filled with such necessary articles as she was obliged to take with her, she added a few trinkets, and other possessions, which had been hers before her marriage, to its contents, and then drawing a table towards her, she unfastened her desk, in which some letters and papers had been stowed away, which she did not choose to fall into other peoples' hands, and proceeded to look them over ere she threw them into the grate, and set fire to the whole. From one of the drawers she took a packet of letters, written many years ago, in a small feminine hand, which had come into her possession after her grandmother's death, having probably been preserved from some feeling of sentiment at the time, and overlooked altogether afterwards, and which were addressed to her father "Lieutenant Geoffrey Lennox," at some out-of-the-way station where he had once been quartered. Barbara had always intended to destroy them without looking through them, but a lingering affection for her father's memory, and a reluctance to part with what had belonged to him had hitherto restrained her from carrying her intentions into effect. Now, however, she decided that they must be summarily disposed of, and having unloosed the packet which was tightly fastened together, she was about to set light to them with a match she held in her hand, when something in the character of the hand-writing arrested her attention, and made her examine it more closely. The ink was faded, and the paper in many places yellow with age, but she was certain that the hand was one she was familiar with, and had even seen somewhere else quite lately. She opened one of the letters, written on the old-fashioned square sheets of paper, and smiled involuntarily as her eye glanced over the contents. It was evidently the letter of a young girl whose heart was given to the person to whom it was addressed. In short, it was a packet of her father's old love-letters !

But who was the writer ? Who were they from ? Her father, Lieut. Geoffrey Lennox, had been the recipient, that was quite clear, but she had seen her mother's hand-writing often, and the letters were certainly not from her. She glanced at the signature—and then an exclamation of astonishment burst from her lips. Each letter was signed in the same way, by two initials, A. J. Those initials were familiar to her, and the sight of them recalled the person whose hand-writing resembled so strongly that before her. She had had a farewell note from her only a few days before, signed in the same way, and written, allowing for the lapse of time and difference of age, in the same hand. Her father's correspondent—her father's old love—probably before he had ever seen or become acquainted with her mother—was her old friend Miss Jones of Wentmore !

It was a curious discovery, certainly, and Barbara, if she had not had other things to think about just then, would have sat and pondered over it, but hastily thrusting one of these old tell-tale letters into her pocket, she threw the others into the grate, set fire to them, and

watched them as they flared up and were con-
sumed in the flames.

It flashed across her as she did so, that there
was something very singular, something almost
ominous in her meeting with these letters at this
moment. Out of the past in the history of her
own family—from the life of her own father, a
warning seemed to hold itself up to her of the
evanescent, perishable end of all earthly loves.
Yes; but in her case, love was an item which did
not intrude itself. Henry Lucas professed unbounded devotion, undying love for her, that was
all as a matter of course. She was not flying
with him because she loved him, but because in
her blindness and infatuation, alas! she thought
that she had only that way open to her for escap-
ing from her present life of misery.

No warning or reflection, therefore, was of any
avail now. She had made up her mind, the die
was cast, and she would give herself no time or
place for repentance. With her, there could be
neither hesitation or delay; so hastily resuming
the dress which she had taken off, and putting on
a bonnet and cloak, she fastened down the bag
she intended to take with her, and advancing
towards the window she waited for the signal which
was to inform her that all was in readiness for
her flight below. A quarter of an hour of silent,
breathless watching, during which the only sounds
Barbara heard were the ticking of the clock on the

chimney-piece and the beating of her own heart—
then half an hour—passed, and after that a low
knocking sound reached her from outside.

The window opened upon a balcony, and gently
unfastening it, she stepped out and looked wistfully round. No one was to be seen. It was a
dark night, and the street seemed deserted, whilst
the few lamps which stood at long intervals, only
just lighted up the space immediately round them.
She leaned over the balcony. Someone stood
underneath it, who seeing her, came forward.
Not a word was spoken, but the person, whoever
it was, beckoned with his hand, and Barbara
retiring again into the room, closed the window
noiselessly, seized her bag, and opening the door
gently, descended the stairs with a soft and silent
tread. At the foot of them she paused and listened. Not a sound was to be heard, and advancing breathlessly, she undid the fastenings of the
hall door. As she did so, the chain in her hand
rattled, and the key, in turning, made a noise
which she thought must be heard all over the
house. She started, and trembled from head to
foot. What if the servants were to be alarmed,
and she was discovered? Had she not better
return? It was not even now, too late.

She listened, but all was silent, and just outside
the door she caught a hurried impatient whisper
urging her to make haste. A cold shivering seized
her from head to foot, but she hesitated no longer.

She turned the handle of the door, and the cold air blew in upon her from the street.

Another moment, and Barbara Graham had left her husband's roof, and her place in social life—for ever.

END OF VOL. II.

RICHARDSON AND SON, PRINTERS, DERBY.

www.ingramcontent.com/pod-product-compliance
Lightning Source LLC
Chambersburg PA
CBHW021720110726
47902CB00005B/1270